POI PAMPERINGS

SARA GODDEN

APS BOOKS
YORKSHIRE

APS Books
The Stables,
Field Lane,
Aberford
West Yorkshire,
LE25 3AE
www.andrewsparke.com

APS Books is a subsidiary of the APS Publications imprint

©2025 Sara Godden

Sara Godden has asserted the right to be identified as the author of this work in accordance with the Copyright Designs and Patents Act 1988

All rights reserved.

First published worldwide by APS Books in 2025

No part of this publication may be reproduced, stored in or introduced into a retrieval system, or transmitted, in any form, or by any means (electronic, mechanical, photocopying, recording or otherwise) without the written permission of the publisher except that brief selections may be quoted or copied without permission, provided that full credit is given.

A catalogue record for this book is available from the British Library

POISONOUS PAMPERINGS

For Richard and the boys

With love

Chapter One

"Welcome back sleepy head" Claire giggled.

Dee awoke abruptly and appeared disoriented. However, upon feeling the softness of the towelling robe wrapped around her, she quickly remembered where she was.

"Sorry, I think I nodded off. Those exams have exhausted me," Dee said, looking embarrassed. "Please tell me I didn't snore?"

"No, I wouldn't have let you do that or not for too long anyway," Claire replied, smirking.

They both laughed together as Dee turned a nice shade of pink.

As Dee took in her surroundings, she felt the warmth of the sun on her face as it filtered through the window, framing the meticulously maintained gardens of Wellsdale Hall. Originally established as a pioneering health farm, Wellsdale Hall was now a retreat offering guests five-star accommodation, award-winning cuisine, and an extensive array of spa treatments. The Victorian Hall was comfortably nestled in twelve acres of countryside and featured a large indoor and two outdoor pools as well as several tennis courts.

Dee reclined in the comfort of the poolside sun lounger; she watched fellow guests in the garden through the window. Some were engaged in pleasant conversation, others read quietly on benches or bean bags. She noticed that a few guests were wearing gym attire, but the majority were cloaked in the warmth of their luxury robes.

"Penny for them?" Claire asked.

"Enjoying the view." Dee pointed to the gardens. "It's so lovely here, I can't thank you all enough."

Alison, Helen, and Claire, who had become close friends with Dee following the murder of Muttering Margo and her breakup with the self-absorbed Edward, had all recognised Dee needed a well-deserved treat. She had started to look exhausted. At Christmas, not only had her boss Peter given her the keys to his flat - he had moved into Gaitley Manor with Helen his new fiancé and her daughter Clara - but had enrolled Dee in a four-month National Investigator Exam course. Dee's friends knew she had thrown herself into her studies, but she had also spent all her spare time decorating her new home.

"There's no need to; you've been studying so hard, you deserved a little pamper," Claire said sitting up from the rattan sun lounger and looking over her shoulder.

Dee copied her actions. Near the waterfall cascading down a rock formation into the kidney-shaped pool, Alison sat on the pool steps, chatting with two half-submerged women. Alison turned, waved at her friends, and wished the women a pleasant day.

Dee and Claire exchanged smiles.

"That's Brenda and Pauline; they're members here. I'd love to be a member here, wouldn't you?" Helen asked her two friends while drying her legs with a towel from the empty sun lounger next to Claire's.

"Police officer salaries don't stretch that far," Claire said glumly.

"Mine doesn't either," Dee said.

"I can't imagine how many scones and cups of tea I'd need to sell. But let's relax, get pampered, and enjoy an amazing lunch. The buffet is supposed to be phenomenal!" said Alison, waving her towel.

"Ooh now you're talking. What time are we eating?" Dee asked.

"Not till twelve-thirty" Alison replied and then asked, "Anyone fancy a few minutes in the sauna and steam room?"

Dee and Claire agreed and the three of them made their way towards the area off to the right from the pool that held a number of different types of sauna, steam and wet rooms all promising to relax mind, body and soul.

"That sounds unusual," Dee said nodding in the direction of a sign saying *Cave Pool*.

"Shall we do that at the end?" Alison said as she opened the door to one of the steam rooms offering a lavender sensory experience. Once seated inside the girls relaxed and the room with its scented steam and coloured images on the ceiling sent them into a dreamy silence.

The silence was broken as the door opened to admit Brenda and Pauline.

"Hi, you two - we meet again," Alison said cheerily.

"There's such a hullabaloo going on in there," said one of the two ladies.

Dee could see two individuals, one wearing a dark swimsuit and the other a pink one. The rising steam made it difficult to identify who was speaking. Unable to curb her curiosity, she inquired, "What's happening?"

Alison intervened "Brenda, Pauline these are my friends I was talking about earlier." Alison pointed out Dee and Claire.

Brenda – the one in the dark blue swimsuit - asked, "Didn't you solve the Gamblewood murder?"

"We helped along with the police," Dee replied tilting her head towards Claire.

"Are you a police officer?" Pauline - wearing the pink swimsuit - asked.

Claire smiled as a response.

"She's a Detective Constable," Alison gloated, "…and Dee's a Private Detective."

"Well, I never. You two might be needed later. There's two girls in there going at each other hell for leather!" Brenda said.

Pauline tutted. "That's not quite true. One's shouting at the other who's sat quietly taking it. I would have given her as good back if someone was speaking to me like that!"

"In the pool?" Dee asked.

Brenda jumped in. "No, in the sauna. We could hear them as we opened the door. They stopped as we sat down but there was an atmosphere, so we left pretty quick. No sooner had we closed the door, you could hear them at it again!"

"Well one of them!" Pauline chipped in.

"I'm sure it's nothing major," Alison said.

"No, I'm sure it isn't, but I think it's time for a sauna," Dee declared, standing up and heading out of the door.

Claire followed leaving Alison with her new acquaintances.

They didn't encounter any arguments in the saunas or steam rooms, and spent the rest of the morning swimming, finishing in the jacuzzi overlooking the pool area.

"Time to get dry for lunch," Alison announced as she made her way towards the steps to climb out of the jacuzzi.

"I'm starving!" Dee declared.

"You always are. I don't know how you do it; look at your amazing figure!" Alison turned towards Claire and said mockingly, "Along with Albert, Dee's one of my best customers. Keeps my little Cafe in business, they do!"

They all laughed as they headed towards the changing rooms.

Neatly nestled at a corner table in the dining room wearing dry swimsuits covered by their towelling robes the opulent catering of Wellsdale Hall did not disappoint.

"It's like something out of Downton Abbey" Claire whispered.

"It's stunning, how did you know about this place?" Dee asked Alison.

"Lots of customers have mentioned it over the years. I've always wanted to come here but I never seemed to have a reason or excuse till now." Alison placed the white napkin upon her knee.

"We should come here for Helen's hen do," Claire said.

"Gosh, with my exams I forgot about the wedding. Please don't tell me it's next week or something!" Dee sounded genuinely shocked.

"Course not, the way that's going there'll be no wedding at all, poor Helen," Alison said looking up at the ceiling.

"Poor Helen? What have I missed?" Dee's eyes were inquisitively wide open.

"Helen and Peter want a quiet wedding with close family and friends. Lord Henry on the other hand wants a full on lavish one at Gaitley Manor with too many guests." Alison paused to take a breath. "Helen says she doesn't know half of them. Why would she? They're all Lady this and Lord that. Not what Helen wants at all!"

"Oh, I didn't realise," Dee said wondering why Peter, her boss and the groom, hadn't mentioned anything.

Claire spoke quietly, leaning across the table "As you all know, DI Jones doesn't say much but as he's the best man, he did tell Tom and me that he wouldn't be surprised if they eloped and then told us all about it after the event."

"I hope not. I love a good wedding." Alison looked forlorn.

"I'll ask Peter on Monday," Dee said.

"I wouldn't," warned Claire. "My best advice is wait for him to tell you."

They all nodded in agreement as the waiter approached the table to take their drinks order.

The buffet lunch offered a variety of nutritious options. A made-to-order hot stir fry was available alongside enticing salads and delectable low-calorie desserts.

Alison had served herself for the third time. "You won't believe who I've just seen" she whispered as she sat back down at the dining table.

"Go on then, who?" Dee giggled.

"Vicky!" Alison said tauntingly, "…and guess who's she with?"

"Who?" Claire piped up.

"Hang on. Vicky as in Jake's neighbour?" Dee asked before Alison could answer.

"Yes, and she's only with the Queen of Hair," Alison said flicking at her own.

"No idea who you're talking about," Dee said, exasperated.

"Sofia Bailey owns the best salon around here for miles. She's won lots of awards for hair and beauty. Wonder how Vicky knows her?" Alison puzzled.

"Probably because she frequents there," Claire said not bothering to look up from her tuna pasta salad.

"Hm," was Alison's reply.

Following a magnificent lunch the three friends had spent the afternoon in the treatment area and were now manicured, pedicured and massaged from head to toe. They had all agreed to meet after their treatments for a prosecco in the cocktail lounge.

"How amazing was that?" Claire asked.

"Very," Alison said, nodding.

"Thank you, girls, I've had the best day. I was just thinking about Helen. It's a shame she couldn't make today." Dee looked thoughtful.

"I know, but Clara had those horse trials - the gymkhana thing today," Alison said, taking a sip of her prosecco.

"We should definitely come here again with Helen; hen do or not!" Claire stated raising her glass in the air.

Dee stood up with some sense of urgency and evenly poured the remainder of her prosecco into Alison's and Claire's glasses. "I've just remembered we never went in the Cave Pool. I'm going to go and have a quick dip before we leave!" She didn't wait for a response but was already making her way to the door.

Alison and Claire exchanged a glance and clinked their glasses together as Claire said, "That girl never sit's still!"

Dee hung her robe on one of the many pegs opposite the entrance to the Cave Pool. On opening the door, the heat hit her. The entrance was lit by candles placed in alcoves flickering away. There was a sign that asked for silence. Dee took her time entering the pool as she didn't want to disturb any other guests who were enjoying one last moment of peace before returning to the onslaught of the outside world.

The water became deeper the further Dee headed into the cave. Dee could feel herself starting to float naturally and without effort. She moved towards a tiled seat positioned under the water. There were tiny jets of water soothing her neck as she lay down. She couldn't resist a quick glance round before closing her eyes; she was all alone.

Dee sat bolt upright, the sudden movement creating ripples in the water. Something had touched her leg. Realising she had become unaware of the time, she immediately began to apologise, "Sorry, I didn't realise the time, I'm…"

There was no one there.

Interpreting it as a sign to leave, Dee chose to swim through the water towards the candlelit steps rather than walking. Once again, there it was - just the slightest of touches. Dee paused. As she stopped swimming and put her feet down to stand up, she noticed that the water only came up as far as her waist.

"Who's there?" she shouted breathlessly.

No answer came. Dee looked all around her. She was alone. Scaring herself she made a hasty retreat to the steps, splashing her way through the water as she went.

Breathing heavily, she turned to take one last look behind her and, to her consternation, in the candlelit cave under the water, Dee could just make out what appeared to be a shape.

Her curiosity compelled her to investigate when others would have fled. She waded closer until she could clearly see the body of a woman wearing a green bikini. Her blonde hair trailed behind her in the water like seaweed.

Dee knew she was dead.

She launched herself out of the Cave Pool. Struggling to speak, she managed a gurgling, "Help." That got the attention of a young girl replacing white towels and plastic embossed water cups in the spa area. The girl ran over to her asking what was wrong and Dee instructed her between deep gasping breaths to be as quick as she could in fetching her two friends from the cocktail lounge and the manager.

The girl sensing the reality of an emergency did not argue.

Dee straightened up, watching the young girl exit the spa, proceed past the pool area, and make her way to the lobby.

Standing guard at the entrance to the Cave Pool, Dee could feel vomit swirling in her throat. Her hands shook uncontrollably as she filled a plastic cup from one of the water fountains hidden conveniently in little alcoves outside every sauna and steam room so as not to spoil the aesthetic.

The reality of the situation struck her, and trembling, all she could hear was her own voice in her head saying, "This can't be happening, not again!"

Chapter Two

Detective Inspector Jake Jones walked back and forth within his office, occasionally pausing to glance out the window at the car park of Gamblewood Police Station.

Gamblewood was a village of quaint cottages, a park with a duck pond and a high street lined by quirky old buildings that housed a few shops a café and a bank. There was, however, a new housing development near the local school, discreetly hidden on the other side of the park to preserve the village's picturesque setting.

Apart from the odd burglary between Christmas and New Year there had been nothing to pique the DI's interest. Despite keeping himself busy updating the kitchen in the cottage he had purchased from Helen following the murder of her aunt, Jake was starting to become a little bored.

"Sir; Sir!" Tom shouted as he came bundling through Jake's office door.

Jake turned. "Yes," he replied noticing that his Detective Sergeants face was alight with excitement.

"We've got another one!" Tom blurted out as he closed the door behind him.

"Another what?" the inspector asked in an irritated tone.

"A dead body, Sir," Tom replied.

Peter and Helen had spent the day accompanying Clara at a gymkhana held on the outskirts of Amberleigh.

"How did Dee find the exams?" Helen asked him as they climbed into the Land Rover to drive home.

He laughed. "You know Dee. Doubting herself but she'll be fine, I'm sure."

A voice piped up from the back seat. "I hate exams mummy."

"We all do Clara, but it's the way of the world. We all to have sit them," Helen soothed.

"I wish I was a horse then I wouldn't have to!" Clara shouted so they could hear her over the start of the engine.

Helen was just about to say something else when Peter's mobile rang. Helen could see it was Alison calling as Peter turned off the engine and removed himself from behind the steering wheel to listen. He was now pacing alongside the car, with his mobile phone pressed firmly to his ear.

"Wonder what Auntie Alison is ringing about?" Helen said pulling a puzzled face at Clara.

"Is Alison really my Auntie?" Clara asked.

"No, but Alison, Claire and Dee are going to be the nearest you ever get!" she laughed.

Ruth tapped her long fingernails on her desk. It irritated the junior journalist whose desk was next to hers, and Ruth knew it. Throwing her a sly smile out of the corner of her eye she noticed the editor beckoning her into his office.

"Just come in. Something's happened at Wellsdale Hall."

"That health spa place? Really? What sort of something?" Ruth asked the obvious questions without showing overmuch interest. "Don't tell me someone broke a nail!"

"More than that; they've dragged a woman out of some sort of fancy pool!" he answered.

"A dead woman?" Now Ruth was interested.

"Who knows?" he shrugged.

Ruth didn't want to waste a second. She knew if she wanted the scoop, she had to act fast. With a nod back at her editor who had already moved on to something more important on his mobile she left his office, picked up her jacket from the back of her chair and fled out of the front door of the Amberleigh Gazette.

All she could think about as she dashed to her car was that with a bit of luck the woman would be dead and in unusual circumstances. Not only would she have another great story to report on but more importantly the dishy DI Jones might already be on the scene. Unfortunately for Ruth the last time their paths had crossed it hadn't ended on the friendliest of terms.

Ruth undid one more button on her blouse and rolled her skirt over at the top to show off more leg. She smiled to herself. She was going to get his attention this time one way or another!

Back at the spa, Dee's friends were huddled around her.

"Dee I've phoned Tom; they're on their way." Claire spoke softly.

"I've phoned Peter too; thought you might need him here," Alison said placing her arm around Dee's shoulder.

"Why me? Why is it always me?" It was a rhetorical question.

A slender woman dressed in a plain navy-blue dress with a yellow and blue spotted scarf tied at her neck ran across to the trio followed by several members of staff.

"I'm the manager. What on earth is going on here? You can't stop people using the Cave Pool. Move away or I'll have you removed!" she shouted at the trio as several of the staff members surrounded them.

"Detective Constable Brown," said Claire stepping forward. "May I have a word with you over there?"

The manager followed Claire to a quieter spot. Guests as well as staff were starting to congregate.

"We can't let anyone enter. There is a body of a woman in there and until we know any further details I have had to secure the Cave Pool. It might be a crime scene," Claire whispered. "I've phoned the police station, and my Inspector will be here any minute."

The enormity of the situation hit the manager like a ton of bricks. She swayed as she blurted out a little too loudly, "Crime scene? Are you telling me there's a dead woman in my Cave Pool?"

"Yes, I checked. She's dead. Please don't go anywhere I need to take your name and find out as much as I can from you shortly." Claire paused. "For now could you please ask all guests and staff to leave the area. That would be most helpful."

"I'm Angela Myers. Yes I'll sort it." She looked ashen.

Dee watched as the manager summoned her staff and they efficiently formed a blockade preventing guests from entering the spa area from the pool. Other members of staff calmly asked the guests who had gathered to leave.

Angela approached Claire who had gone back to stand at Dee's side. "Do you think she drowned? Who is it? Do we know? Oh my god this is awful," she stammered.

Claire was just about to answer when she heard Tom's voice.

"Police, let us through!"

Helen was glad the call had come after the gymkhana had finished for the day. She knew the look on Peter's face. He could say a thousand words to her without saying anything at all. "Problem? Alison, okay?" she asked.

Peter turned to look at her but shifted his eyes in Clara's direction. "Alison's fine. I'll drop you two back at the Manor. Then I have to go out for a little while."

Helen mouthed, "Has something happened?"

Peter nodded.

"Where are you going?" Clara shouted from the rear seat of the Land Rover.

"I'm just popping to see Auntie Alison and Auntie Dee," he answered with raised eyebrows that only Helen could see.

"They aren't my real aunties you know," Clara replied.

Detective Inspector Jake Jones surveyed the scene. Although the staff had formed a human barricade, the onlookers were now three or four people deep and growing.

"Get police back up here immediately," Jake said to Tom who did as he was ordered.

Jake made his way over to the detective who had her back to him. "Claire; who found the body?"

Claire didn't answer, and Dee moved forward so he could see her with Alison behind her.

"That would be me!" Dee looked straight into his eyes.

Jake was surprised. Tom hadn't mentioned that Dee and Alison had accompanied Claire to the spa.

Jake took Dee by the elbow and moved her to a spot away from onlookers. Claire and Alison exchanged worried glances.

Jake had not seen Dee since the party Lord Henry had held in December at Gaitley Manor. It had not only been to celebrate Christmas but also the solving of the murder of Muttering Margo. He felt a pang of something he could not quite put his finger on. He looked at her, wisps of red curly hair spiralling around her face. She was as pretty as he remembered. Her green eyes looked up at him in anticipation.

Shaking his head, Jake said irritably, "It would have to be you, wouldn't it?"

Ruth had arrived quicker than she'd thought she would. The traffic had been light. Although she might hate to admit it, the grandeur of Wellsdale Hall intimidated her a little. She steeled herself. "Amberleigh Gazette," she announced showing her press badge.

The tall thin man, highly polished, looked up from behind the desk. He took one look at Ruth knowing instantly she was trouble. "And," was all he said.

"I'm here to report on the woman who died," Ruth replied, trying her luck. She wasn't sure if anyone was dead or not.

"Who said anyone has died madam?" The man's voice could not be any more sarcastic if he tried "The police and ambulance are dealing with the situation. I have not been informed of any death here. Now please leave."

Ruth was about to make a scene but thought better of it. Sticking her nose in the air and swearing under her breath she made her way towards a seating area in the lobby. The man watched her sit down and returned to his duties. He would keep an eye on her.

Ruth was rapidly hatching a plan. She had already spotted two robes resting on the top of suitcases by the ladies' toilets situated under the grand staircase. She waited until Mr High and Mighty was engaged on a phone call and quickly made her way to the loo, grabbing a robe as she went. The man at reception finished his call. He looked over to the seating area pleased with himself that she had finally given up and left.

Angela had been escorted by Claire to her own office. As forensics, ambulance and the sight of crime tape had descended upon the spa, the manager had experienced what could only be described as a meltdown.

Recovering somewhat she said to Claire, trying to be helpful, "I'll try and get any CCTV we have to you. I can't believe this has happened. We've never had anything like this happen here before, never. I just want to know who it is!"

"Angela it's fine. I'm going to leave you here. PC Stanner will stay with you. Do you need to call the owners?" Claire tried to be gentle with her as the spa's manager had turned into a dithering mess.

"Yes, sorry I can't think!" Angela was going paler by the second.

"PC Stanner, cup of tea for Ms Myers here; two sugars," Claire ordered. "And be quick!"

Back at the spa, Alison sat with Dee holding her hand.

"He was his usual charming self," Dee said to Alison rolling her eyes.

"I know, but it is his job. Jake is nice you know," Alison replied.

Dee nodded in agreement. She was sure he was. Dee always felt herself go shy when he was around. It unnerved her. The two women watched together as the body of a young woman was carried out on a stretcher. Strands of wet blonde hair could just be seen hanging down from under the blanket that covered her.

"Dee," DI Jake shouted across at her.

She let go of Alison's hand and went over to him.

"You know the protocol. Will you be okay to come and make a statement tomorrow morning?"

"Yes, of course. Who is she?" Dee asked fiddling with the belt on her robe.

"We don't know yet but it's only a matter of minutes. The locker band we have removed from her wrist was assigned to her on arrival by reception. One of my officers has taken it up to Claire who's with the manager now. Drowning is such a horrible death."

"Is that what you think happened?" Dee tried not to seem too eager for information.

"On the face of it, but forensics will tell us more," Jake sighed.

"At least I won't be a suspect this time!" Dee piped up.

Jake stared at her. "Really, who's to say you didn't hold her under the water!"

Just as Dee was turning an angry shade of red and about to give the Detective Inspector a piece of her mind he was saved by a scuffle breaking out in the crowd gathered behind the crime scene tape.

"What the…!" Jake managed to spit out as he manhandled Dee out of his way.

Alison was quickly at Dee's side. "What's going on?"

They both strained to see what was happening. Two women had jostled their way through the crowd and were now trying to get under the tape. Officers and staff were pushing them back.

"Jake, Jake!" wailed a familiar voice.

"God it's Vicky. What's she doing!" Alison said. The two friends looked dumbfounded at each other.

"Detective Inspector Jones," Jake said sternly to the pair as he pushed officers aside to let them through.

"Jake - Detective Jones," Vicky was clearly out of breath. "Was the woman in the pool wearing a green costume?"

Jake turned his back on the crowd and walked away gesturing for the two women to follow him. Lowering his tone he replied, "Yes Vicky, but so do many other guests. Why do you ask?"

"Our friend…we thought she'd gone home after her treatment but…" Vicky stammered.

Jake interrupted her. "What treatment?"

"Her massage, but we've just heard that a woman was found dead in the cave pool, and you know, what if it's Lucy and she didn't go home!" Vicky's eyes were on stalks.

"I think you need to take a deep breath. Let's get you some water," Jake soothed putting an arm around her.

"I'll get you one," the lady following Vicky said solemnly.

"Sorry, I missed your name?"

"No, you didn't. You haven't asked. I'm Sofia Bailey."

Jake watched as the tall woman elegantly made her way towards the water fountain.

"Jake, did she have blonde hair. I'm worried. We've tried phoning and Lucy's not answering She just left without saying goodbye…" Vicky babbled on.

Turning his attention back to her, Jake was just about to ask Vicky what time her friend had left and why would she leave without saying goodbye when DC Claire Brown came running over.

"Sir, Sir, I've got the name. We know who the dead woman is. It's a Lucy Walker."

Wellsdale Hall came to a halt as Vicky let out a spine-curdling shriek.

Chapter Three

Jake was fuming. His crime scene at Wellsdale Hall was turning into a farce. He'd already lost his temper and shouted at officers to remove guests from the spa and pool area once and for all. Now he watched as Vicky, his neighbour, had to be ushered away by her two friends and Alison after throwing herself at the doors of the ambulance insisting on seeing her friend who lay dead behind them. Angela the Manager had reappeared and refused to leave until she knew what was going to happen next as the Hotel's legal team were on their way and, to top it all off, he had seen Ruth, who for some reason was wearing a robe over her day clothes and making a nuisance of herself trying to get as much information out of anyone as she could.

Jake felt a welcome hand clap on his back. "Okay, so what do we have here?"

"Peter!" Jake spun around. "Am I glad to see you. You know I can't talk to you here, though. Meet me later in the Star and Crown?"

Peter noticed that Jake looked tense. Sensing the effect of the environment and the amount of people milling around, Peter knew how frustrated Jake must be. "You're a good detective. I'm sure it's just a drowning, nothing more. Who discovered the body?" Peter asked calmly as Alison hadn't said.

"Dee!" Jake replied, looking Peter straight in the eyes.

"Bloody hell, here we go again!" he said with a shake of his head.

Alison returned to the Spa looking flabbergasted at what she had witnessed as she searched for Claire. She could see Tom and Jake in the corner talking to what she thought must be someone from forensics and then she spotted Dee and Peter sitting upright on a sun lounger, deep in conversation.

"How is Vicky?" Alison heard Claire ask from behind her.

"They're all in what they call the Quiet Room along with the manager who's waiting for her lawyers or someone." Alison shook her head. "Vicky's really upset to be honest as are her friends. It must be such a shock."

"Very," Claire nodded. "See Peter's arrived. I'll go over and say hello."

Peter stood as he saw Alison and DC Claire Brown making their way towards him.

"Hello ladies, seems we have a drowning on our hands," Peter said lightly.

"Looks that way," Claire agreed,

"It had better be otherwise I'm in for it!" Dee exclaimed, taking the three by surprise.

"What do you mean?" Peter asked.

Pointing over at the Detective Inspector, Dee said loudly, "He implied that just because I found her doesn't mean I'm not involved somehow. Involved in what? Killing her? It's ridiculous! I've never seen her before in my life!"

Peter had to hide a smile. "Dee, Jake's just doing his job."

"He said who's to say I didn't hold her under the water until she drowned!" Dee's voice was getting louder by the second.

"And did you?" Alison asked straight-faced.

Dee scowled at Alison as they started to laugh. "It's not funny!" she yelled.

"You're coming with me!" The thin man from the reception desk said as he took a firm hold of Ruth's arm.

"Get off me, you pompous sod. I'm doing my job!" she spat back at him.

"And so am I. We don't need your type in here," he replied in a deliberately demeaning tone.

"My type? You're so far up your own arse with self-importance, I bet…" Ruth didn't get to finish her sentence.

"I bet? Bet what?" He glared at her and lowered his voice. "Watch your step. You're wearing a Wellsdale Hall robe but you haven't paid to be here. Shall we look at trespassing or stealing, madam?"

Ruth knew when she was beaten. She pulled her arm from his grasp. "I'm leaving," she declared.

"Yes, madam, you are." He spoke haughtily, his eyes burning into hers.

Upon hearing laughter in the spa area, Detective Inspector Jones spun on his heels. This was no laughing matter. He strode across to the group, Tom following quickly behind. Jake was disappointed with his Detective Constable and was about to tell her so.

"Jake, sorry, we should know better. We all apologise," Peter spoke up instantly, seeing the disgruntled look on the DI's face.

"You can all leave. Please come to the station tomorrow to give statements. Talking of statements DC Brown shouldn't you be in the Quiet Room with Ms Walker's friends and Angela Myers taking them?" Jake spoke with authority as he scowled at them.

Claire did not argue. She nodded in agreement and, with a slight wave of her hand, left them to it. Tom felt embarrassed for her.

"You didn't need to talk to her like that. We're all friends," Dee said annoyed.

Jake couldn't bring himself to look at Dee directly. He was ashamed of how he had just pulled rank. "That's my job," Jake sighed. "Please leave and we'll see you all in the morning. Alison we'll come to you; I don't want you to have to close Coffee Creams."

Alison managed a smile.

Peter ushered the two women towards the exit from the spa and pool area. Jake couldn't help watching as Dee's ponytail swished from side to side.

Dee turned back to look at him as if she knew he'd be watching her.

He turned away.

Ruth had arrived swiftly back at the offices of the Amberleigh Gazette and her nails were once more irritating the junior journalist as they tapped away on the keyboard.

"I have no idea how you manage to type with them things. Ever think of chopping them off?" she asked sarcastically.

Ruth smirked; she loved to annoy the youngster with her flat stomach and smooth face. "Ever thought of minding your own business before I have you thrown out of here!" she retorted, not looking up from her computer.

The young journalist was fully aware that Ruth could have her dismissed at any time. After breaking a major story at Christmas and earning multiple awards, Ruth was the editor's favourite.

"Ruth!" The shout came right across the newsroom.

"Just finishing it up, one minute!" she yelled back to the editor.

"We don't have a minute. It's going to press now; I want to see it."

"It's with you - you've got it - you're going to love it!" she shouted back smiling.

"I'd better do!" He slammed his door shut.

"You will," she shouted at the closed door.

Jake was tired. It had been a long day and it was getting late. As he entered the Quiet Room police officers and DC Brown stiffened. He dismissed them all but ordered Claire to stay behind. He wasn't going to apologise but he hadn't meant to upset her and explained as much. The DS watched as Claire nodded; he couldn't help feeling she might burst into tears at any moment.

Jake checked his watch. The day had run away with him. It was already nearing seven in the evening. He needed to head off to meet Peter. "Let's call it a day. It's been a tough one. Hopefully nothing sinister but we'll wait for the autopsy report. I suggest if you two have nowhere to be, you both go to Mr Wangs for a Chinese on me." He was trying his best to make it up to Claire.

"Thank you, Sir," Tom beamed.

"Yes Sir, thank you; that's kind of you," Claire said looking at the floor.

"It's the least I can do.".

Claire lifted her head and smiled at him.

Peace within his team was restored.

Peter entered the Star and Crown with a bit of a crash bang wallop.

"Steady there!" shouted the Landlord.

A few drinkers turned to stare at the commotion.

"Sorry, lost my footing," Peter explained as he approached the bar.

"It's been a while since we've seen you." The Landlord knew all his customers and the last time he'd seen Peter in his pub was just before Christmas. "Never forget a face."

"Yes, it's been a while. Well remembered," Peter praised.

The landlord knew the man who stood before him was a copper if not a detective as was the younger man who usually joined him. He decided against any further prying. "One pint or two?" he asked

"Two, please. Meeting a friend." Peter spoke while looking around the pub for a quiet table.

"Round there. Out of the way," the landlord said gesturing with his head.

Peter nodded as Jake too fell through the door.

"You two haven't already been on the sauce, have you?" the landlord joked.

Although Peter laughed, Jake didn't see the funny side and went back to check the carpet. "You need to get that sorted. You'll have a claim against you if you don't," he said.

Peter grabbed the two pints and headed over to the table that the landlord had suggested before any further exchange occurred. "Bit of a day then?" Peter was trying to be breezy. He knew Jake well.

Before leaving the force to set up and work alone as a private detective, Peter had taught Jake all he knew. He instinctively recognised recruits with a natural talent for detective work and Jake always showed plenty. Peter was secretly proud of the young man who sat before him.

"Hasn't it just? I can seriously say that was hard to deal with." Jake picked up his pint and took a large gulp. "Too messy for me, Peter. Too many people all over the place.

This better be a simple drowning. Lord only knows how forensics are going to handle this one!"

"Water is a problem. I dreaded any case that involved the sea or a river," Peter paused remembering a specific difficult case. "Washes away too much evidence."

"Yeah," Jake agreed unknowingly thinking of the same case as Peter.

"Haven't seen you in a while. Kitchen coming along?" Peter enquired.

"Really good actually. I'm rather enjoying installing it myself. Mind you with work, it's taking longer than I thought it would, but I'll get there." Jake sounded pleased with himself.

"Well, I know you didn't want to meet me to talk about your new kitchen. What's going on Jake?"

"I lost control today and I didn't like it, not one bit." Jake lowered his head as he spoke. "I'd already shouted at the officers before you arrived and then I go and upset Claire. I've sent her and Tom out for a meal at Mr Wangs to try and make it up to her!"

"Jake, it happens to the best of us. You're overthinking it." If he could he would have put an arm around him, he would have. "You're highly thought of Jake; so what if Mr Cool lost his temper. You're not the first and won't be the last. It was a difficult situation for anyone to handle. Personally I thought you handled it well."

Jake finally had a smile on his face. "Mr Cool?"

"Well, you were always a hard nut to crack. Helen says you have a handsome, steely exterior." Peter laughed. "It's nice to know my best man is human after all."

The landlord interrupted them. He was carrying two more pints. "On the house. Apologies for the trip hazard. All taped up now."

They thanked him and Jake shifted in his chair.

"What else?" Peter could see he had something else he needed to get out.

"I have that itch, Peter. You know what I mean. When something looks one way but it's another. I have an uneasy feeling about this one."

"Is it because Dee found the body? You do know that's all she did, Jake. She was angry at you for insinuating otherwise."

"I know; someone else I took my frustration out on. Looks like I owe Dee an apology too." Jake looked fed up.

Peter took his opportunity. "Better still why don't you take Dee out for a meal at Mr Wangs. I think she'd like that."

"I'll think about it," was Jake's reply as he moved on to his second pint.

Dee had arrived home. She was fuming. She was annoyed at her friends for laughing at her expense and even more annoyed at the Detective Inspector. She was stomping around her apartment having a hissy fit when her mobile rang. It was her Gran.

"I missed your call love."

"Oh, Gran, I've had an awful day!" Dee was on the cusp of tears.

"Love, get yourself a wine, sit down and you can tell me all about it. It can't be that bad. It's not as if you've killed anyone." The soft tone of her Gran's voice cajoled.

"That's the problem, Gran. They think I have!!"

In the Star and Crown Peter and Jake had finished their drinks and were ready to leave. They thanked the landlord for his generosity as they passed him on their way to the door, exchanged glances as they stepped gingerly over the taped carpet and went out into the night air. Peter commented on how long they must having been chatting in the pub after checking the time.

Just as they were about to part ways, Jake's mobile rang. He reached his hand into his jacket pocket and checked to see who was calling. Peter sketched a silent goodbye, but Jake gestured for him to stay.

When the call was finished, Jake turned to Peter. "You know that itch that I couldn't shake off."

"Yes." Peter had experienced that instinct on numerous occasions throughout his career.

"That was forensics. It's early days but they can confirm that Lucy Walker had no water in her lungs."

"Meaning she was dead before she went into the water."

Jake whispered, cautious of nearby open windows and passersby. "Exactly!"

Chapter Four

Dee hadn't exactly bounced out of bed the next morning. She was trying to justify to herself that it was all the stress of the day before. Finding a dead body floating in a pool with you could upset one easily but she knew deep down it was the bottle of wine she had drank during the phone call with her Gran that had her feeling a little the worse for wear.

She stood up and made herself a promise to drink only water for the remainder of the day. She took a shower, and walked around the apartment in her pink fluffy dressing gown, eating yogurt with muesli and honey. Both actions comforted her and made her feel better.

Breakfast completed and the dishes washed up, Dee sat staring into her bedroom mirror. She applied a little makeup and pinned back the top section of her red curly hair.

Knowing that she had to go and give a statement at Gamblewood police station, she decided to wear an old favourite - her green trouser suit. She paired it with a little white t-shirt and a thin green necklace made from beads. As She looked back at her reflection, she heard a noise from inside the office of the detective agency attached to her flat.

There was only one other person who had a key.

"Just coming!" Dee shouted as she unlocked the adjoining flat door.

Peter sat at his desk opening and closing drawers. "Hurry up Dee, we've got loads to do."

She joined Peter in the office, shocked to see him there so early.

"Surprised to see me, eh?" he asked still searching through the drawers.

"Just a bit, Peter. You're never here this early. You do know it's not even eight yet?"

"Yes, but you've got to give a statement this morning, Dee and I need to do a little research before we go."

He finally looked at her.

"What are you looking for? What research?" Dee looked confused and went to sit behind the new white office desk that was part of the office refurbishment she had in hand. She had hated the dull brown of the office and at the first opportunity had repainted it apple white, placed plants here and there and overall made it look much brighter.

"I'm looking for a brown notebook; it's seen better days. We had a difficult case involving a boy drowning in the local canal, long time ago, but I made lots of notes. Just can't seem to find it. I was convinced it was here." Peter looked perplexed.

"I haven't touched your desk, Peter," Dee said, opening her laptop to type up her statement. Then the thought occurred to her. "Peter what has a boy drowning in a canal got to do with a woman drowning at a health spa?"

"Nothing much. Apart from the same unusual circumstances. That boy had no water in his lungs either," Peter said nonchalantly, now perusing the new bookshelf that Dee had put up.

"Are you saying what I think you're saying?" Dee quizzed.

"What are you saying?" Peter didn't stop what he was doing.

Dee sat back in her chair. "That she was already dead before she went into the Cave Pool."

"Yes. Like I say, I made lots of notes at the time. Where has it gone?" He was partly speaking to Dee and partly to himself.

"Let me look. My Gran always says men can't find anything even if it's under their nose!" Dee pushed past him. She ran her finger over the many books placed neatly on the floating shelf but there was no brown notebook hidden among them. "Let me check the filing cabinet. What was the boy's name?"

"Hmm…now you're asking. Carl something – no, not Carl." Peter was back at his desk with his hands behind his head. "Robert. Robert Carlson. That's it. Carlson!"

Dee went through the grey metal filing cabinet that her predecessor Mary had meticulously maintained in an organized manner. There it was a file clearly marked *Robert Carlson*. Dee retrieved it and handed it to Peter.

"Well, there you are."

Peter looked as if he'd won the lottery. In a moment he was holding a brown tatty notebook in the air.

"Type up your statement as quickly as possible, Dee. You know not to leave any little detail out," he said thumbing through the notebook.

"Yes, okay I'm on with it. Why such urgency? Jake won't want us there too early. It's not as if this Lucy woman was murdered…" Dee's voice trailed off as the realisation hit her.

Alison was busy filling up the coffee machine with coffee beans.

"Morning Albert," she greeted her first customer with a cheery smile as he came through the pink door of Coffee Creams. "Usual?"

"Aye lass." He nodded.

Albert was Alison's most devoted customer. He arrived at the same time every morning, carrying the local newspaper, and always sat at the same table in the corner so as not to be bothered by anyone else.

Alison could hear Albert tutting and talking under his breath as she approached his table with his usual tea and toasted currant teacake. "What's wrong, you're all a bit of a bother this morning?" she asked him, concerned.

"It's not me you need to worry about. It's Dee. Look at this." Albert spread the centre pages of the Amberleigh Gazette out on the table for her to read "Weren't you there too?"

"Oh no, you've got to be kidding!" Alison turned the newspaper back to the front-page ignoring Albert's question. "Peter's going to hit the roof when he reads this!"

"Look, look at that." Albert read the opening paragraph aloud. "A dead body found in the Cave Pool at Wellsdale Hall by local Private Investigator Dee Firth…" Albert paused "You know it goes on to question if it's a simple matter of drowning or foul play!"

"I'm reading it. This is awful, I bet that cat of a woman wrote this!" Alison managed to get out between gritted teeth.

"Have you got to the bit that says Dee found the body and then goes on to say how she was a suspect in the recent murder of Margaret Darnley. It sort of infers…" Albert took a sip of his tea.

"I know exactly what it infers, Albert. This is not good," Alison uttered as she walked back behind the counter. "I'm phoning Peter."

Gamblewood police station was a hive of activity. The telephones seemed to be constantly ringing, and the noise level was much higher than usual.

"What's going on out there?" Jake was asking Tom as Claire entered his office carrying three hot mugs of tea.

"Lots of guests from the spa yesterday wanting to know if they need to come in and see us, give statements etcetera," Claire said .

Tom chipped in, "It's not helping, Sir. As it turns out one of Lucy Walker's friends - a Sofia Bailey and her husband - are some sort of minor celebrities around here."

"Really?" Detective Inspector Jake Jones rolled his cool blue eyes. He heaved a heavy sigh and ran his hand through his dark curly hair "That's just what we need!"

In the office of the Private Detective agency, Peter had been busy scribbling down notes from the old brown notebook Dee had eventually found.

Dee on the other hand had run into the bathroom to throw up.

Peter knowing full well that once again his secretary now turned super sleuth was once again embroiled in a potential murder smiled at her and gently asked if she was okay on her return to the office. He was met with a nod and not much more. Changing the subject Peter mentioned the décor and how the office was looking much brighter and more inviting. "You've done a great job with the office, Dee. Can't wait to see what you've done with the flat." He was trying to be as perky as possible.

"Hopefully you'll see it soon - just a few final touches, then you can all come over for a meal or drinks," Dee said, focusing on her computer to avoid eye contact.

Dee was checking the words she had typed as her stomach did another flip. Watching as she gulped hard, Peter's attention was suddenly diverted as his mobile rang. It was Alison. "I'll take this outside - wedding stuff," he lied.

Dee thought it was probably Jake asking them to come in sooner rather than later to make her statement. She couldn't help but have thoughts of how much Jake was going to enjoy accusing her of this one.

Peter stood outside the door of the agency. Paula from Flowering Fancies waved at him from the other side of Gamblewood High Street as she popped a bouquet of flowers into the back of her van. Peter returned the wave as he thanked Alison for the heads up on the newspaper article. Replacing his mobile back into the pocket of his jeans he found himself pacing up and down undecided on what to do next.

"You'll wear a hole in your shoe doing that," a male voice announced. It was Doctor Glen.

"Good morning, Doctor. Just thinking somethings through. Helps to clear the mind," Peter said only half joking.

"Yes, and from what I've read this morning in the Amberleigh Gazette you have a lot to think about." Dr Glen gently placed a hand on Peter's arm "Messy business."

Peter answered with a wordless smile.

Dr Glen took his leave waving goodbye cheerily as he asked to be remembered to Lord Henry and Helen.

Peter took a deep breath. He'd decided they should go to Gamblewood police station as soon as possible before any press arrived.

Gaitley Manor looked magnificent in the May sunshine. Helen had dropped Clara at school and was having a morning cup of tea and a catch up with her newly rediscovered father.

"Well, I say, looks like Dee has got herself involved in a drowning at Wellsdale Hall." Sir Henry was fishing for gossip as he placed the newspaper down on the side table.

"Now Henry, behave. Dee found the body of…who was it again?" Helen asked.

"A Lucy Walker," Sir Henry replied.

"You do know that I would have been there too if Clara hadn't had that Gymkhana yesterday. Sort of wish I had been." Helen whispered the last part.

"I know dear; so much more exciting than young girls riding about on horses isn't it." Sir Henry couldn't wait any longer "Helen tell me all you know."

"Me? I don't know anything." She smirked, trying to look as if she didn't know what he could be referring to.

"I heard you on the phone this morning with Alison and Peter was back late last night. Come now," he teased.

"You've got me." Helen rolled her eyes and took a sip of her tea. "Alison said it's a friend of Vicky's, Jake's neighbour. They think she drowned in the Cave Pool."

Sir Henry interrupted her. "A Cave Pool? Whatever will they come up with next?"

Helen continued "Unfortunately for Dee she went into the Cave Pool after her treatments and the body of the poor woman touched her as it floated past." Helen shuddered at the thought. "According to Alison, Vicky and her friends were all distraught. They thought she had gone home. Horrendous, isn't it?"

Sir Henry nodded in agreement. "I understand Peter left early this morning."

Helen replied, "Yes he did. I think he wanted to accompany Dee to the police station. She has to give a statement this morning."

"Yes, yes," Sir Henry said rising to his feet. "I will look forward very much to catching up with Peter's news this evening!"

"Henry you are a card," Helen laughed.

The police station was swarming with members of the public and a couple of reporters.

Jake sat calmly in his office with Claire and Tom.

"Just to clarify, we have my neighbour Vicky; dreading interviewing that one." Jake pulled a face "The other friends of the victim are a Louise Smart and the infamous Sofia Bailey. What do they do for a living? Not Vicky - we already know she's a stay-at-home mum."

Claire opened her notes. "Louise Smart is an estate agent - works for Blacks in Amberleigh and Sofia owns the largest Hair and Beauty salon - also in Amberleigh."

"What's the name of the salon?" Jake questioned.

"It's called Bailey's after their surname, Sir," Tom explained.

Jake wanted to say he could have worked that out for himself but didn't. "And Lucy Walker. One of you mentioned earlier she works at the bank here in Gamblewood?"

"Yes, Sir she did but she was only covering while the deputy manager's away. Lucy Walker worked mostly at the branch in Amberleigh. Is that where we're starting?" Claire asked.

"No, I'd like to start with her family. I feel we need to know more about her as a person," Jake said tapping his pencil against his lower lip.

His thoughts were interrupted by a knock on his office door. One of the PCs popped their head round the half-opened door announcing that Dee Firth and Peter were in reception.

"Good timing," Jake said. "Tom, are you okay to go fetch them. We can take Dee's statement here."

Ruth sat nursing her latte in the office of the Amberleigh Gazette. She was watching the time and twisted on her office chair deep in thought.

"What are you thinking about?" the junior journalist asked.

"What to do next," Ruth replied tapping her long red nails on the coffee cup.

"What do you mean?" asked the girl.

"Let this be a tip for you. After my article yesterday where do you think the majority of any other press might be?"

"At the spa I imagine," she replied.

"Maybe, or maybe at Peter's." Ruth looked meaningfully across at the junior.

"Who's Peter?"

"He owns the private detective agency here in Gamblewood. I wrote about his assistant yesterday, Dee Firth. She was the one who found the body in the Cave Pool." Ruth paused as she was becoming irritated with the girl. "Don't you know anything about Gamblewood? You'll make a pretty useless investigative journalist if you don't know who people are!" She grabbed up her car keys from the desk.

"I'll try harder. Can I come with you?" The girl was crossing her fingers.

"Not a chance in hell!" Ruth replied.

Dee sat in the Detective Inspector's office. Every now and again she would look from Claire to Peter but made no eye contact with the Inspector himself.

"Very concise, Dee," Jake praised as he read the statement she had already written.

"Thank you," Dee said, finally looking at him.

"Just to confirm the time, are you saying you went into the Cave Pool at quarter past three?" Jake asked her.

"That's what I think the time was, give a minute or two."

"The CCTV we hopefully get today can confirm the time," Tom chipped in.

"Sir, if I may I have a receipt from the spa bar when I ordered the glasses of prosecco. It might still be in my handbag," Claire interrupted.

"Explain how that helps," Jake asked a little snappily.

"It should indicate the time I ordered drinks for the three of us; then allow a few minutes for service, plus additional time since Dee didn't drink hers but poured it into my glass and Alison's before heading to the Cave Pool." Claire paused for a moment needing to draw a deep breath.

"You can go check; however, Dee could have been delayed for some reason, DC Brown, after leaving you and Alison. You would not have been witness to that. Therefore the only proof we really have will be the CCTV if there is any," Jake said.

Dee noticed Claire looked upset.

"I'll go with you, Claire." Tom piped up.

Once the pair were outside and Jake's door firmly shut Tom asked if his colleague was okay.

"I can't seem to get anything right at the moment. I don't think Jake…sorry, the Inspector, likes me any more," Claire said shrugging her shoulders and looking downcast.

"He can be like that you know. Don't worry about it," Tom said popping an arm around her shoulder then removing it quickly as one of their fellow officers walked into the corridor.

Inside his office, Jake had positioned himself by the window.

"Still being hard on Claire I see," Peter said with raised eyebrows.

"Not intentionally. She's a clever one. Claire's going to be a great detective one day. She needs to realise it," Jake said staring out into the car park.

"If you carry on treating her like that, she'll be a great detective for someone else!" Dee said sarcastically.

"Point taken," Jake said as he turned back to face into the room. He paused briefly. Sunlight from the window illuminated Dee's red hair making her emerald eyes, enhanced by her matching trouser suit, appear even greener. He looked away quickly aware that she might notice he was staring.

"So, do you still think I had something to do with it?" Dee asked nonchalantly.

"No Dee, I don't believe you do - never did. We still don't know if it is murder. There are other possibilities." Jake spoke calmly, returning to the chair behind his desk.

"Are you thinking she might have slipped and fallen; banged her head?" Peter asked.

"Or the heat from the pool," Dee chipped in. "It really hit me as I opened the door. If she'd been drinking who's to say she didn't pass out."

The conversation was brought to an abrupt by the ringing of Jake's phone on his desk. Peter made a movement towards Dee to usher her out but as Jake lifted the receiver, he told them to stay and they watched as Jake scribbled down notes as the person on the other end spoke.

"Anything else, anything at all," Jake asked into the phone. "…I see, I know, I appreciate it's a difficult one and will take time. Thank you." He replaced the handset and looked directly at Peter. He swallowed hard. "This has taken a turn. That was forensics." Jake paused and shook his head.

Dee was about to say something but thought better of it.

"She definitely hadn't been drinking." Jake looked like he was struggling for words.

"No alcohol found in her system?" Peter interjected.

Jake looked visibly shaken. "Absolutely not. Lucy Walker was six weeks pregnant!"

Chapter Five

Jake had promptly turfed Dee and Peter out of the police station, just managing to thank them for coming in as he had grabbed his jacket and ordered Tom and Claire back into his office.

"I take it he's off to Lucy Walker's' house?" Dee asked Peter.

"That's where I'd be going," Peter answered as they crossed to his car.

"At least he doesn't think I'm involved this time. Hopefully I'll be able to sleep tonight," Dee said as she climbed in.

Peter shut the car door behind him and started the ignition. "About that Dee…"

"About what?" She looked puzzled.

"Jake doesn't think you're involved but Ruth's written an article that infers you might be." He waited for her reaction.

"*Might be!* I need to read it - stop at the garage on the way back to the office - I'll get a copy!" Dee shouted at him.

Peter took a deep breath. "Let's go straight to Alison's for some breakfast. You can read the article there, okay?"

"No, it's not okay!" Dee stammered "Alison knows all about this?"

"Yes, she gave me the heads up this morning. Albert had the Amberleigh Gazette and showed her the article."

"Albert? This is getting worse. So, basically the majority of people in Amberleigh think I'm now involved in the drowning of Lucy Walker!"

Peter started driving without replying. There was nothing he could say.

The bell over the door at Coffee Creams tinkled.

"Helen, lovely to see you!" Alison was surprised to see Helen and hugged her friend as she entered the café.

"Doesn't do that to me!" Albert shouted across before ducking behind his newspaper again.

"Morning, Albert," Helen shouted. "Sir Henry would love a rematch sometime. He said you beat him at dominoes last week?"

"I did," Albert replied, looking pleased with himself "I'll pop up to Gaitley Manor soon."

"He'd like that very much," Helen said taking a seat at a table in the window.

Alison came over to take her order. "I can join you in ten, is that alright?"

"Sure, I'll wait for you. Can I have a tea and piece of your flapjack? "Helen asked looking past Alison at all the cakes on display.

"Absolutely, I'll be over as soon as I can," Alison replied.

Back in Jake's office at the police station, Jake had informed Tom and Claire of the latest report from forensics. "There's still a lot to do. We don't have a toxicology report as yet and forensics are saying they haven't found anything conclusive as to how Lucy Walker died but it's early days."

"Are we going to Lucy's home? I understand her husband returned a week ago," Claire stated.

"Returned from where?" Jake questioned.

Claire answered, "I'm not sure, Sir."

"Very well. Let's go and find out shall we," Jake stated and left his office with such a sense of urgency, that Claire and Tom had to run to keep up with him.

Alison had managed to find five minutes between customers to join Helen. They'd exchanged the usual pleasantries, and Helen had asked Alison not to ask about her wedding plans as there weren't any.

"I take it you've read about Lucy Walker and Dee finding her in the Cave Pool this morning?" Alison asked in hushed tones.

"I've just read it while I was waiting for you. Albert lent me his paper." Helen lowered her voice. "Does Dee know about it?"

"I phoned Peter as soon as I read it, but in all honesty, I don't know?" she replied.

The little bell over the door tinkled so Alison turned to greet her new customers but was taken aback as Dee barged in and stormed her way over to their table.

"Can you believe it? Have you read it as well Helen?" Dee looked flustered to say the least. Her cheeks were as red as her hair.

Helen nodded.

"Dee, sit yourself down and I'll get you a drink," Alison ordered, pulling out a chair for her.

"One for me too please," Peter said arriving in Dee's wake.

"It's all happening in here today," came the comment from Albert, hiding behind his newspaper.

"Morning," Peter said as he made his way over to Albert's table. "Do you mind if we borrow your paper just for minute or two?"

"Keep it. Read it inside and out," Albert stated as he handed it to him. "I'll be getting off. Plenty to do. See you tomorrow, Alison."

They watched as Albert left with a wave of his hand.

"Here you go." Peter handed Dee the newspaper and, went to peck Helen on the cheek.

Alison returned with mugs of hot coffee for everyone, a plate of cookies and a flapjack for Helen. "Give me a second or two then I can join you all," Alison whispered taking a bill out of her pocket and promptly placing it on the occupied table behind them.

The couple took the hint, and Alison put a sign up on the door saying *back in thirty minutes* as she closed it behind them. "Are you okay, Dee?" she asked.

"She just had to drag up Muttering Margo didn't she? That bloody Ruth woman doesn't bother to mention I helped to solve the case though does she?" Dee handed Peter the paper.

"Dee, it does say that she probably drowned. It's just awful that you had to find her body," Helen said soothingly as Peter read the article.

"I know. It would happen to me wouldn't it?" Dee said with a shiver remembering how she had felt as Lucy Walker's body touched hers. "It really was awful, Helen. I didn't get much sleep last night."

"No, I imagine neither of you did," Helen said calmly looking first to Dee and then at Alison.

"I was fine. Jim told me to shut up and go to sleep - I guess I was talking too much about it," Alison said, grimacing.

Dee and Helen giggled.

"Interesting, she's just clutching at straws, Dee. Was it an accident or not? That's what we're all asking," Peter said folding the newspaper. "Ruth knows no more than we do."

"That's not exactly true, Peter," Dee said looking across at him. "We do know something she doesn't."

"Why? What do you know?" Alison was literally on the edge of her chair.

"You have to keep this to yourselves," Peter said to them.

"Yes of course." They both agreed.

Peter nodded at Dee.

Dee took a sip of her coffee before announcing, "We know she had no water in her lungs which means she didn't die by drowning, and Lucy Walker was six weeks pregnant!"

Jake sat behind the steering wheel of his car outside Lucy Walker's' house taking a few deep breaths. He hated dealing with the families especially with something as delicate as this. For all he knew, Lucy's husband might not even know she was carrying his child. He got out of his car as Tom and Claire pulled up behind him in a police car.

"Nice neighbourhood," Tom declared looking around.

Jake noticed a few faces at windows looking out.

"Never been here before," Claire stated.

"Me neither," the Detective Inspector said as he pulled on his jacket.

Tom and Claire followed him to the front door and waited patiently a few steps behind as Jake introduced himself to the man who had opened the door. He invited them in, and Jake noted that he looked upset and as if he hadn't slept.

"Firstly, we want to say how sorry we are for your loss. If you're up to it, we'd like to ask you a few questions about Lucy?" Jake asked gently.

"Yes…yes; do you want a drink?" he asked.

"No thank you," Jake replied for all three of them. "David how long have you and Lucy been married?"

"Five years." David passed them a wedding photo that was displayed on the mantlepiece.

Jake looked at the picture and handed it to Claire to replace. "Thank you. Any children?"

"No. We had talked about it, but I'm away a lot. We hoped to try in the next few years though." He looked down at his hands.

Jake changed the subject. "I understand Lucy was having a spa day with her friends. Have they all known each other long?"

"Sofia and Lucy have been friends for ages. They knew each other before we met, but I don't know one of them that's been mentioned - a Vicky?" David looked up at Jake. "Louise helped us find this house. I think she's a good friend of Sofia's too."

"We'll be speaking to all three of them, Mr Walker and we'll endeavour to find out what happened to Lucy or how this occurred," Jake said in a determined tone.

"I've not heard anything. No one is saying a word. Lucy is – sorry - was a good swimmer. I just don't see how she could have drowned!" David put his head in his hands.

"As you know a post-mortem is being carried out as we speak and as soon as we know anything we will be straight back to inform you, I promise." Jake knew he was looking at a heartbroken man.

Claire asked, "Mr Walker just for the record can I ask what it is you do for a living?"

"I'm on the oil rigs; away weeks if not months at a time," he answered her.

Claire continued. "When did you get back Mr Walker and how long have you been away working this time?"

David took a deep breath. He looked as if he was counting in his head before answering the question. "Yes, this stint was just short of nine weeks. I said I would do some holiday cover. Pays well, you see. I'm here for two weeks, but they've said I can have as much time as I need due to what's happened. Then when I'm ready, I'll be back on a four-week shift pattern unless someone's ill or there's an emergency."

There was a knock at the door.

David said he was expecting his mother and Jake gave Tom the nod to go check. The Detective Sergeant came back followed by a lady in her seventies neatly dressed who flung her arms around David and they both began to sob.

"David, thank you for talking to us today. We'll leave you now, but we'll come back as soon as we have any further updates. Once again, thank you," Jake said.

As the trio exited, Claire glanced back to observe David and his mother still sharing a close embrace and discreetly brushed away a tear.

They reached their cars in silence until Tom felt the urge to say, "Sir, you didn't mention the baby."

"No. Think about it Tom. Why didn't I?" Jake didn't look at his Sergeant.

"Because there's a good chance it isn't his, Sir," Claire chipped in.

"Exactly, Claire," Jake said as he opened his car. "That man is heartbroken enough without us dropping that particular bombshell today."

At Coffee Creams the *back in thirty minutes* sign still hung on the cafe door.

Helen felt like she was repeating herself. "There was definitely no water in her lungs?"

"No," Dee answered her.

"Well, I agree with Dee, she could have passed out and banged her head, especially in the early stages of pregnancy. I used to feel quite dizzy at times when I was carrying Clara," Helen told them.

"It's a possibility, that's for sure. I'm hoping Jake has had an update from forensics," Peter said.

"I can't help thinking you think there's more to this, Peter?" Alison said picking up the finished mugs of coffee and the empty cookie plate.

Peter replied as casually as he could, ignoring the itch he felt when something was amiss. "No not at all, I'm sure there will be a simple explanation."

They women exchanged glances. They all knew when Peter was lying.

It was just after lunch. Ruth had arrived at Bailey's Hair and Beauty salon where the décor was as outrageous as the prices they charged. She had booked herself in for a wash and blow-dry in the hope that Sofia Bailey would be there and she could pry a little further about the dead friend, Lucy.

"She's not here." The girl towelling her hair announced.

Ruth was gutted.

"Her friend drowned yesterday - it's awful, but since we all knew Lucy, I think we should have closed today, out of respect," the young girl announced loudly.

"You knew Lucy?" Ruth asked as the girl finished towelling her hair dry and started to run a brush through it.

"Yes, she came here often, always having her hair done. Sofia and Lucy were always trying the latest Bailey products from the shop on themselves." The girl stopped talking as a strand of Ruth's hair got caught on the brush.

"Close, were they?" Ruth prompted her.

"Very." The girl stopped brushing and picked up the hairdryer. Just before she turned it on, she gestured towards a man who was wrapping a lady's hair in foils. She whispered in Ruth's ear as she bent over to change the brush she was using. "All three of them!"

Chapter Six

"Sir, are we going to Wellsdale Hall now?" Claire asked the Detective Inspector as they finished eating their lunch in the police station canteen.

"Not just yet. Maybe tomorrow. We've got officers over there collecting CCTV, interviewing staff and forensics are still at the pool. I want to do some more digging on Lucy first," he replied.

"So, it's the bank next then?" Tom piped up.

"No, we're going to see my neighbour Vicky, the one person who can tell us much more about Lucy. After all they're friends. Meet me there," Jake ordered his Sergeant and Constable.

They nodded in agreement and all three headed towards their respective cars.

At the Detective agency, several journalists had left messages for Dee, but one missed phone call caught their attention as they listened to the voicemail.

"Mrs Walker here. I am calling to confirm that you're open as I plan to visit at two-thirty to speak with you. Should you be unavailable at that time, please feel free to contact me on my mobile number, which I have provided." The voice was very matter of fact.

"Connected to Lucy Walker. Must be," Dee said looking mystified.

"I would think so. But let's see, we have forty-five minutes before she arrives. Let's collate what we already know," Peter said excitedly.

"Wonder why she wants to talk to us and not the police," Dee thought aloud.

Ruth was on her way back to the Amberleigh Gazette. Apart from a little gossip she had not learned very much and felt disappointed. All the employees seem to like Sofia and Lucy, so she had drawn a blank on that line of enquiry. Most of the staff thought it was a tragic accident except for one who thought it seemed odd but when pressed for further information said she shouldn't have said anything in the first place.

On leaving the salon Ruth had decided to make another appointment for the end of the week with the male stylist. She was surprised to find out that the man was Jett Bailey the husband of Sofia Bailey. Ruth had commented to the receptionist that she thought he would have been at home comforting his wife after losing her friend yesterday. Her words were ignored, and she was simply asked how she would like to pay.

She tapped her long nails in annoyance on the steering wheel as she drove. Ruth hoped she could justify the cost of two hairdressing appointments in one week to her editor and, more importantly finally gather some form of information from the hairdresser about his wife and Lucy Walker.

"Here we go," DI Jake Jones said looking glumly at Claire and Tom as he knocked on Vicky's front door.

The door opened and Jake's neighbour practically dragged him in.

Claire and Tom followed.

Once inside Vicky launched herself into Jake's arms. "It's been awful, Jake. I couldn't sleep. How could this happen to Lucy. She's the most wonderful person. I'll have to go and see David. Have you seen David?"

She spoke far too quickly and Tom and Claire were unimpressed with Vicky's performance.

Jake felt the same way. "Yes, we have. Can we all sit down, Vicky. We would like to ask you some questions about Lucy." He virtually had to peel Vicky off him.

"Yes, yes of course. It's just so upsetting, isn't it? Have you ever lost a friend?" Vicky looked at all three of them.

Even though Jake had lost a good friend and colleague in Cami during a bank robbery, he chose to ignore the question. "We could all do with a cup of tea, Vicky. Is that okay?"

Vicky didn't need asking twice. She had been dressed up to the nines all day wearing full make up and the highest of heels hoping her dishy neighbour with his dark curly hair and steely blue eyes would be popping in to interview her, but although she was happy to see him, she felt a little put out that he'd brought his sidekicks with him. "Sugar?" she asked.

They all declined but as she passed the Inspector his cup of tea, she flirtingly commented on how he was probably sweet enough. Tom and Claire shook their heads in disapproval whilst trying to hide their sniggers.

"I would like to start at the beginning, Mrs Wright. How did you know Lucy Walker?" Jake asked sternly.

"Jake, it's Vicky to you; you know that," she said tilting her head to one side as she sat down.

"Can you please answer the question, Mrs Wright," Jake said putting a steely authority into his voice.

Tom and Claire locked eyes, while Vicky was taken aback, visibly stunned by the Inspector's tone.

Exactly forty-five minutes later Dee and Peter swapped glances as they heard the outer door to the Private Detective Agency open, followed by a knock on the office's internal door.

Dee went to open the door to find a neatly dressed woman in her seventies standing before her.

"Please come in - take a seat." Dee gestured towards an empty chair placed between her desk and Peter's.

"I didn't know what to expect. This is much nicer than I thought it would be," Mrs Walker declared, looking around at the office.

"Thank you. I've just decorated it myself," Dee said happily.

Peter didn't want to waste any time. "How can we help you, Mrs Walker?"

Mrs Walker took a deep breath in and explained her connection to the late Lucy Walker.

"Does your son David know you're here?" Peter asked.

"No," she answered. "And I would rather it stayed that way for the time being. My son works on the oil rigs and is away for months at a time. He's absolutely heartbroken and I can't help feeling that something more happened to Lucy that day."

"What do you think could have happened?" Dee pressed.

"I don't really know. I never liked how close her and that fancy hairdresser Sofia were. It seemed too cosy for my liking. When David was away, Lucy would spend most of her time with her and some other friend who's an estate agent, but she never had any spare time for me." Mrs Walker looked down at her hands.

"Sorry to hear that," Dee chipped in.

Mrs Walker continued. "I may seem silly, but since David is my only child, I always hoped my daughter-in-law would be like a daughter to me - and Lucy was, until recently when things seemed to change."

"Towards you?" Peter asked.

"No, not really." Mrs Walker shook her head. "More in general; keeping a low profile, busy working on her hobby that sort of thing - felt like she was avoiding me if anything."

"Would Lucy have a reason to avoid you - like a little argument for example?" Dee quizzed.

"Not at all. I adored Lucy. I would do anything for her and David. "Mrs Walker paused but continued, "We did have a little fall out about grandchildren. I suppose I did tend to go on a bit asking her how much longer I had to wait to become a grandmother. Do you think that has something to do with it?"

Dee and Peter exchanged a knowing look. Dee was about to say something, but Peter interrupted her. It was obvious to him that the Walkers had not been informed of Lucy's pregnancy and he wondered why. "No, Mrs Walker, I don't believe so, but I hope you don't mind me asking? Apart from saying that Lucy was busy at night and weekends with friends, and not spending time with you, I'm not sure in what way we can assist you." Peter looked confused.

"You found Lucy in the Cave Pool, didn't you?" Mrs Walker looked at Dee. Her tone had noticeably changed.

Dee nodded and Peter stood, starting to move out from behind his desk. He had a feeling that this was about to escalate.

"As a private detective, I can only presume you didn't kill Lucy. Mind you after reading the local paper it does infer you could be involved," Mrs Walker continued, looking straight at Dee. "However, I'm not that naive and I know you helped the police solve a murder before Christmas."

"Yes, I did." Dee looked at Peter.

"Then help me. David is beside himself with grief and I want answers." Mrs Walker took a handkerchief from the bag she had placed on her lap and dabbed her eyes.

"Mrs Walker, we don't know if there's anything to investigate. Lucy could have simply had an accident or passed out in the Cave Pool and drowned." Peter tried to keep his voice as neutral as possible as he knew the latter could not be the case.

"Yes, but someone could also have pushed Lucy or held her under the water," Mrs Walker stammered in obvious distress.

"Mrs Walker, why would someone do that? Lucy was having a nice day out at the spa with friends. There is no reason to suspect foul play at this moment in time. I'm sure it will be nothing more than a tragic accident," Dee said trying to be as understanding and as convincing as possible.

Mrs Walker stood up and passed Dee a piece of paper. "Read that!"

Helen and Sir Henry were enjoying a wander around the rose garden at Gaitley Manor.

"Tell me what happened this morning, dear?" Sir Henry probed.

"It's so sad," Helen said linking her arm through his. "Lucy was pregnant; early days but still that's horrific for her husband and her family."

"Yes, dear, very sad. I do hope they find out what happened," Sir Henry said stopping to smell a delicate yellow rose.

"I've been thinking, everyone presumes it might be connected to the pregnancy; dizziness that kind of thing but you know I've been wondering," Helen said.

"Go ahead, dear, enlighten me!" Sir Henry urged as he resumed walking.

"What if it was some kind of aneurysm and nothing to do with the pregnancy at all. That could be another explanation." Helen looked thoughtful.

"That's very true, you are so clever, dear." Sir Henry patted his daughter's arm and changed the subject. "Can we talk about wedding plans?"

"Do we have to?" Helen asked rolling her eyes.

"I need to pick up the boys from school soon," Vicky declared.

"Just a couple more questions, Mrs Wright. You have done so well answering everything we've asked so far," DI Jones urged.

Tom and Claire knew nothing was further from the truth as at every opportunity, Vicky had tried to coerce their boss into coming round for a meal whether her husband was going to be there or not. They were impressed with how Jake had kept her on track.

"Mrs Wright, just to confirm, you met Lucy at Pilates as she's a friend of Louise who's a friend of yours." Jake looked at Claire who was writing everything down.

"Yes, that's what I'm saying, Jake. I met Lucy at Pilates through Louise. She introduced us." Vicky smiled fluttering her fake eyelashes.

"And you say you didn't know Sofia Bailey until you met her at Wellsdale Hall yesterday?" Jake enquired.

"Well not exactly. As I said before I knew who she was. Everyone round here does but did I know her personally? No I didn't, but she was lovely - very friendly. Louise liked her very much and I got the impression they had all been friends for a long time."

Vicky checked her watch.

"Do you have any reason to think that your friend Louise and Sofia Bailey might have had a falling out with Lucy?" Jake probed carefully.

Vicky was out of her chair. "Absolutely not. We were all having lots of fun together. Why would you ask that? Anyone would think you thought it wasn't an accident." Vicky's eyes were bulging.

"We just have to ask; nothing more," Jake stated calmly.

"Jake, you could ask me the same question. Did I have a fallout with Lucy?" Vicky stood with her hands on her hips.

"I could, Mrs Wright, Vicky, but I don't need to," Jake said trying to smooth over what was becoming a tense situation.

Vicky smiled and edged towards Jake as he rose from the chair he'd been sitting in. She placed her hand on his and looked into his eyes. "Yes Jake, of course you know me so well. No, is the answer to your question. I don't know of any fallout between them."

Claire couldn't stand another minute of what she was witnessing and came to Jake's rescue. "Sir we need to be heading back to the station and Mrs Wright needs to collect her children from school."

"Yes, DC Brown." Jake gave a sigh of relief as Vicky let his hand go and made her way towards the door.

"You're welcome to come back anytime, Jake. Maybe we can have a glass of wine next time. Remember I'm only next door!" Vicky was gushing as they left.

Under his breath the Detective Inspector said, "How can I forget!"

Peter and Dee looked at each other in silence. Mrs Walker had left after asking them to keep her informed and mentioned that any expenses would be covered before saying goodbye.

"We have our next real case, Peter. Not a cat or dog in sight!" Dee was excited.

"Dee, I'm not sure we have a case at all to investigate but we can most certainly ask around and that throws an interesting element into it doesn't it?" Peter said pointing at the piece of paper now sitting on Dee's desk.

"Can we talk to anyone at the bank. Do you think they'll talk to us?" Dee asked.

"Probably not, but we can try. I think I need to phone Helen. I might be late back tonight," Peter said removing his mobile from his pocket.

"Are you going to meet up with Jake?" Dee enquired.

"If he's around. Do you want to come too?" he asked her.

"Should I? Or will he talk more openly with you if I'm not there?" she asked, looking up from her computer as she tapped away.

"It's Jake. It can go one of two ways. I think you should come, Dee," Peter said as he went to get the white evidence board that sat neatly tucked away in the corner of the office.

"You're not bringing that anywhere near my desk," Dee laughed.

"No, it can stay here," Peter said taking a quick glance over Dee's shoulder at what she was looking at on her screen on his way back to his desk. "Dee, we've just been given a case; you can't possibly be thinking of going on holiday, are you?" He sounded worried.

"No, of course not. What's made you ask me that?" she answered, keeping her eyes on the screen before her.

"If you're not going on holiday, why are you looking at bikinis?"

Dee smiled at Peter. "Lucy Walker was pulled out of the Cave Pool wearing one."

Peter found himself at a loss for words, feeling more puzzled by Dee than ever.

Tom and Claire were in their office busily going through the statements made by guests.

Jake stood at his office window overlooking the police station car park. He was starting to doubt his gut instinct but still felt sure there was going to be more to this case.

His mobile vibrated on his desk. "Hi Peter, to what do we owe the pleasure?" Jake was trying not to sound as miserable as he felt. "…Yeah sure, usual time and place. Okay see you there."

Claire stuck her head round the inspector's door as Jake popped his mobile back on his desk. "Sir, I'm sure it's something and nothing but two of the guests say they heard people arguing in one of the saunas. Any thoughts?"

"I don't want this to be made out to be more than it is, until we know more, Claire. I think we should leave it for now." Then as an afterthought Jake added, "Sitting in a sauna is enough to make anyone tetchy!"

Claire didn't answer but closed the door behind her.

Jake sat down at his desk and opened his bottom drawer. The letter he had received a few days ago stared back at him. He had instantly recognised the handwriting. He touched the envelope briefly before firmly slamming the drawer shut.

"Gosh he's in a bad mood today!" Claire said to Tom on her return.

"He's definitely not himself," Tom agreed. "Fancy going to the new wine bar tonight?" he asked Claire.

"I can go straight from work, if we ever get out of here, but I can't stay long," Claire told him. Looking up from the two statements in front of her.

"That's okay. You know I think he's bored," Tom said

"Who's bored? Jake?" she asked looking up again.

"Yes, there hasn't been much happening here in Gamblewood. Perhaps it's a bit too quiet for him."

"Are you saying what I think you're saying?" Claire stared at Tom.

"Maybe." He shrugged.

Peter and Dee were happily chatting at the fish and chip restaurant in Amberleigh when Helen and Clara arrived to join them.

"Gosh I had to go all in to persuade Henry not to join us. He's desperate to know about this Lucy Walker. By the way, Henry says he hasn't seen you in a while, Dee. Maybe you would like to come to the Manor for dinner sometime soon?" Helen said as she sat down.

"Please, Auntie Dee, please come," Clara chirped in.

"Of course, I'm sorry I've not been to see you all sooner. I've been so busy with my exams," Dee said pulling a face at Clara.

"I hate tests!" Clara announced.

"Please don't start that again!" Helen said promptly placing a menu in Clara's hand as a distraction. "Now this is a lovely change."

"We're meeting Jake shortly so we thought we would have a quick bite to eat beforehand, and I thought this would be a nice change for Clara," Peter said patting Helen's knee underneath the table.

Helen giggled. "You know we both love fish and chips, Peter."

Jake wondered if he had time to go home before heading off to meet up with Peter.

Tom and Claire were finishing up too. "I'll go say bye from both of us," Tom said as he was halfway out the door. However, he practically bumped into Jake in the corridor as he was locking his office door behind him. "Sorry, Sir, we are…"

"I know I heard you. You're both just leaving. I'll see you in the morning early," Jake said solemnly.

Tom nodded an acknowledgement and returned to the office he shared with Claire.

"He needs a stiff drink or two. He's like a bear with a sore head," Tom said, revealing just how fed up he was.

"Or a good murder to sink his teeth into!" Claire responded.

Peter and Dee said goodbye to Helen and Clara. They waved as they drove away.

"You're so lucky, Peter," Dee said.

"You will be too one day," Peter said nudging her.

"Chance would be a fine thing!" Dee said laughing as they made their way towards the Star and Crown.

Jake had already left but as Tom and Claire passed the station reception desk one of the officers shouted them back. "Can you give a message to Jake?"

"He's gone home. Unless it's really urgent, with the mood he's in, I'd leave it till tomorrow," Tom replied.

Against his better judgement Jake decided to go straight to Amberleigh. He was unsure why Peter wanted to speak to him but hoped it wouldn't take long. His stomach rumbled reminding him it had been a while since he had eaten. He decided to pull over and pop into one of the convenience stores on his way where he picked up a French stick, ham, bits of salad and a large packet of crisps. As he headed towards the checkout he was distracted by a nice bottle of red. After paying he threw his purchases on the back seat of his car and drove at speed towards the carpark near the pub.

"Two visits in two days. We are honoured," joked the landlord. "And you, young lady are welcome anytime."

Dee felt herself blush.

"At least we didn't fall through the door this time," Peter said with raised eyebrows.

"All fixed. Danny has sorted the carpet," The landlord said as he poured Dee a glass of white wine.

As they sat down Jake came in not immediately noticing Dee's presence. "Peter, I've had a shite day. I'm not going to be the best of company." Only then did he see Dee sitting next to Peter.

"Hi," she said sheepishly.

Having seen the whole encounter, the landlord smiled to himself.

Once pleasantries had been exchanged and they were settled, Peter spoke in a low voice. "Jake, Dee and I had a visit today from a Mrs Walker, David Walker's mum. She's asked us to investigate Lucy's death as she thinks she's has been acting out of character. Her mother-in-law doesn't seem to have much time for her friends either."

"Really, that's odd. We've not heard from forensics today or the forensic pathologist. I was really hoping they would have given us an update," Jake said taking a sip of his beer.

"Lucy might have been acting out of character especially if she was having an affair and then ended up pregnant," Dee offered.

"Maybe that's why she'd been avoiding her mother-in-law too," Peter put forward.

"It's all plausible but let's pretend she was killed, and it wasn't an accident, why would someone want to kill Lucy Walker?"

Jake looked fed up.

"Ah well, we might have the answer to that. Look at this." Dee handed over the piece of paper Mrs Walker had given to her earlier.

"A bank statement. Where did you get this?" Jake said almost spitting his drink out at the same time.

"Mrs Walker…now there's a motive if you need one." Dee looked at him.

Jake made eye contact with Dee. "I've known people kill for much less!"

Peter dropped Dee back at her flat attached to the Detective Agency in Gamblewood. Following Ruth's article he wanted to ensure that no one was hanging around and that she was safe. Once he saw the light of his old flat spring into life, he started the ignition and headed home to Gaitley Manor.

Peter knew that Helen and Sir Henry would be waiting for him.

The light flashed on Dee's mobile. She had several missed calls. One was from Alison, another from Claire and three from her Gran. They all said much the same thing. They wanted to check if she was okay. Dee returned their calls as she ran herself a bath. All three calls lasted only minutes. Alison was watching a film with Jim, Claire was out with Tom and about to head home and her Gran was just in from line dancing and needed a cup of tea so it was agreed that Dee would speak to them all at some point tomorrow for a more thorough chat.

She tested the water with her hand and then slid into the warm bubbles closing her eyes.

Jake felt as if it had taken ages to get home. The neighbouring cottages twinkled in the night sky as lights shone through the breaks in the curtains. Jake's cottage in comparison sat in darkness waiting to be woken by its owner when he arrived home. Jake was struggling to open the door, carrying the food and wine he had bought earlier when he heard a softly spoken voice behind him.

"Need a hand there?"

Although it startled him, he instantly knew who it was. "Catherine…How? Why?"

"Let me help you in with those and I can explain," Catherine said, grabbing the wine bottle.

They entered the cottage together, and Jake went into the kitchen and then the lounge turning on lights, taking his time as he was trying to get his thoughts together.

"I know it's been a while, Jake, but I needed to see you. I did write to you to tell you I was coming, and when you didn't return my call today…" Catherine was busy opening the wine.

"Sorry, I didn't know you had called," Jake spluttered, handing her two wine glasses.

"Didn't you get my letter?" she asked.

"Yes," he said, looking down at the floor.

"Jake; you didn't open it did you?" She looked upset and disappointed.

Jake didn't answer and, in a bid at diffusing the situation, he held up the French stick and asked her if she wanted to join him for a sandwich.

"No thank you, Jake. We need to talk properly but for now, I'm here on business." Catherine looked at Jake fighting back her tears.

"Business? What business? Aren't you here on holiday?" Jake asked cutting the French stick in half.

"No, Jake. If you'd read my letter, you'd know I'm the new Forensic Pathologist. I've been trying to determine the cause of death of Lucy Walker." Catherine refilled her wine glass with water from the tap as she was driving.

"Catherine, I can explain." Jake felt so awkward.

"There's plenty of time for us to chat, but I want you to read this." Catherine passed over a typed report.

"She died of anaphylactic shock?" Jake looked confused. "Bee sting maybe, what was she allergic to?"

"I'm not sure she was allergic to anything. It looks like she was poisoned!" Catherine watched his reaction.

"Poisoned?" Jake spoke out as he continued to read "This say's *Poison Ivy*. What on earth?" Jake put the report down and picked up his full wine glass.

"It's a highly poisonous plant and in some cases can cause anaphylactic shock," Catherine said calmly.

"Yes, but Poison Ivy? Really? I didn't think it could kill someone; I thought the worst you might experience is a rash."

"That's why I thought you ought to know straight away. If Poison Ivy is swallowed or breathed in, life threatening reactions can occur." Catherine continued to watch the man before her. "I found residue of it on her lips and a very light dust on her skin as if it had been burned near her. Plus there's another thing…"

"What thing?" Jake was struggling to comprehend what he was hearing.

"She had a tiny piece of clingfilm caught in her earring. How odd is that?" Catherine too was obviously bamboozled by that one.

"None of this makes sense. Are you absolutely sure she was poisoned with Poison Ivy?"

"Yes, Jake. After all it's known as *the Kiss of death*!"

Chapter Seven

Tom and Claire had arrived in good time at the police station following a late-night message to arrive early from Jake.

"I hope he's in a better mood than yesterday," Tom said rummaging through his desk drawer.

"Me too," Claire replied. "What are you doing?"

"I need a new notebook; thought I had one in here," he answered without looking up.

"Here, have this one." Claire threw it across her desk at Tom who was unaware the notebook was flying towards him.

"Morning" Jake said and coming through the door, he promptly caught the notebook mid-air as it was about to hit him.

"Sir!" Claire yelled. "That was meant for Tom!"

"What?" Tom finally looked up from his desk drawer.

Jake placed the notebook on Tom's desk.

"Well caught, Sir," he offered.

"Thank you. School cricket captain back in the day," Jake shifted from one foot to the other. "Coffee in mine, ten minutes."

Claire and Tom acknowledged the inspector and Jake closed their office door behind him.

Tom went to make the coffees and as he was leaving; he turned to Claire. "I believe there must have been a further development."

"He seems a lot happier than yesterday, that's for sure!" Claire smiled.

Dee was excited. She finally felt like she had been given her first real investigation. Rising early she had decided to wear white cropped jeans and a pale blue jumper. She checked her reflection but felt underwhelmed. Then she remembered the blue scarf she had bought to wear at Sir Henry's annual garden party. Reaching into her wardrobe she could feel the luxury of the silk as she touched it. She wrapped it around her neck and once again checked her appearance. Sunlight streamed through her bedroom window, making the scarf shimmer with the colours of the sea. She nodded at the girl who smiled back at her from the mirror and said, "Just perfect."

Peter was already on his way into the office of his private detective agency. He knew Dee would be up and eager to start investigating. Following a late night with Sir Henry and Helen, Peter had expressed his gratitude to Mrs Wood, the housekeeper, for preparing him a substantial breakfast of bacon and eggs.

Now as he drove along the country lane, the picturesque village of Gamblewood emerged below him. The morning sun illuminated the rooftops causing Peter to smile. As he continued, suddenly the warm feeling of Gamblewood was abruptly replaced by a sense of urgency. Peter couldn't shake off the feeling, and he didn't like it.

He promptly put his foot down.

Alison had arrived at Coffee Creams later than usual. She was running around at a speed of knots to get everything prepared. She had just over an hour before Albert arrived, and she needed to make more cookies before she opened. She regretted letting Jim talk her into another film and more wine. As the coffee machine started, she rubbed her forehead and gave herself a talking to as she went to find her handbag, hoping it would contain some paracetamol.

Ruth sat on the edge of her bed rubbing body lotion into her long legs. Her mind was elsewhere. She hadn't gained any meaningful information about Lucy Walker and Sofia Bailey from talking to the staff at the salon. Her appointment with Jett wasn't for a couple of days so she was wondering where and what to do next when suddenly it came to her.

She grabbed her phone from the bedside cabinet.

"Good morning, Wellsdale Hall. How can we help you today?" the voice on the other end shrilled.

"I'd like to come as a day guest if that's possible either today or tomorrow?"

"Today is perfect. Can we take some details?" The high-pitched voice went straight through Ruth.

She finished her call, pleased with herself and started to pack a bag, putting in her favourite swimsuit and book. After all she needed to fit in.

Back at Gamblewood Police station, Tom and Claire sat open-mouthed in the Inspectors office.

"Sir, where did you get this?" Tom asked bewildered.

"Mrs Walker, Lucy Walker's mother-in-law has asked Peter and Dee to investigate Lucy's death. She gave it to them. This is a copy."

"Really. Why?" Claire interrupted.

"She said that Lucy hadn't been herself recently. She is however unaware of the pregnancy, so we need to tread carefully. Also she has a dislike for her friends," Jake said, pacing up and down behind his desk.

"Why would the mother-in-law have access to Lucy's bank statements?" Claire asked.

"Dee asked that very question. Apparently, she found it hidden behind the microwave when she was cleaning the kitchen. I believe David is struggling to come to terms with Lucy's death, so she's moved in." Jake turned to look at them both.

"A bank statement hidden behind a microwave. I doubt it!" Claire said.

"Me too. I bet she was snooping," Jake agreed "However that's a lot of money."

"It sure is!" Tom heaved a sigh "Wouldn't mind being a penny behind her. Didn't know assistant bank managers earned that much."

"They don't!" Claire rolled her eyes at him.

"Those deposits have come from somewhere," Jake said looking at both his sergeant and constable.

Tom jumped up from his chair. "I'll get the team straight on to tracing them, Sir."

"Good idea, Tom," Jake said smiling to himself wondering when the penny was going to drop. "…and you, Claire, are coming with me."

"To the bank, Sir?" Claire asked.

"No, we're going to Wellsdale Hall to talk to the Head Gardener."

"Sir, you've lost me now. The Head Gardener?" Claire shook her head as she spoke.

"One little detail I haven't mentioned," Jake paused and held out a piece of paper. "I have a report from forensics."

Claire took the report from Jake, read it, and handed it to Tom.

"What? Are they sure? No way!" Was all that Tom could manage to say.

"Sir, Poison Ivy?" Claire couldn't believe what she had read "Is that even possible?"

"Yes," Jake replied, grabbing his jacket. "We have a murder to solve!"

Dee had already watered the office plants and was busy sticking a copy of Lucy's bank statement to the white evidence board when Peter arrived.

"All okay here? Any calls?" he asked out of breath.

"It's only just after eight, Peter. What's wrong? Are you expecting a call?" Dee asked turning back to the white board.

"No, nothing's wrong. Just had an odd feeling. Something and nothing, I'm sure," he said sitting down at his desk. "How far have you got?"

"Well, we haven't got a lot to go on. I think we need to go back to where it started maybe someone at Wellsdale Hall saw something." Dee tapped on a picture of the hall that she had printed from the internet and stuck at the top of the white board. "Plus I think we should speak to Angela Myers."

"Angela Myers?"

"Yes, the manager." Dee turned and stared at him. "Peter, are you alright? I think you need a coffee and an iced bun from Alison's. This diet is doing you no good."

"I don't think it's the diet, Dee," he said solemnly.

"You think this is murder?" Dee could hardly contain herself. "So do I. How does someone working in a bank have all that money if they're not stealing it and then there's the baby. Maybe the baby's dad killed her and…."

"Dee stop. I know you're excited, but we need to stick to facts." Peter smiled.

"I know, just throwing scenarios out there, but I think she was murdered too. Question is how, when and by whom?" Dee pointed at a black faceless figure she had drawn on the white board.

Peter laughed aloud at the drawing. "Come on let's see if Alison will let us in for an early coffee before we head to Wellsdale Hall."

Sir Henry and Helen were having a morning cup of tea in the orangery. Mrs Wood was busy baking as Sir Henry had invited Albert over in the afternoon for a game of dominoes.

"Re-match, is it? "Helen smiled.

"I think we'll play five and three's this afternoon. See if the old man has his wits about him," Sir Henry said fondly.

"Albert always has his wits about him. Talking about that, what do you think about the death of Lucy Walker and her mother-in-law asking Peter and Dee to look into it? Very strange isn't it?" Helen looked out into the garden as she spoke.

"Very strange indeed, my dear Helen. We too could use our wits and do a little investigating ourselves." Sir Henry had a glint in his eye.

"What do you mean?" Helen looked at him.

"You are getting married my dear girl. I think you might want to make a few enquiries about having your hair done for the wedding by the infamous Bailey's," Henry said with a raised eyebrow.

"Ooh I see." Helen placed the teacup and its saucer gently on the coffee table, "…but I'll never get an appointment today."

"Mention you are my daughter. I feel sure you will be given an immediate appointment." Sir Henry had a twinkle in his eye.

"I can't do that. That's not right." Helen looked at her father. Excitement showed on his face. "Well I suppose I could. Shall I call them?"

Sir Henry didn't answer. He watched Helen google the salon and then call the number. He listened as she made the appointment.

"Well handled, dear girl. Now shall we make a list of questions that you're going to ask."

Alison opened the door of Coffee Creams to let Peter and Dee in. "You do know I don't open till nine o'clock," she asked them.

They both smiled at her.

"We do," Peter said as he took a seat at one of the tables in the window.

"Coffee? Anything to eat?" Alison asked.

"Coffee for me please," replied Peter.

"And an iced bun, Alison. He needs some sugar!" Dee winked at Alison. "Can I have a latte please? Have you given your statement to the police yet?"

"Sure. Just let me get the cookies out of the oven and I'll be with you," Alison said running into the kitchen, shouting over her shoulder. "Yeah, the police came here yesterday afternoon!"

"She's a little frazzled this morning," Peter whispered over the table.

Dee didn't answer. She just pulled a face and nodded.

"Jake seemed shocked about the amount of money Lucy had in her bank account," Dee mentioned breaking the silence as Alison approached from the kitchen with two broken cookies.

"Money? Who has a lot of money?" Alison asked as she placed the cookies on the table. "They're on me."

"Lucy Walker," Dee answered.

Alison was already over by the coffee machine making Dee's latte.

"Lucy Walker? Wouldn't think so. I know she had a good job at the bank, but I wouldn't think it pays that well. Maybe she's inherited it or better still stole it!" Alison's voice had taken a sinister turn as she handed them their coffees.

"You're as bad as Dee!" Peter laughed "No one's stolen anything."

"We don't know that for sure. Just another line of enquiry to follow," Dee said.

"Exactly how much are we talking?" Alison asked.

Dee looked at Peter for approval and then beckoned to Alison to bend down so she could whisper in her ear.

"How much?" Alison shouted louder than she thought she had as the little bell tinkled over the door of and Albert arrived with the daily local newspaper in his hand.

"Good morning. How much is what?"

"The price of food!" Alison jumped in. "Usual Albert?"

Albert nodded. Peter and Dee watched him thumbing through the pages of his newspaper. Peter shouted over "You're either a quick reader or there's nothing of interest in there today."

"No there's not. I was hoping this young lady might be in it." He nodded in Dee's direction and then muttered under his breath, "Fancy being murdered in a Cave Pool"

Dee and Peter exchanged glances. They immediately knew that, at this point, it was not yet known publicly that Lucy had died prior to entering the pool.

Dee felt the need to ask, "Albert why would you think it's murder. It could just be a simple accident."

Albert looked over the top of his paper. "Because murder follows you around!"

Detective Jake Jones and Detective Constable Claire Brown sat in the office of Angela Myers. The walls were adorned with pictures of Wellsdale Hall, staff members and certificates of awards that Wellsdale hall and Angela herself had won.

"Sorry to keep you waiting, I had to finish up with the staff. Our legal team will be here shortly if you wish to question me." Angela sounded very matter of fact.

"We're not here to interview you, Angela." Jake had a soothing tone to his voice. "I see you've won lots of awards"

Angela looked over at the wall. "Yes a few. Why are you asking me about them?"

"I'm not; it's merely an observation." Jake smiled at her and continued, "Can you tell me the name of your Head Gardener please and where we can find him."

"Eric, why?"

Jake didn't like Angela's tone and Claire could see it. "We need to talk to him; nothing more than that," she butted in.

"If you wish to talk to any members of my staff, you can wait for our legal team to arrive." Angela was if anything even sterner as before.

"If we've upset you, we'll give you a minute or two, then pop back," Jake said as he rose from his chair.

"You haven't upset me." Angela glared as her phone rang.

"We'll leave you to it." Jake smiled as he opened the door.

Once they left Angela's office and the door clicked shut, Claire said, "I presume we'll go and find him on our own."

"Too right," was Jake's reply.

Ruth was having a swim in the kidney-shaped indoor pool. A few guests wished her a good morning as they swam past. The pool girls hadn't been very helpful and neither had the girl on reception. Any questions Ruth had asked about the incident in the Cave Pool fell on deaf ears. It was becoming apparent that all staff had been informed not to discuss it with anyone.

Ruth convinced herself to swim two more lengths before heading into one of the saunas.

Jake and Claire were sauntering around the outside of Wellsdale Hall. The gardens were extensive, and Jake was trying to spot any sign of a greenhouse or of ground staff working.

"It's pretty quiet; not many guests out here and I haven't seen one member of staff. Jake, look there's the tennis courts." Claire pointed them out in the distance.

"Let's see if we have better luck down there," Jake said striding ahead.

"Yes, Sir," Claire said struggling to keep up.

In the manager's office inside Wellsdale Hall, Angela was all a fluster The legal team had arrived and were firing so many questions at her, most of which she couldn't answer. "Can we just stop for a moment please; I've already had the police here this morning and I've no idea where they've gone and all these questions are too much. I can only tell you what I saw and experienced on that day. I know nothing about Lucy Walker and as I've told the police, and I'm now telling you, I never met her. She was just one of many guests here at Wellsdale Hall that day. It's all so unfortunate."

"Yes, Ms Myers it is," said the young man in the grey suit sat opposite her. He leaned forward. "We're here to protect you, your staff and the reputation of Wellsdale Hall. No one is accusing you of anything. We're all on the same side."

"I wish you would tell that to the Inspector that was here earlier. He makes me feel like this is all my fault," Angela blurted out. Tears started to fall.

"As long as all procedures have been followed and checks regularly done and recorded you have nothing to worry about," the young man said, tapping away on his iPad.

Angela suddenly sat bolt upright as she recognised that, should Lucy Walker's death be deemed accidental and any health and safety guidelines found lacking, responsibility would fall upon her. Indeed, she realised she could be facing the sack.

Jake waved at a couple enjoying a morning game of tennis as he made his way towards them.

The couple promptly stopped playing and came over to the netting.

"Hello, Jake. I thought it was you."

"Hi, Nigel. Haven't seen you for a while," Jake replied.

"No, I've left the gym and joined here. You should do the same. Never know who you're going to meet." Nigel wrapped his arm around the shoulders of the pretty brunette next to him. "Guess you're here about the drowning the other day. Such sad news."

"Yes - we are - it is. I was trying to find a gardener or any maintenance worker," Jake said nonchalantly.

The brunette spoke cheerily. "You'll find Eric doing the plants in the courtyard. That's where he was when I came out of the changing rooms about ten minutes ago."

"Eric? Is he one of the gardeners here?" Claire asked.

"Eric looks after all the grounds here. He's the one in charge; been here a long time." The brunette smiled nudging into Nigel.

"Thank you, we'll let you return to your game. We'll have to have a pint sometime, Nigel," Jake said starting to walk away.

"They seem a nice couple, Sir," Claire said chasing after her boss.

"She might be nice, but he's a womaniser. He had to leave the gym as he'd run out of ladies to try his luck on!" Jake said as he quickened his pace.

"Will you meet him for a pint then, Sir?" Claire struggled to say as she was now running to catch the inspector up.

"Absolutely not!" came the reply.

Peter and Dee had also arrived at Wellsdale Hall. "Looks like we're not the only one's here," Peter said pointing at Jake's car. "I think we should wait till they leave."

"I don't." Dee sounded cross. "We're doing our own investigation on behalf of Mrs Walker. What's that got to do with Jake?"

"Nothing, when you put it like that, but let's just collect our thoughts," Peter said.

Dee was already getting out of the car. "I have many thoughts, and I don't have to collect them!" She had already closed the car door and was striding towards the entrance as Peter locked the car and set off casually behind her. He knew from talking to Helen that this had more to do with Dee's personal feelings towards Jake than it did with the case.

Dee was chatting away to a girl on reception when he caught up with her. He took a seat on the comfy flowered sofa and a girl dressed in a white uniform asked him if he would like a cup of cucumber water. The thought made Peter wince, and he declined.

"Ms Myers is tied up now, but she knows we're here. She said if we could wait, she'll see us shortly." Dee looked pleased with herself.

"It's a nice day. Fancy a walk round the gardens?" Peter asked Dee.

"Why not? They did say it might be sometime before she's free. She's in a meeting with a legal team." Dee shrugged.

"I bet she is," Peter said, raising his eyebrows.

Ruth had moved from the indoor pool to the saunas and was now sitting in the courtyard on a lounger, drinking a glass of iced water. Although it was May and the sun was shining, there remained a slight chill in the air so Ruth was using the blanket that had been hanging over the arm of the lounger. With the sun on her face and the warmth of the blanket on her legs, Ruth rested her head back and briefly closed her eyes. She froze suddenly recognising a male voice - Inspector Jake Jones. She placed her water down on the little table nestled between the loungers and grabbed her book quickly. Covering her face, she opened it at random and pretended to read.

Jake looked around him. There was a person lying on a lounger reading a book, a couple sitting on a wooden padded bench both on their phones, and two ladies chatting happily on bean bags. No one seemed to notice their presence.

"Eric, can we speak to you please. I'm Inspector Jones and this is DC Brown." Jake was being almost excessively polite.

"Urh yeah, sure," Eric said, removing his gardening gloves. "Is everything alright?"

"Yes, Eric. We'd just like to ask you about the beautiful gardens," Jake continued smiling.

"They are stunning a credit to you," Claire said beaming.

As Eric thanked them, they manoeuvred him towards a table with four chairs under a gazebo.

"Thank you, but how can I help? What do you need to know?" Eric looked worried.

"Please don't be concerned. Have you ever had to deal with Poison Ivy here in the gardens at Wellsdale Hall or have you ever come across it?" Jake kept his questioning light.

Eric looked thoughtful. "We only have English Ivy here. Completely harmless. Grows on the walls, see." He pointed to the wall at the rear of the courtyard.

"It's Poison Ivy we;re interested in learning about," Jake continued.

"You won't find that here, young man, I'm sure of that." Eric smiled back.

"Why?" Claire interrupted.

"It grows in North America," Eric said slumping back in his chair.

They expressed their gratitude to Eric for his time before proceeding to the reception area. Upon arrival, a woman carrying a tray offered each of them a glass of water and inquired if she could be of assistance. Jake flashed his badge and asked to speak to the manager if she was now free.

Ruth had overheard the whole conversation. Her mind was going into overdrive. There was only one reason the inspector was asking about Poison Ivy and that was that they believed someone had been poisoned with it. Was that someone Lucy Walker?

Peter and Dee had seen enough of the gardens and in any event Dee was starting to get a little cold. They headed back towards reception.

Claire spotted Dee first. "Sir, Dee and Peter are here."

Jake turned round to see Peter giving him a wave. Dee did likewise.

"Peter, Dee; hello, what brings you here? Oh don't tell me. Mrs Walker?" Jake said.

"Yes, she has," Dee replied through gritted teeth. "Hope the inspector is treating you well, Claire?"

"Yes, Dee." Claire's eyes were on stalks. "Very well. In fact he treated Tom and I to a Chinese the other day at Mr Wangs."

"Yes, I did, and I owe you one too by way of an apology." Jake smiled at her.

"You do?" Dee's cheeks were taking on a rosy tinge.

"Yes, I do." Jake was just about to continue when Angela Myers appeared at the side of them accompanied by a young man in a grey suit. Jake instantly knew he was a lawyer.

"Ms Myers is happy to answer any of your questions. Who would like to go first?" the young man asked.

"Please do" Peter gestured towards Jake and Claire "We can wait."

"Thank you," Jake replied.

Dee watched as Jake, Claire, Angela and the young man disappeared into a side room.

"I know what you're thinking," Peter said to Dee.

"No, you don't" Dee replied sheepishly. She was pleased he didn't, or he would have known she was thinking how handsome Jake looked in the pink shirt he was wearing.

Ruth needed to reach the dining room as her table was ready for lunch, but the only route was through reception. Not only was she trying to avoid been seen by Inspector Jones, she had also spotted Peter and Dee. She asked a staff member if there was any other way. It was her lucky day. There was another entrance at the rear of the building near the treatment rooms. Hoping Peter and Dee hadn't seen or recognised her she made her exit. The last thing she needed was an argument in front of guests about the article she had written.

While waiting for Jake and Claire to finish interviewing the manager, Dee had become bored and was perusing the clothes shop attached to the reception area.

"Can I help you with anything?" a trendily dressed lady asked her.

"I'm okay, thank you. You have some beautiful swimwear," Dee replied.

The assistant smiled and made her way towards another customer returning a moment or two later to say, "I recognise your scarf. Did you get that from Natalie's shop in Amberleigh?" She reached out to touch the silk of the scarf.

Dee was slightly taken aback. "Yes - yes I did. I love it." She patted her scarf.

"If we don't have your size or the right colour, I shouldn't be telling you, but Natalie is a good friend, and she also sells those bikinis," the woman whispered. "Might be cheaper there too."

Dee thanked her and when she rejoined Peter she was scrolling down her phone. "Hope you're not looking at bikinis again." He laughed.

Dee turned her phone around to show him. "Indeed I am." She smiled as Jake and Claire came out of the side room followed by the young lawyer.

Jake made a gesture that he would call him as Peter and Dee were ushered away by the lawyer usher.

Angela Myers stretched out a hand to greet them both. She looked exhausted.

Peter explained that they were there on the behalf of Mrs Walker and the lawyer made it very plain that in his opinion this had been nothing but an unfortunate incident. He continued to explain that all health and safety regulations at Wellsdale Hall were fully checked, met and regularly updated. Unless they could help in any other way he said he felt that Ms Myers should be allowed to continue with the rest of her day.

Peter and Dee took their leave. They both knew they weren't going to achieve anything by arguing with the lawyer.

Dee looked disappointed. "That was short and sweet."

Peter checked his phone. "Cheer up. We're meeting Jake for lunch in Amberleigh. Sometimes a police badge helps to obtain more information than we can. Let's see what they found out."

Jake sat staring at the menu in the little teashop in Amberleigh. He didn't want much as he'd arranged to meet Catherine at Mr Wangs early evening. His thoughts were interrupted by Dee and Peter's arrival.

"Take a seat." Jake gestured to them noticing the way Dee's outfit complemented her red hair. "That's a lovely scarf, Dee."

"Thank you," Dee replied feeling annoyed that he had not remembered her wearing it at the garden party. She had then to ask herself why she felt this was so annoying.

Peter noticed that Dee had gone off into one of her daydreams and nudged her to bring her back to reality.

"We learned nothing, Jake. Just short sharp thrift from the lawyer. Angela Myers never said a word," Peter said as he passed Dee the menu.

"We weren't much more successful. She answered some basic questions but nothing more. Like you say, the lawyer spoke more than she did." Jake beckoned to the waitress to come and take their order.

"Have to get back?" Peter asked Jake.

"Yes; there was a development last night." Jake lowered his head so as not to be overheard. "It looks like Lucy Walker was poisoned."

"What with?" Dee piped up.

"Poison Ivy."

"Well, I never. That's a first. Poison Ivy, how unusual." Peter lapsed into deep thought.

They placed their order as Jake checked the time on his watch but in fact their sandwiches arrived very promptly.

They ate asking Jake their further questions, but he apologised, saying he was sorry, but he really had to leave. He left more than half his food behind.

"Doesn't he eat much when he's on a case?" Dee asked Peter looking at Jake's plate.

"Can't say I've ever noticed, but murder by poisoning can do that to a man's stomach," Peter answered.

Dee put down the sandwich in her own hand. "And a woman's!"

Chapter Eight

Jake was behind his office desk back at the police station. He had just finished an important phone call and was thinking about his next move when Tom knocked on his door.

"Ah," said Jake. "Can you and Claire come in please. We're going to need a cup of tea too. We have something important to discuss."

Within minutes Claire and Tom were sitting in Jake's office waiting in anticipation. The inspector was sipping his tea, deep in thought.

Tom broke the silence. "Sir, you mentioned something important to discuss?"

"Yes, sorry. There's so much going on," Jake said apologising into his teacup.

They watched him gather his thoughts and took a huge deep breath.

"We have it from above, we're now officially investigating the murder of Lucy Walker. She died of anaphylactic shock from being poisoned with Poison Ivy. Further traces of Poison Ivy have been found in her throat and ash on her torso. It's an unusual method and poison to use to say the least, but someone knew how to use it and where to obtain it from." Jake paused and took another sip of his tea.

"Sir, do we presume they did it for the money. The husband for example?" Claire asked.

"We have the unfortunate job of telling Mr Walker and his mother Lucy's death is now a murder enquiry and is no longer being treated as a potential accident. It will be interesting to find out what he does know about the money. If anything - after all it's all in Lucy's name," Jake said.

Tom cleared his throat. "They're still tracing the money at the moment, Sir. Might not be as easy as we first thought, as it might be from a few overseas accounts, but the team are dealing with it."

"How are we on CCTV from Wellsdale Hall," Jake asked.

"They're stalling," Claire replied. "I thought you might have chased up the CCTV footage this morning and mentioned about the poisoning from the forensic report."

"I wanted to let them stew for a little longer. The manager is panicking about her job, and the lawyer is worried about them being sued to high heaven hence not answering any questions," Jake said.

"They will have to now!" Tom replied.

"Sir, are you going to make the Walkers aware of Lucy's pregnancy?" Claire asked intently.

"I think we have to," Jake said grabbing his jacket. "Time to go."

Dee and Peter were nearly back in Gamblewood when Peter took a detour.

"Where are we going?" Dee asked.

"Who do we know with an extensive knowledge of plants?" Peter asked her.

"Paula. I thought we were going to Flowering Fancies to ask her," Dee said looking down at her phone.

"Henry," Peter said taking a left rather than heading into the village.

"Sir Henry. Yes of course and he has that amazing library. I bet we'll find some information in there too!" Dee had put her phone down and was now excited again.

"What have you been thinking about?" Peter quizzed "I've never known you so quiet."

"It's Jake," Dee pulled a face. "It irritates me that we gave him Lucy's bank statement but at lunch he gave us no information in return. It just seems one-sided to me."

Peter took a different tack and jokingly said, "Seems our handsome detective irritates you quite a lot. I wonder why?"

"Give over Peter. Grow up," Dee chided him. However, Peter did have a point. Why did he annoy her so much?

Alison was having a quiet afternoon when Brenda and Pauline from Wellsdale Hall walked in.

"Hello ladies. What do you fancy this week?" Alison asked cheerily.

"Just tea for two please. We can't stay long. We're on our way to Wellsdale Hall" Brenda answered.

"Ask her. Go on." Pauline was nudging Brenda in the side.

"Ask me what?" Alison said grabbing a teapot from the side.

"Can you spend ten minutes of your time with us?" Brenda asked.

"Course I can, ladies. I hope it's nothing major?" Alison joked.

"Pauline thinks it is," whispered Brenda across the counter.

Peter and Dee walked into the library to find Sir Henry and Albert playing a game of dominoes.

"He's a sharp one, Henry. I hope you're not playing for money," Peter teased.

"Peter! "Sir Henry rose to his feet. "What a pleasure. Dee too. Come in, come in." At that, Sir Henry placed a firm kiss on Dee's cheek.

Mrs Wood had heard the door and came rushing in. "Sir Henry - oh Peter. I wondered who it was. I thought I hadn't heard the doorbell ring," Mrs Wood put her hand on her chest. "Dee, lovely to see you. It's been awhile."

Dee adored Mrs Wood and went over to kiss her. "I hope Peter thanked you for that quiche you made me last week. It was lovely. Thank you once again."

"You've been studying hard, girl. It's the least I could do. It's no bother for me to rustle you up a little something from time to time," Mrs Wood beamed. "Now then, are we all having a fresh pot of tea?"

The question was met with enthusiasm all round and Mrs Wood left them saying she would be back shortly.

"Henry, we need some help. What do you know about Poison Ivy?" Peter asked forgetting that Albert was sitting there.

"Gives you a nasty rash; I know that much," Albert piped up placing a domino down.

"Ever know anyone die from it?" Dee asked a little too directly.

Albert and Sir Henry turned to look at her. Sir Henry spoke first. "Die from Poison Ivy? Of course not."

Then Albert said, "I do but it was a dog. The silly bugger ate the stuff!"

"In Gamblewood? Albert; the dog ate it from somewhere around here?" Dee's eyes were huge.

"No of course not. It was my Annie's brothers' dog. They live in Canada. Moved over there years ago," Albert answered and Dee looked disappointed.

Sir Henry went over to a bookshelf. "Peter, can you reach up there please. You will find a book or two on poisonous plants. Maybe that will help you."

Peter went over to the bookshelf, but he needed to use the ladder to reach the shelf Sir Henry was pointing to. He retrieved the books and passed them down to him.

"These haven't been out for a while," Sir Henry said, brushing dust from their covers with his hand.

"Is it okay if we borrow these for a while?" Peter asked.

"Yes of course you can, Peter. You don't need to ask. Everything here is yours and Helen's as much as it is mine, but I do want you to tell me one thing?" Sir Henry passed Peter the books. "Why do you need them? Is it to do with the girl Dee found in the Cave Pool?"

Peter nodded. "Yes. It looks like she might have been poisoned then dumped in the pool to look like a drowning."

"I knew it," Sir Henry said.

"Me too," Albert chipped in and then pointed at Dee. "I told you; murder follows you around!"

Mrs Wood returned to the library carrying a tray laden with a huge pot of tea and biscuits. "You all seem very excited in here. Excuse me for asking but did you just mention murder?"

"Mrs Wood, we believe so, but Jake hasn't said it's officially a murder enquiry yet," Dee said. "You know the body I discovered at Wellsdale Hall. They think she might have been poisoned with Poison Ivy."

"Well, I've never heard of that before. A friend of mine who works in Scotland was poisoned with mushrooms. There was a mix-up in the kitchen, and the wrong ones were used in the soup," Mrs Wood said as she handed around the plate of biscuits.

"Did anyone die?" Dee asked her.

"No," came the reply, "but they were all very ill."

"We need to keep this to ourselves at the moment and that includes you Albert until Jake makes an official statement," Peter warned them all.

"Of course, we fully understand." Sir Henry nodded as did Albert and Mrs Wood.

"Is Helen at the stables?" Peter asked as they finished their tea.

"No," Sir Henry replied. "She's paying a visit to the hairdressers."

In Bailey's Hair and Beauty salon Helen sat in the purple chair in a gold cape having her wet hair brushed through by Jett Bailey. Helen had asked the shampoo girl a couple of questions, but she hadn't been very forthcoming.

"I hear we have a wedding on the horizon. What are your thoughts; up or down?" Jett said, his hands constantly touching her hair.

"I think up," Helen replied. "I was surprised to get an appointment at such short notice."

"I moved a few people for you. No one is as important as a bride to be. Are you having the wedding at Gaitley Manor?" he asked.

"Maybe. In truth it's still all up in the air." Helen watched his expression change.

"Is it not imminent?" He looked at her face in the mirror.

"It could be." Helen sighed watching Jett's face. "It's just who to invite? I'd like a small wedding. However my father, Lord Gaitley, wants a huge one."

Jett seemed more impressed when she dropped the word *Lord* into the conversation, as she'd thought he might.

"Every bride should have a huge wedding. After all it's only once," he laughed, moving his head in the direction of another woman having her hair blow waved. "Or, in some cases, three times!"

Helen giggled politely. "On behalf of Lord Gaitley and I – we're sorry to hear about your wife's friend. I read about it in the paper."

Helen saw Jett bite his bottom lip and look away for a second. "Yes, she's very upset. Lucy was a good friend to me and my wife. I must call to see David her husband; he must be so upset."

"Were Lucy and your wife friends for a long time?" Helen asked.

"Yes, we all were. I knew Lucy before I met Sofia. Lucy introduced Sofia and me. They met at university and as they say the rest is history. Jett looked down at his feet.

"I'm so sorry. How is Sofia?" Helen had a mental list of questions to ask but looking at how upset Jett appeared it didn't seem appropriate to ask any of them.

"Very upset. Such a tragic accident. We loved her." Jett paused then his voice and demeanour changed back into hairdressing mode. "Now let's get this gorgeous hair dry and pinned up in a few styles for you to try. Sofia is a wonderful make-up artist, and we can offer a full bridal make-up and beauty service for you and your bridesmaids."

Helen smiled as Jett turned on the hairdryer.

When they were on their way back to the office, Dee asked Peter if it was okay to be dropped at Alison's. She wanted to check in on her. "Think I might grab one of Alison's breakfast muffins for the morning," Dee thought out loud.

"You're planning ahead. Thought you were a yogurt girl?" Peter said sarcastically.

"I am. Just fancy a change. Actually I have nothing in for tea tonight either!" Dee giggled as Peter pulled over to drop her off.

Dee said goodbye as Peter drove away, mentioning she would return to the office shortly. When Dee entered Coffee Creams, Alison invited her to join herself and two women Dee thought she might have seen before.

"Dee, this is Brenda and Pauline from Wellsdale Hall - the women I spoke to in the pool?"

"Yes, yes - and if I remember rightly, you heard two people arguing in one of the saunas?" Dee said as she sat down to join them.

"That we did and that's why we're here," Brenda said looking around her.

Dee looked around the café too. "What do you mean?" she asked.

"They came to tell me to tell you, but they can tell you themselves now," Alison said. "Are we having a latte?"

"Well, Alison, I actually came in for a breakfast muffin for tomorrow morning and to see if you're okay. You were a bit flustered this morning."

"Jim's fault. Made me watch two films with too much wine!" Alison shouted over the noise of the coffee machine. "Go ahead, ladies. Tell Dee what you told me."

Dee listened intently as it was explained in detail what Brenda and Pauline had heard and seen.

"Are you sure it was them? Lucy Walker and Sofia Bailey?" Dee asked for the second time.

"Yes, we recognised her from her photo in the paper, and we both said that's the two girls we saw arguing in the sauna that day", Pauline said calmly.

Brenda was much more excitable and asked Dee, "Do you think she pushed her, and she banged her head or even worse drowned her in the Cave Pool?"

"These are all possibilities." Dee took her latte from Alison as she sat down to join them.

"Now ladies, we can't go round guessing or accusing people of drowning their friends. Best to keep things to ourselves for now. After all, it could just have been an accident," Alison warned.

Dee was grateful for Alison's wise words. They were perfectly timed.

"Ladies can I ask one more question? What colour swimsuits were they wearing?"

Alison looked at Dee strangely.

"I don't know. You couldn't really see. Did you see Pauline?" Brenda asked her friend.

"No, but I think they were both wearing bikinis not swimsuits," Pauline said putting her finger on her chin with a quizzical look.

"Well thank you, ladies. You've been most helpful. I must get back to work. Peter will be wondering what happened to me."

Alison walked over with Dee towards the door. "What's that about swimsuits and bikinis? You know what Lucy was wearing. You saw her," Alison whispered.

"I know. It's nothing. Nothing at all." Dee shrugged and waved them all goodbye.

Alison turned towards Pauline and Brenda as she closed the door behind Dee. "Sometimes that girl confuses the hell out of me!"

Ruth had enjoyed a pleasant lunch and was now having a session from a masseur called Will.

"I didn't know men worked here. How come I ended up with you?" she asked between winces.

"There's a couple of us, but you asked for a hard, strong one and that's what you're getting," he replied in a deliberately sexy tone.

For once Ruth wasn't in the mood to play. Her mind was racing as to why the inspector was asking the gardener about Poison Ivy. She wanted to find Eric herself and ask him some questions.

Ignoring the inuendo Ruth told him to hurry up and he could cut the crap she wasn't interested. In the next second she let out a yelp of pain as Will dug his fingers into her back.

"What is that?" Peter asked Dee.

"It's a picture of Sofia from their webpage. Her and Lucy were seen arguing in one of the saunas by Pauline and Brenda." Dee carried on sticking the picture to the white board.

"Pauline and Brenda? Who?"

"Alison's friends from Wellsdale Hall. They're members. They heard them arguing in one of the saunas the morning that Lucy died." Dee replied .

"And how do you know this?"

"They've just told me all about it at Alison's. They'd come to tell Alison to tell me but then I…."

"Yes, Dee, I've got it. So, we have a potential suspect?" Peter sat back in his chair and folded his arms.

"Yes, we do!" Dee said tapping the picture of Sofia.

Jake hated this bit and asked David and his mother if it was alright for them to go and make everyone a cup of tea in the kitchen to give them a few moments alone to take in the news of Lucy's murder.

"They're clearly devastated," Claire said as she joined Tom and the Inspector in the kitchen.

"Very," Tom said.

"Should we come back another day about the money and the baby, Sir?" Claire asked Jake.

"No, we need to do this now, especially as Mrs Walker suspected foul play."

They made the tea between them, putting some sugar in Mrs Walker's and David's.

"Here we are, get that down you. It will do you both good," Tom said as he carried the mugs of tea into the lounge.

"Mrs Walker, we're aware that you've instructed Peter Gill and Dee Firth to look into Lucy's death. Can you tell us why?" Jake was smiling as he spoke.

"Yes, I did. Shall I tell them to stop?" Mrs Walker looked Jake in the eye before continuing. "You see it was the money; I know they don't have that much money or didn't and while David's been away working, Lucy was acting oddly, avoiding me and I just didn't want her to get into trouble. I thought they might find out where it's all come from. I don't like her friends, Inspector. What if they have made her do something she shouldn't have. Oh, I don't know." Mrs Walker put her head in her hands as she turned a flustered bright red.

David put his arm around her. "It's okay mum. Thank you for doing that, but what are you talking about money? How much money?"

Jake passed David a copy of his wife's bank statement. He went ashen as he looked at it.

"David, we have something delicate to tell you. Please understand this is not pleasant for us by any means as it won't be for you." Jake tried to keep his voice level.

David and Mrs Walker stared back at Jake. Neither of them spoke.

"Lucy was six weeks pregnant." Jake said it slowly so they'd take it in.

"Pregnant. I so wanted a grandchild. Why didn't you tell me?" Mrs Walker said sharply to her son.

David didn't answer her. They could see he was doing the maths.

Suddenly Mrs Walker stood up and shouted at David. "It's not yours. How can it be?"

Claire went over to Mrs Walker and urged her to sit down.

After a quiet moment or two David looked straight at the Inspector. "It all makes sense," he said.

"What does?" Jake asked encouragingly.

"The money and the baby. No, mum, it's not mine." David didn't look at her as he spoke "We were having money troubles. Well, I caused them - gambling."

"Gambling? You're just like your father!" Mrs Walker spat at him.

David ignored her and spoke under his breath. "I didn't think Lucy would go through with it."

"With what?" Jake urged looking at Claire first and then Tom.

"Being a surrogate mother," he replied.

"A what? To who?" Mrs Walker was back on her feet again.

David took a deep breath. "Sofia and Jett Bailey."

Chapter Nine

Ruth had been walking through the gardens, searching for Eric, the Head Gardener. She had had no luck finding him and decided to return to the courtyard garden to relax before it was time to leave. She had only been sitting for a couple of minutes when Eric entered the garden through a back gate carrying a set of shears.

"Excuse me; excuse me!" she said waving at him.

"Yes, is something wrong?" Eric asked her.

"No, it's just that I overheard you talking to the police about Poison Ivy this morning." Ruth put on her best smile.

"Did you now," Eric replied doing his best to edge away.

"Yes, I did. Do you think it's connected to that girl drowning in the pool?" Ruth had her hand on his arm.

"You can remove that. None of my business or yours, I need to get on with my job. Go bother someone else!" He snapped, pulling his arm away from her and walking briskly off.

Ruth's face changed. "Yes, and I'm trying to do mine!" she shouted back at him.

Peter and Dee were busily typing up and making notes on everything they had learned about Poison Ivy.

"It's a nasty thing," Peter stated tapping one of the books in front of him. "It says here it can sedate people and cause paralysis."

"Peter but why would someone use it? Surely there are easier poisons to use." Dee tapped the pen on her chin.

"Yes indeed, why would someone use it?" Jake said as he came through the door.

Peter stood up and shook the Inspector's hand. "Sit down Jake. What brings you in to see us?"

Jake took the chair nearest to Peter's desk. "It's changed a bit in here, Peter. Looks great; didn't know you'd been decorating too," Jake said looking around him.

"Not me; it's all Dee. Have to say she's done a great job."

"That you have, Dee; I know where to come when I need some interior design tips." Jake smiled at her.

"Anytime," Dee answered pleased that he liked what she'd achieved.

Peter interrupted them, coughing a little as the two of them continued to look at one another across the office. "Jake, any reason for your call or were you just passing?"

The Detective Inspector suddenly felt embarrassed. He sat up straight in the chair, messing with the lapels of his jacket.

Dee smiled to herself.

"Yes, Peter. I thought you would both like to know we're officially treating Lucy's death as murder. I've got to do a rotten press conference tomorrow morning." Jake pulled a face.

"We'll go see Mrs Walker," Peter announced. "She might want us to stop investigating."

"I hope not. We already have a suspect!" Dee jumped up out of her seat to point at the white evidence board.

"I've just come from David's house; I'd leave it till tomorrow, Peter, they were very upset." Jake looked across at the evidence board.

"Claire and Tom not with you?" Dee asked.

"No, I've sent them to Wellsdale Hall to inform Angela Myers that this is now a murder enquiry. Her and that lawyer will be happy," Jake said smirking.

"Sure will," Peter said with raised eyebrows "One gets to keep her job, and the other doesn't have to worry about a lawsuit."

Jake smiled at Dee. "What suspect then?"

Dee was just about to tell him when she had a change of mind. "To be honest Jake why should we tell you. We seem to be forever telling you what we know but you don't seem to be doing the same in return."

Peter scowled at Dee. She stood defiant with her arms crossed.

"I don't see it like that," Jake answered her.

"Neither do I," Peter interrupted "Jake tells us what he can, when he can, Dee. Jake doesn't have to speak to us at all!"

Dee went to sit back at her desk. "I suppose," was all she could muster.

Jake looked across at the dejected woman. "Dee does have a point, Peter. Maybe this has been a little one-sided." Jake winked at Peter. "Dee they found traces of Poison Ivy on Lucy's lips and in her throat. They also found ash on her body as if it had been burned near her."

"Ash?" Dee stopped looking sorry for herself "Seriously someone burned Poison Ivy next to her? Why?"

"According to forensics if you swallow or inhale it, it can cause a serious reaction resulting in death." Jake made his way over towards the evidence board.

Dee looked at Peter, who could almost see her mind racing.

"Maybe someone made an innocent mistake. They burn sage and things for cleansing people's auras," Dee said closing the book in front of her. "Like what happened with the mushrooms."

"Mushrooms?" Jake asked peering at a picture stuck on the evidence board.

"Never mind the mushrooms," Peter interjected shaking his head.

"Peter, why do you have a picture of Sofia Bailey on here?"

"Dee would be better answering that than me." Peter came over to join Jake by the board.

"Dee, care to explain?" Jake smiled.

"She was heard arguing in a sauna with Lucy on the morning of her accident - sorry - murder," Dee corrected herself.

"How do you know this?" Jake asked retrieving his notebook from his jacket pocket.

"I can't reveal my sources!" Dee said stubbornly.

Peter let out a howl of laughter as did Jake.

"You don't need to know, but it's true and if you don't believe me ask Alison. She knows all about it too." Dee stood up and made her way out from behind her desk, clearly peeved.

"Okay Dee, we're only messing," Peter said holding his hands up. He turned to Jake. "That's the only reason we have to suspect Sofia Bailey might be involved."

"Any idea what they were arguing about?" Jake asked them.

"No," Peter replied.

Dee shook her head.

"Dee I'm sorry for laughing just then." Jake took a deep breath. "I want you to know and to save you both some time, you can cross Sofia Bailey off your suspect list."

"And why is that?" Dee asked and continued before he could answer. "Maybe Lucy was having an affair with her husband and that's why they were arguing. After all she was pregnant."

Jake looked into her green eyes then away as he felt an uneasy pull. "Dee, that's why she can't be a suspect - because of the baby."

Peter said, "Was the baby Sofia's husband's?"

Jake nodded.

"Sofia knew that Lucy and her husband were having an affair and that she was having his baby!" Dee blurted out. "Sounds like a motive for murder if you ask me!"

"No, it's not, Dee. Lucy was carrying their baby."

"Their baby?" Peter's eyebrows were raised. "Oh, I see."

"I don't, I don't understand. What do you mean by their baby?" Dee looked as confused as she sounded.

Jake explained. "Lucy was acting as a surrogate mother for Sofia and her husband."

Helen had returned home from the Bailey's Hair and Beauty salon to be met by Mrs Wood as she came through the door.

"Your hair looks lovely, dear; beautiful."

"Thank you, Mrs Wood. A little practice for the wedding day. Do you really like it?" Helen asked checking her restyling in the hallway mirror.

"Yes, dear, it's very you. You can always wear it down in the evening if you preferred, but if I were you, I would keep it like that all day. Have we set a date then?"

"No, Mrs Wood, Henry asked me to do some investigating. One of Lucy's friends owns this hair and beauty salon in Amberleigh, and Henry thought we could help Peter by doing a little investigation of our own," Helen explained quietly.

"Do you mean Sofia Bailey?" Mrs Wood asked her.

"Yes, Mrs Wood. Do you know where I mean?" Helen was surprised.

"I do dear, Sofia and her husband have won so many awards. He's an amazing stylist, isn't he?"

Helen patted her restyled locks. "Yes, he is. Mrs Wood do you…"

Mrs Wood interrupted her. "Sir Henry is in the lounge, and I must warn you, he's a little grumpy. He lost to Albert again."

Helen thanked her and made her way towards the drawing room door. Before she could open it, Mrs. Wood called out from the kitchen doorway. "It was a pleasure to see Dee today. I hope they were able to find what they were looking for."

Helen smiled. She wasn't sure if she had heard Mrs Wood correctly. She opened the door to find Henry sitting on the sofa with his eyes closed.

"I see you've had a busy day?" She nudged him "What's all this about Dee being here?"

"Oh Helen, Peter and Dee called in to find out about Poison Ivy," Henry said suddenly becoming alert.

"Poison Ivy, whatever for?" Helen asked as Mrs Wood brought a tray of tea and biscuits in for them.

"Let me explain dear," Sir Henry said gently patting her knee.

"It reminded me of my friend and the mushrooms," Mrs Wood said as she poured the tea.

Ruth had enjoyed her swim and was getting ready for afternoon tea. Two ladies joined her in the changing room and were busily chatting away about Wellsdale Hall.

"Hi, sorry, I couldn't help but overhear you. I'm thinking about joining. Are you two members?" Ruth put on her most innocent smile.

"Yes, dear. We've been members for some time. Are you here as a day guest?" one of them said.

"Yes, I am. I thought it would be a good idea to try out the facilities before taking out a membership especially as it's so expensive."

The blonde lady said, "I know it is but if you're going to come regularly and use the spa, it's worth it. Are you staying for afternoon tea or do you need to rush?"

"No rush and yes I'm just on my way to have afternoon tea," Ruth replied.

"Why don't you join us. We can tell you all about Wellsdale Hall. Did you hear about that young lady who died here in the Cave pool?" the other one asked.

Ruth played it down. "I heard a little something but it's not enough to put me off joining."

"No dear, such a kerfuffle," the brunette one said as they made their exit out of the changing rooms.

Ruth followed quickly behind. "I'm sorry ladies I didn't catch your names; I'm Ruth."

The blonde lady turned around. "I'm Pauline and this is Brenda."

Tom and Claire were sitting patiently waiting for Angela Myers to put her office phone down.

Finally, she hung and announced, "I have the go ahead from the powers that be to help you in any way I can, and you have full access to Wellsdale Hall."

"Thank you, Ms Myers. As this is now a murder enquiry please can we have full lists of all employees and those who were working on May the seventeenth," Tom requested.

"We'll be needing all your CCTV footage immediately too," Claire chipped in.

"Yes, absolutely. That's all going to take me at least half an hour. Would you like to join our fellow guests for afternoon tea in the dining room while I gather all the information you need?" Angela was beaming.

Tom nodded at Claire.

"That's very kind of you," Claire answered.

In her high heels Angela Myers crossed her office and led them out into the hall. "Follow me, I have the perfect table for you."

Claire and Tom ignored the stares as they entered the dining room. Angela seated them at a table out of the way but with a perfect view of the gardens and a young boy came over carrying two menus and asking if they had any allergies.

Once they had selected their preferred type of tea, they were able to sit back and relax.

"My mum would love to come here," Claire said .

"Bring her for her birthday," Tom suggested.

"I might but it would be so expensive. I don't think I could afford it." Claire looked out at the gardens as she spoke.

Tom was just about to say something more when an array of beautiful sandwiches, scones and cakes were placed before them. As the young man poured the tea, Tom stretched his neck to look behind him.

After he had gone, Claire said, "What are you looking at?"

"I think I might be wrong, but does that look like who I think it is."

Claire turned and instantly recognised Ruth. "Yes, it's that journalist."

Tom shrugged as he took a mouthful of cream cheese and cucumber sandwich.

"Wonder what she's up to?" Claire said.

"Enjoying her afternoon tea. Eat up, Claire; this is unbelievable!" Tom waved another sandwich at her.

Peter and Dee sat quietly digesting the latest update from Jake.

"Imagine how Mrs Walker and David must be feeling. They must be as shocked as we are," Dee said breaking the silence.

"What at the pregnancy or Lucy's murder?" Peter questioned.

"Both," Dee said thoughtfully. "Although Jake said David was aware of a possible surrogacy, it must have been shocking for him to learn Lucy had gone through with it."

They both sat thinking quietly until the internal door of the private detective agency flew open. Peter jumped to his feet. Dee shocked quickly grabbed her mobile from her desk. There, before them, were a raging Mrs Walker and a heartbroken David.

"We don't care what it costs. You know we have the money. You two need to find out who killed our Lucy. What the hell is that?" Mrs Walker pointed at the evidence board as she shrugged her coat off and slammed herself down onto one of the spare office chairs."

Dee quickly flipped the evidence board over. "It's another case we're working on." She had to almost sprint across the office to take Mrs Walker's coat.

"David, have a seat." Peter offered him a chair next to his mother, "Could we all please take a minute."

"We don't have a minute. Get out there and find her killer, Mr Gill," Mrs Walker ordered.

"Yes, Mrs Walker, but I suggest we calm down for just a second so we can discuss things in finer detail. I know you're both upset."

Dee disappeared into her flat, returning with tea and biscuits. "Always helps, my Gran says," Dee said with a smile.

"Clever lady, your Gran," Mrs Walker said. She took several deep breaths and then a sip of the tea Dee set before her.

Peter went to sit behind his desk. Dee at hers, took out her notepad from her top drawer.

"Mrs Walker," Peter started.

"Please call me Jean," Mrs Walker said with the slightest of smiles.

"Jean, we've been informed that this is now a murder enquiry. The police are good at their job. I'm not sure you need to employ us to look into it any further."

Peter waited for Jean's reaction.

"Yes, we do. You…" She pointed at Dee. "I know you solved that murder before Christmas. Even though the police took the credit, everyone around here knows it was you."

Dee smiled and nodded to her. She was still in disbelief at the utter rubbish Peter had just spoken.

"Jean, we'll do everything we can to find Lucy's murderer," Peter said. "You both have to start at the beginning. We'll have a lot of questions, and I feel it's late in the day to be doing that. Would it be alright if we pop round tomorrow to talk to you both."

David finally said something. "I have to be at a press conference in the morning,"

"As do we, David. We'll come round to yours straight after. Is that okay?" Dee smiled at him.

David replied with a mere nod.

"I've written some things down. Lucy was pregnant too." Jean grabbed a tissue from her bag.

"We're so sorry for what you're going through. Dee and I will endeavour to do everything we can to make this right," Peter said, coming around the side of his desk to put his hand on hers.

David rose to his feet. "Come on Mum. We can sort it tomorrow. They've said they'll look into it. Come on."

Jean and David made their way to the door. "I'll walk out with you," Dee offered.

"No need," David said raising his hand. "We'll see you tomorrow."

They watched the door close and Peter settled back at his desk. "Looks like we have our first paid murder case."

Dee was beyond herself with excitement. "Yes, we do indeed!"

Claire checked the time. It was heading towards four thirty.

"That manager is slow," Claire said, sinking back into the chair.

"I'm pleased she is," Tom said. "Are you as full as me?"

"Tom, you ate most of it, but yes I am. Now I think we should go and check on our Ms Myers." Claire was already on her feet.

Tom grumbled and pulled a face but followed her as she walked between the tables, coming to a sudden stop at the table Ruth was sitting at. Smiling sweetly, Claire asked the trio, "Have you enjoyed that as much as we have, ladies?"

Brenda responded promptly and positively, receiving enthusiastic support from Pauline. Only Ruth remained silent, offering only a polite smile to the officers.

"I didn't know you were a member here?" Claire asked Ruth, politely.

"I'm not but these two ladies are. I'm here with them," Ruth replied, haughtily.

Pauline frowned. She didn't like Ruth's tone and felt a correction was needed. "No she's not. We just met in the changing room. We were discussing the death of that young lady. Is there any news?"

"I'm sorry I didn't catch your names?" Claire continued to be ultra polite with Tom standing quietly behind her.

The ladies introduced themselves and Claire answered their question by saying she had no further updates, but a press conference was to be held in the morning. To her surprise, Ruth jumped up, grabbed her bag and left without so much as a goodbye or a thank you.

Brenda spoke tutting. "How rude is that? Wonder what got under her skin to make her leave so fast?"

"The words *Press Conference*," Claire said looking at the duo.

"Why?" asked Pauline.

"I hope you were both careful with what you discussed. There's a chance you might find yourselves quoted in the Amberleigh Gazette." Claire waited for the penny to fall.

Pauline and Brenda looked at each other in dismay.

"I'm sure no harm's been done," Claire said.

As Claire and Tom departed, Brenda took Pauline's hand and whispered, "Alison and her friend Dee were right. We should have been more cautious. We've been targeted, Pauline."

Back at the police station, Jake was reading his press statement for the umpteenth time. It was one of the downsides to being an Inspector. His mobile buzzed. It was a text from Catherine making sure he was still okay for tonight. He wanted to keep it casual and replied with a thumbs up.

"Hi, Sir. Finally got what we needed from Angela Myers and the CCTV footage has been downloaded," Tom declared as he popped his head around Jake's office door.

"Come in. Where's DC Brown?" Jake asked.

"On her way. She stopped to pick up a message left at the desk."

"Hi." Claire knocked on the Inspectors door but came straight in without waiting for an instruction to do so.

"How was this afternoon? Any developments?" Jake asked.

"No, Sir," Tom answered, his hand across his stomach and something like a wince on his face.

"Are you alright, Tom?" Jake asked, mildly concerned.

Claire provided the explanation. "Ms Myers was so relieved to hear it's a murder enquiry, she gave us afternoon tea while she got all the information for us. This one ate most of it!"

"Tom, honestly, you'll need to run that off and I suggest you don't have anything else to eat today," Jake said laughingly.

"No, Sir, please excuse me?" Tom didn't wait for an answer but raced out of the office towards the loo.

Ruth went directly to the offices of the Amberleigh Gazette.

"Where have you been?" her editor bellowed as she flew past his open office door.

"Doing my job. I just need to get this typed up," she hollered back.

Everyone else seemed to have gone home except the new photographer who was bent over swearing with his head in a cupboard. "Can you find what you're looking for more quietly please," Ruth shouted across at him.

He banged his head again on the top of the cupboard as he turned around to see who was shouting. "Well, if it isn't the infamous Ruth Watkins." He straightened up. Rubbed his head and, walking over to Ruth's desk, he held out his hand.

Ruth was taken aback but shook it only now noticing his rugged look, his eyes – brown - and his face - chiselled and handsome. She asked, "And you are?"

"Robert Harrison; nice to meet you."

She couldn't help but spot the gleam in his eye.

"I don't want to be here all night, and you've got a press conference in the morning. Wrap it up!" The editor yelled.

"Right you are," Ruth shouted back. Until that moment, she hadn't let go of Robert's hand.

Peter had arrived home to a warm hug from Clara, who was already undressed in pajamas, and a kiss from Helen.

"We're going to pop Clara into bed. She's tired and Henry wants us to have dinner together. I believe you've had a busy day." Helen winked at him.

Mrs Wood appeared with three crystal wine glasses on a tray and a bottle of red wine.

"Mummy, can Mrs Wood tuck me in. She tells me the best stories," Clara pleaded.

"Give me that tray, Mrs Wood," Peter said taking it from her.

"Of course she can." Helen smiled at her daughter.

Clara grabbed Mrs Wood by the hand and dragged her towards the staircase. "Night Mummy. Night Peter," she shouted, blowing kisses at them.

Peter and Helen laughed and blew kisses back.

"I'm not the only one who's had a busy day. Your hair is as beautiful as you are," Peter said staring at his future wife.

"I'm glad you like it. Henry suggested that I should go and have a trial before the wedding…" Helen's voice trailed off.

"I bet he did, and I bet I know where!" Peter said as they entered the dining room.

Tom and Claire were both making their individual ways home when Tom remembered that Claire had had a message left for her at the station and realised he had not asked her what it was about. He pressed the bluetooth button on his car and asked it to call to her.

"Tom, hi. Are you okay? Feeling any better?" Claire asked him.

Just hearing her voice made Tom feel better. "Struggling a bit. No one to blame but myself."

"You'll be fine. Take care of yourself and I'll see you tomorrow."

"I will. Look, Claire, I forgot to ask. That message you received at the station. Anything to do with the case?"

"No Tom, and I'm home now. Got to go; bye." With that, Claire cut him off immediately.

Dee looked at the clock on the wall. It was a little after seven. She was showered and dressed in clean jeans and t-shirt. She checked her cupboards and her fridge; nothing inspiring to cook. The breakfast muffin sat on the countertop starring at her.

Dee addressed the inside of the fridge. "That's it. I'll have to do a supermarket shop tomorrow."

She extracted her head and closed the fridge door. Searching through the kitchen drawers, she found Mr. Wang's takeaway menu, picked up her mobile phone and called to place an order for prawn toast and a chicken Chow Mein to be delivered.

Jake was seated in Mr Wangs when Catherine returned from the toilet. She looked just as he remembered, and she smiled at him in the same way too.

"There's no need to look like that Jake. I'm not here to rekindle anything. Quite the opposite in fact." Catherine took hold of Jake's hand.

"I'm sorry, Catherine. I shouldn't have run off to North Yorkshire like that but after Cami's death I had to leave. I couldn't put you in danger like that." Jake didn't look at her as he spoke.

"I know, Jake. Let's face it, we only got together through grief. We'd both lost our best friend."

Jake looked hard at her. "It was more than that, Catherine. You know it was, but I had to leave."

"I know. Maybe it was but that was then and this is now. Jake, look at you, an Inspector. Cami would be so proud of you," Catherine said, staring back into his eyes.

"As she would have been of you too." Jake removed his hand from hers. "Why here in Amberleigh? I thought you always wanted to work at the Met."

"I did, I still do. This is only temporary. I'm here for four months – another twelve weeks now. If you'd bothered to read my letter, you'd know why." Catherine shook her head.

"I know, I should have read it. Sorry." Jake smiled.

"Stop apologising. I'm covering for Ann while she's over in Australia. Her daughter had twins," Catherine explained "And then I'm taking a year off myself."

"Wow a year. Where are you going for a year?" Jake asked her.

"Maternity leave, Jake!" Catherine announced as she stood up. "I need the toilet again."

"Oh my. I didn't know you were…married," Jake stuttered.

"I'm not, Jake. We may do one day but not right now. This one is more important than any wedding. Ben and I can get married anytime," Catherine laughed at him as he rose to his feet.

"Ben? Ben as in Cami's brother?" Jake questioned her.

"Yes, Jake. I put it all in my letter." She wagged her finger at him. "I really need to go to the loo, Jake."

As Catherine made her way past him Jake grabbed her and pulled her in for a hug and kissed her on the cheek. "I'm so pleased for you both, I really am."

"Good but you have to let go; right now."

Mr Wang was at the restaurant's reception desk apologising to Dee. "I'm so sorry Miss Dee. We have no driver tonight. I have given you free prawn crackers and a voucher for your next visit. So sorry you had to come and pick up your order."

Dee smiled at Mr Wang and told him it was fine, but she wasn't really listening. Her attention was elsewhere. She had witnessed Jake hugging an attractive brunette in the restaurant and her heart stopped as she saw Jake kiss the woman's cheek.

She returned to her car, placed her takeaway on the passenger seat and sat outside Mr Wangs for a while watching the rain run down her windscreen.

Chapter Ten

"Good morning!" Peter greeted Dee as she emerged through the connecting door from her flat into the office.

"Is it?" Dee said sarcastically under her breath.

"Pardon?" Peter said.

"Yes, it is," Dee answered him, inwardly telling herself off for being grumpy.

Peter realised that Dee must have got out of the wrong the side of the bed that morning and suggested a reviving coffee at Alison's followed by a trip to Wellsdale Hall. He felt that would cheer her up but Dee continued to look down in the dumps when they arrived at Coffee Creams.

"Morning," Alison greeted them cheerily.

Dee went straight over to sit at their usual table in the window leaving Peter at the counter to order rather than waiting for Alison to come over.

"What's wrong with her?" Alison whispered.

"Lord only knows. I'll go to the gents. Have a word with her, will you?" Peter asked Alison, feeling concerned. "I'm hoping it's not her Gran."

"Sure, Peter," Alison nodded.

Alison plated a couple of slices of banana bread and took them over to Dee as Peter made his way to the toilet.

"How are we?" Alison asked as she sat down opposite Dee. "I need you both to try this. I've made it this morning, and I want an honest opinion."

"I'm alright," Dee responded. "That looks nice."

"Do you want to come over later or I can pop into yours once I've closed for the day?" Alison pressed gently "Is it your Gran, or your Mum?"

"Oh no, they're absolutely fine. It's just me. It's annoying when you think you might have something, but then you find out you haven't and probably never did in the first place," Dee said looking out of the window.

Alison could see Peter making his way back over to join them. "Let me know what you think." Alison pointed at the plate of banana bread. "I'll go make your coffees, Message me if you want to talk later."

Dee smiled at her and said she would be fine. She was annoyed with herself for showing other people how she felt.

As Peter passed Alison, he enquired, "Any luck?"

"It's not her Gran or her Mum. She said they're fine. If anything she seems angry with herself more than upset."

Peter changed direction and followed Alison back to the counter. "Wonder what about?" he said.

Alison shrugged. "Whatever it is, I'm sure it'll pass."

"I know she's not had her exam results yet, so it's not that." Peter was trying to whisper to Alison over the noise of the coffee machine.

"I wouldn't worry, Peter. I've said for her to message me if she'd like to talk later." Alison smiled at him as she handed him their drinks. "I've made some banana bread this morning – new recipe and I need you to try it. Let me know what you think."

Peter carried the coffees over to Dee. "Have you tried that yet?" he said.

Dee shook her head as she thanked him for the coffee.

The bell tinkled over the door heralding Albert's arrival.

"Morning all," Albert grinned. He glanced over to Peter and Dee. "You two are here as much as I am. Thought you'd be on your way to Amberleigh to the press conference."

"How do you know about that?" Peter asked as he took a bite of the banana bread.

"You don't need to know how I know anything," Albert smirked, opening his paper to use it as his customary shield.

Dee rolled her eyes smiling as she tried the banana loaf.

"Albert, I want you try this while I make you your tea and toasted teacake. Will you?" Alison asked.

"If it's free, lass, I'll try anything," Albert said putting his paper down.

Dee and Peter looked at each other and turned to watch Albert as he tried the banana bread.

"What on earth is this? Alison, I need my tea and now - that's disgusting!"

"What?" Alison looked alarmed. "What's wrong with it. It can't be that bad."

"You won't have any customers if you serve that rubbish. It's so salty!" Albert said, pulling a face.

"Alison turned to ask Dee and Peter. "Is it too salty?"

They both nodded, deciding it was best to make a hasty exit.

Alison took Dee's plate and trying it for herself, she spat it out. The others watched astonished as she ran into the kitchen cursing as she went only to return, moments later, frustrated with herself. "It's all Jim's fault. I've put the salt and the sugar in the wrong canisters. We are never having two bottles of wine in one night again!" she shouted, gathering up the rest of the banana bread and throwing it in the bin, swearing under her breath.

Albert disappeared behind his newspaper.

Dee waved goodbye and, as Alison looked up, Peter said to himself, "Whatever it is, it's catching!"

Angela Myers had arrived early at Wellsdale Hall. She was pleased that her staff had already set out chairs in neat rows in one of the lounges and had placed a long table at the top in preparation for the press conference.

"Morning. Nice and early I see," praised the lawyer.

"As are you. Didn't think you would need to be here today." Angela tried not to show how concerned she was that he was there. She had not been informed he would be in attendance.

"Last minute decision. Nothing for you to worry about. Them above are just looking after their investment, nothing more," he said checking his mobile.

"That's okay then. I'd hate to think they thought anyone here could possibly be involved in a murder," Angela retorted.

The lawyer didn't reply.

Jake, Claire and Tom had decided to travel together in a marked police car to the press conference. Jake usually preferred to drive his unmarked vehicle but today he had Claire drive. She turned to her front seat passenger and said, "Sir, it's unusual for you to come with Tom and me. Any particular reason?"

"Yes, I might need to make a quick getaway. That's why I wanted to come in a police car. If we do, you two know what to do.".

"Yes, Sir," they replied at the same time.

Ruth and Robert were travelling separately despite spending the night in bed together. Ruth tapped her painted fingernails on the steering wheel as she waited to park. In her rear-view mirror she watched the police car pull in behind her, manoeuvre around her and head towards the main entrance of Wellsdale Hall. Ruth thought she would do the same. She had smiled at Jake as the police car went past. She wasn't bothered that he had not returned her smile. Suddenly the thin, haughty employee from the other day was standing in front of her bonnet blocking her way.

Jake and his colleagues had parked outside the main entrance door. All three stopped before entering the hotel to watch the well-dressed man with the highly polished shoes that glistened in the morning sun tell Ruth to turn round and go back to the carpark. They watched as she promptly gave him the finger out of her car window. The three officers responded with laughter to the scene before them, finding it particularly amusing when the man raised his hands in a display of arrogance and gave her two back.

A couple of hours later, to Jake's pleasure, the press conference had gone well. Ruth had asked a couple of questions as had other journalists but in the main she had behaved herself.

On their way out the three officers bumped into Dee and Peter.

"Where are you heading off to?" Peter asked Jake.

"Sofia Bailey is next on the list. She's had a few days to process what's happened. Interesting to see what she has to say for herself. What are your plans?" Jake asked in return.

"We need to spend some time with David and his mother. We were going to call on them after this but as they're both here, it makes sense to speak to them now. I wonder if there's somewhere quiet, we could talk?" Peter asked Jake.

The manager was walking past so Jake hailed her and she stopped in her tracks.

"Angela, can you help Peter and Dee please. They need somewhere quiet to talk to Mr Walker and his mother in private."

"I thought these two were Private Investigators. We don't need to get involved with them. I only need to accommodate the police," Angela said folding her arms.

"The only advice I can give you, Ms Myers, is that you should help these two in any way you can. If anyone here is involved in the murder of Lucy Walker, I'd rather be talking to them than me!" Jake said sternly as he watched Dee slipping quietly away.

"Oh yes, yes, I see. Please bear with me," Angela stuttered looking around her. "I'll see if one of the lounges is free."

"Thank you," Jake said politely.

"Sir, we really need to get going," Claire urged.

"Catch you later?" Peter shouted after him as the police officers headed for the door.

He turned to see where Dee had gone and found her inside the spa shop talking to a sales lady.

"Honestly!" he tutted as he ran over to rescue David and his mother from journalists.

Henry and Mrs Wood sat enjoying a cup of tea together in the orangery at Gaitley Manor.

"You're blessed, Sir Henry," Mrs Wood said.

"That I am," Sir Henry replied and then looked aghast as Helen came in from the garden covered in dirt. "What on earth? Don't you walk another step, you're bringing it all in with you!"

Mrs Wood looked equally horrified at the messy footprints on her clean floor.

"I'm so sorry, Mrs Wood. That flipping pig is nothing but trouble!" Helen declared rubbing her hands together.

"Are we talking about Big Bertha?" Sir Henry asked, trying to hide a smile.

"You may laugh; I've dealt with hundreds of pigs but that one gives me the right run around!" Helen retorted "I'm going for a shower!"

"Fancy a day at Wellsdale Hall tomorrow? You're looking for a venue for your hen party, dear," Sir Henry cajoled.

"I am?" Helen looked at them both quizzically.

"We've been talking," Sir Henry said.

"Less of the *we* and more of the *you*!" Mrs Wood interrupted.

"I think," he corrected himself. "We think a little more investigating is in order."

"Oh, you do, do you. Well I wasn't successful last time. What makes you think I'll find out anything this time?" Helen was shaking her head.

"Because you are taking Mrs Wood with you!" Sir Henry announced.

"Me, why would I go?" Mrs Wood exclaimed, looking a bit shocked.

"To keep Helen company, Mrs Wood," Sir Henry said beaming at her.

"I'll book us in," Helen said with a sigh, knowing there was no point in arguing.

Alison had spent the remainder of the morning checking that everything she had done the day before was now right. Not only had she put salt in the sugar cannister she had also misplaced the walnuts in the almond jar.

She was treating herself to a latte and a piece of Victoria sponge while the café was quiet when the little bell tinkled over the Coffee Creams front door.

"Hello again. You two can't stay away!" Alison greeted the two arrivals.

"We need tea for two and two minutes of your time," Pauline said looking back at the door.

"Everything alright, Pauline? You seem all of a dither" Alison asked her, popping two teabags into a pink teapot.

Brenda stood on her toes to reach over the counter "We need to talk to your friend Dee; something happened yesterday and we're in big trouble!"

"Blimey, I didn't even know there were houses this big in Amberleigh?" Tom was bewildered as he took in the enormity of the Bailey's home, a modern version of the palatial architecture of two centuries earlier, with pillars outside and a grand black door.

"It's not as big or as nice as Gaitley Manor," Claire corrected him.

"Yes, but that's Gamblewood. This is in Amberleigh," Tom said, trying to be clever.

Jake ignored the two of them as Sofia Bailey opened her front door and invited them in.

Inside, the atmosphere balanced contemporary elegance with a sense of warmth, the sunlight pouring through expansive windows illuminating polished surfaces and soft furnishings. Tom kept glancing around, still impressed by the sheer scale of the place while Claire lingered near the doorway, clearly uneasy in such surroundings. Jake, however, remained focused on Sofia Bailey, whose quiet grief seemed to fill the place.

"I thought you might have been to see me before today. Do you want tea or a coffee?" she asked them as they followed her through to the kitchen.

The kitchen was as modern as the rest of the house. Everything looked brand new and large bi-folding doors spread across the back of the kitchen inviting the garden in. Claire counted sixteen chairs around a white table at one end of the kitchen with several comfy chairs and sofas scattered at the other.

"No thank you. We've had more than enough after the press conference," Jake answered. "Lived here long?"

"A few years now. I knew about the press conference, David and Louise phoned me last night to let me know. I couldn't face it. She was our best friend. I can't believe anyone would do that to Lucy." Sofia sat down on one of the cream chairs and offered the others to her visitors.

Jake took one of the chairs, and Tom sat on one of the sofas, but Claire remained standing.

"Oh, do sit down. You're making me nervous," Sofia chided her.

Claire looked at Jake, and he nodded in agreement.

Claire took out her notebook as did Tom.

"Please can you introduce yourselves, I know we spoke briefly at the spa but…" Sophia's voice trailed away.

"I'm Detective Inspector Jones. This is Detective Constable Brown, and this is Detective Sergeant Tom…" Jake didn't get to finish his sentence.

"Smith!" Sofia quipped.

"Beckford," Tom said solemnly not finding her funny.

"Sorry," she said apologetically.

The room fell silent for a moment or two.

"Mrs Bailey you mentioned Lucy was your best friend. When did you first meet and is there anything that could be of significance that you think we ought to know?" Jake enquired.

"That's years ago. We met at university and have been close friends ever since. All I can tell you is that Lucy was the most caring, loving person you could wish to meet."

Jake pressed a little harder. "We have witnesses who heard you both arguing in one of the saunas on the day Lucy died."

"Lucy and I arguing? We did no such thing. We might have a little tiff every now and again, but I was not arguing with her in the sauna. Your witnesses are mistaken!"

"They're reliable," Tom interjected.

"Don't care if they are or not. It wasn't me!" Sophia retorted.

Jake could see she was becoming agitated. "Can you tell me about Lucy's husband. Was she happy?"

"As far as I know, she was." Sofia looked down at her nails. "She wasn't happy about his gambling habit - that had reared its ugly head again - but other than that... He was away a lot with work, but overall, yes, she loved David."

Jake questioned her further. "What about Mrs Walker, David's mother?"

"This is ridiculous. I don't know David's mother. Lucy never talked about her, apart from saying she was pushing them to have children. That was all." Sofia looked at Jake and promptly looked away again.

"Talking of children; do you have any?" Jake asked her directly.

"No, I don't, but we did try." She answered again without making eye contact.

"Ah yes, Mr Bailey. Was he a close friend of Lucy's?" Jake looked over at Tom and Claire.

Tom was busy writing in his notebook and Claire was looking over at a wedding picture on the side table.

"That's a beautiful photo. Is that Lucy in the background?" Claire asked.

"Yes, she was my maid of honour."

After a pause Sofia asked, "Why are you asking about Lucy and Jett?" Finally she was looking toward Jake.

"You mentioned they were best friends. I just wondered how close?" Jake pried.

"If you're inferring what I think you are, you couldn't be further from the truth. Lucy went to school with Jett, here in Amberleigh. Lucy introduced us because she thought we would make a great couple and we do!" Sofia paused to regain her composure. "If you're thinking anything else, you're more stupid than you look."

Jake winced a little at the put down, but calmly continued. "I'm not inferring anything, Mrs Bailey; just merely trying to understand your relationship with Lucy."

"We had a great relationship with Lucy and David. I would have done anything for her as she would have done for us. There is nothing more to tell you!" Sofia was almost shouting at him now.

Claire could feel the atmosphere change. Tom nudged her. They knew what was coming.

"We feel there's something more you can tell us." Jake looked directly at Sofia. "Lucy was six weeks pregnant. If you were such best friends, I'm surprised she hadn't told you."

"What!" Sofia screeched and immediately fled the kitchen.

At Wellsdale Hall, Dee discovered Peter sitting in one of the lounges with David and his mother. After they had answered all of Dee's and Peter's questions, both looked completely worn out.

"Is there anything more at all you think might help us? Anything?" Peter asked them.

"No, we've told you everything. We've no idea why someone would do this. We just don't," David said.

"Okay, take care getting home and we'll be in touch as soon as we have any news," Peter replied, standing up.

Just as they were about to head out the door Dee spoke up. "Can I ask you where you both were on the seventeenth of May?"

Mrs Walker turned and glared at her. "No, you may not!" and slammed the door on her way out.

Back at Coffee Creams Alison had written everything down that Brenda and Pauline had told her.

"She's a cat of a woman that Ruth, but I don't think you were both targeted; more wrong place for you two and the right place for her." Alison soothed the two women sitting with her.

"We do hope you're right, dear," Pauline said.

"Please pass this on to your friend, just so she knows what happened," Brenda asked her again.

"Absolutely. Now ladies, I hope you don't mind but I need to get on. These pots won't wash themselves." Alison held the tea cups aloft.

"No, dear," Brenda and Pauline agreed.

Ruth couldn't get back to the offices of the Amberleigh Gazette quick enough. She needed to finish her story as soon as possible.

Her editor shouted at her to come into his office as she passed his door. "Is this some sort of joke?" He threw a piece of paper at her across his desk, fuming.

"Is what a joke?" Ruth picked up the piece of paper and read it.

"I can explain!" Ruth said standing her ground.

"You'd better. One hundred and fifty pounds on a hairdo and two hundred and eighty-five pounds on a spa day. Are you taking the piss?" he shouted at her.

"No, I'm not. If you want an exclusive then I need to do my research." Ruth puffed out her chest. "I am an award-winning journalist after all!"

"I don't care what you are!" He shouted back at her "This better be a damn good story!"

Ruth didn't answer him. She went straight to her desk to finish what she had started.

The junior journalist turned to her as Ruth opened her laptop. "He's got it in for you today. What are you working on?"

Ruth didn't look at her as she began typing, her nails click-clacking away on the keys. "I'll give you the polite answer…" She paused. "None of your business!"

"We should go. Claire go find Mrs Bailey and tell her we're leaving but be gentle please," Jake asked, standing as he did so.

Claire followed Jake's instructions, opening the door through which Sofia had fled. She found their witness, sobbing uncontrollably, sitting on the bottom step of an elegant glass and wood staircase.

"Mrs Bailey, we're sorry for your loss. We'll be on our way, but we'll pop back later when Mr Bailey is here." Claire spoke to her softly.

Sofia Bailey nodded but did not look up at her.

"Would you like me to contact Mr Bailey for you? I can sit with you until he arrives," Claire offered.

"No need for that. Give us a moment!" a voice behind her bellowed.

Claire spun round to see a man she presumed was Mr Bailey. He was tall and extremely good looking. Together the Baileys would really make the most attractive couple.

"Yes, Sir," Claire replied heading back into the kitchen where she found Jake looking out onto the garden and Tom on the edge of the sofa looking anxious.

"Mr Bailey?" Claire asked Tom.

"Yes, and he said if we've upset his wife, we'll have his solicitors to answer to. Jake's not happy," Tom whispered to her.

"Well, he might've handled it more gently," Claire remarked. "We should have waited for Mr Bailey before revealing the news about the baby - especially since we know the child was theirs."

"What's ours?"

Jett and Sofia stood at the top of the steps.

Jake turned. "I would personally like to apologise for any upset we've caused."

After a momentary hesitation, Jett and Sofia sat down on the sofa together holding hands.

"I understand you've told Sofia that Lucy was pregnant," Jett said putting his arm around his wife.

"Yes, we did. Did you know?" Jake asked him.

"Of course I knew. It's mine," Jett replied. "Ours," he said tightening his grip on Sofia's hand.

"Mr Walker - David - informs us that Lucy might have been acting as a surrogate for you both. Is that true?" Jake continued standing by the window.

"Yes," Sofia said wiping away tears. "…and it's all above board. We paid her and we had a contract drawn up. You can speak to our lawyer if you have to."

"That's fine," Claire said. "Mr Bailey can I ask if you knew, how come Mrs Bailey didn't?"

"Lucy and I were going to surprise you on your birthday with the scan pictures," Jett said answering Claire's question but directing his response to Sofia.

Jake was about to ask a question when Claire continued. "When is your birthday, Mrs Bailey?"

Sofia replied not looking up. "End of this month."

Once again Jake was about to ask a question but Claire beat him to it. "So Lucy would have been about eight weeks pregnant by that point. We're sorry. This must be so difficult for you both."

Jake coughed to get their attention. "Can I ask how much you paid Mrs Walker – Lucy - please?"

Jett stood up and went over to a sideboard. He opened one of the three drawers and extracted what looked like a contract which he passed to the Inspector.

"Thank you," Jake said, starting to thumb through it.

"You can keep that. It's a copy. We have others as do our lawyers. You will see it was all above board," Jett said firmly.

"Did you not go to any of the appointments?" Claire asked Sofia.

"We all agreed it would be better for me to distance myself from that side of things just in case it didn't work. It's difficult to describe, but after trying for a baby for so long and facing disappointment month after month it's…." Sofia started to cry.

Jake nodded and thanked them once again. As the trio made their exit to the police car, they could hear Sofia screaming at Jett for not telling her she was about to become a mother sooner.

Dee and Peter were sitting comfortably in Angela Myers office.

"What would you like to know?" Angela asked them.

Dee rose and went over to the roster on the wall.

"Do you have any connection to Lucy Walker at all?" Peter enquired.

"Absolutely not!" Angela replied.

Peter continued. "Did you know her friends, Louise, Sofia and Vicky?"

"I know of Louise; she works for Blacks Estate Agency. As a matter of fact I'm on their mailing list," Angela answered him.

"Looking to buy or sell?" Dee butted in.

"Both!" came the reply.

"And the others?" Peter said looking over at Dee who was busily writing something in a pink notebook.

"Vicky, I think you said. No never met or heard of her but everyone knows Sofia Bailey. We sell her hair and skincare range here." Angela pointed towards some poshly labelled jars on the side.

"May I?" Dee asked popping her notebook away as she went over to the shelf and picked up one of the jars "Very fancy."

"Indeed, and expensive," Angela said watching Dee like a hawk.

"Are you the only one to sell it?" Peter asked her.

"Yes, we are. We're proud to support local businesses, and it sells very well. Their products are excellent," Angela gushed.

"They smell lovely too," Dee said as she raised the now open jar to her nose. "Mrs Myers, do the girls ever swap the days they work?"

Peter looked at her, surprised by the change of direction. Dee smiled at them both.

"No, not without my knowledge or consent. I run a tight ship." Angela seemed proud of herself.

"That's great. Can we look at any CCTV you have please on the seventeenth," Dee asked.

Peter started to speak, but Angela interrupted. "Give me your details and I'll send it to you. We made a copy for the police, and since they want us to talk to you, it should be fine for you to have a copy too."

"Thank you," Peter said. "Mrs Myers...Angela, you've been most helpful."

Dee placed a card on her desk. "Most helpful, Mrs Myers. Thank you."

Once outside Angela's office Peter shook his head and said to Dee, "You were cheeky in there, asking for the CCTV."

Dee smiled. "As my Gran says, if you don't ask you don't get!"

Peter laughed. "C'mon; time to get back to the office. I've missed a call from Jake."

Dee said, "I've missed a call from Alison, and I'm hungry."

"Coffee Creams first then," Peter said as they reached his car.

Jake sat in his office, his door ajar. He watched Tom go into the office he shared with Claire followed by a PC. He waited until the constable left and then went across the hallway to join them.

"What did PC Donelly want?" he asked the pair.

"He had a message for me. Nothing to do with the case, Sir," Claire replied.

Jake noticed the odd expression on the Sergeant's face but decided to let it be. "Can you bring Lucy Walker's bank statements into my office please. I just want to check a couple of things with you both," Jake said, already halfway out of the door.

"Sure, Sir," Claire said. She already had them to hand.

They followed Jake into his office where they all sat down.

"Look at this." Jake had already highlighted the amounts due to Lucy on her becoming pregnant, going full term and then the final payment on the day of the baby's delivery.

"Wow. That is just so much money." Tom looked flabbergasted.

"Sure is, but if Sofia didn't know, does that mean that Jett had paid Lucy the first instalment and…" Claire stopped herself mid-sentence.

"And what?" Jake pushed her.

"Sir, this doesn't make sense." Claire looked confused.

"What doesn't?" Tom asked her.

"The money, Tom." Claire looked to Jake. "Sir, if Lucy had received only the first payment from Jett, then where did all the rest of this money come from?"

"Exactly!" was the Inspector's reply.

Chapter Eleven

Louise Smart sat upright in the luxurious office, her eyes fixed on the door, as Inspector Jake entered Blacks estate agency with Tom and Claire following close behind.

Louise smiled and asked them to take a seat. "I presume this is about Lucy and not because any of you're house hunting." She spoke with a sarcastic tone.

It instantly irked Jake, and he responded with a flat, "You presume right."

Claire went over to peruse some of the properties for sale while Jake and Tom took seats opposite Louise.

"Ms Smart, may we ask you some questions about Lucy." Jake grinned.

"You may but please be quick as I have clients due in ten," she said looking at her watch.

"Can you tell us how you met Lucy. Known her long?" Jake asked with raised eyebrows.

"I met Lucy through Sofia. Sofia and I have been friends for ages. Then Lucy joined the same Pilates class that I go to and of course I helped Lucy and David find their home here in Amberleigh, but I guess you already know that?"

Jake nodded. "So how did you meet Sofia?"

Louise checked her watch. "I thought you wanted to know about Lucy?"

Claire turned round and asked, "How did you meet Vicky too?"

"Vicky? I met her at Pilates as well, but now she has kids she doesn't go as much as she used to." Louise rolled her eyes. "Regarding Sofia, I was one of Sofia and Jett's first clients when they set up here in Amberleigh. I've helped them find bigger and better premises as they grew and of course I helped them buy their magnificent home, but I don't see what any of this has to do with Lucy."

"Were you closer to Lucy or Sofia?" Jake asked her.

Louise seemed flummoxed by the question. "I've been friends with Sofia longer, but I was good friends with both of them. They helped me, and I helped them."

Claire jumped in. "What do you mean they helped you and you helped them?"

Louise, annoyed, said, "As friends. What did you think I meant?"

"Do Blacks bank here locally where Lucy worked?" Jake probed.

"Yes. Our bank account is at Gamblewood not here, but we use both branches." Louise checked her watch again.

"Did you know Lucy was pregnant?" Jake asked outright. All three were watching Louise closely.

"Lucy pregnant? Really? I thought her and David were waiting another year or so." Louise sat back in her chair "Hang on, how pregnant was she?"

"Six weeks," Claire announced.

"So, it's not David's." Louise smiled to herself.

"No. Any idea who the father might be?" Jake asked probing to find out if she knew about the surrogacy.

"Probably her boss!" Louise shrugged. "I really do have clients arriving any minute. If there's nothing further, could you please leave."

Jake, Tom and Claire thanked her saying they would be in touch as Louise Smart practically shoved them out of the door.

"Her boss? Where's that come from?" Tom said.

"Let's find out!" Jake said as lead the way across the road, heading towards the bank on the corner.

Dee sat in Coffee Creams reading Brenda and Pauline's account of what had happened with Ruth and how they had been targeted for information. As Peter joined her placing two mugs of hot tea on the table, Dee laughed out loud and passed the page to Peter for him to read.

"Don't laugh, Dee. They're scared and I know how that feels," Alison chided her.

"Sorry, Alison, but it looks like they just bumped into her - not exactly targeted but you're right. They could be in trouble if Ruth prints any of this." Dee looked at her apologetically.

"Their gossip seems to have thrown all of Lucy's friends under the bus," Peter remarked.

"I'd like to ask that Sofia Bailey a question or two and Louise Smart," Dee said taking a sip of her tea.

"I don't see why the ladies are scared Alison. What of?" Peter asked.

"Getting sued, I think," Alison said.

"Ruth won't name them. She's far too clever for that. They have nothing to worry about," Peter stated.

Alison said she'd be back with their sandwiches but shouted across the café, "Dee, won't you have to speak to Jake's neighbour, Vicky?"

Peter suddenly realised that he had not yet returned Jake's call and he indicated to Dee that he needed to step outside to phone him.

Dee nodded at Alison; her mind filled with numerous thoughts and ideas. She too needed to make a call - to her Gran.

Jake's mobile shrilled as they reached the bank and he asked Tom and Claire to go ahead and see if the manager was available as he needed to take the call.

"Peter, hi. Can you meet me at the Star and Crown tonight? Early though. I have some news you might be interested in."

"Sure, Jake. Are you alright?" Peter detected a slight wobble in the man's voice.

"Yes. I'll tell you more later," Jake replied ending the call. He took a deep breath as his hand pushed the door of the bank open. Suddenly memories came flooding back. The robbery, finding Cami clubbed over the head unconscious. He felt sick.

"Sir, are you okay? You look a little pale?" but Claire didn't wait for him to answer. "The manager will be with us shortly."

Peter rejoined Dee at the table in Coffee Creams, Alison had brought their sandwiches over and was now serving two new customers.

"I'm seeing Jake tonight. Well - late afternoon. Do you want to come with me?" Peter asked Dee.

"No, thanks. I've a few things to do, and look what's just come through."

Dee had no intention of seeing Jake. She pushed him to back of her mind as she showed Peter her mobile. "It's the CCTV footage. I'll make a start on going through it if you don't mind."

"No, not at all. Great idea. I think this case is dragging. I hope Mrs Walker doesn't call for an update, Dee. We've nothing to tell her," Peter said biting into his sandwich.

"Not as yet, but we really do need to talk to Lucy's friends."

"I don't think that's going to be straight forward, but we could start with Vicky. I'm sure she'll be happy to speak with us," Peter said.

"I knew you were going to say that!" Dee said looking up at the ceiling.

"Please take a seat," the Bank Manager said as he showed them into his office. "How can I help?"

Claire observed the man before her. He was probably in his fifties, balding and short. Hardly the sort of man that Claire could envisage anyone having an affair with and most certainly not Lucy.

"We've come to speak to you about Lucy Walker," Jake said professionally.

"Yes, I'm surprised you haven't been to see me before now." The manager looked at Jake then said, "I'm sorry; did you say your name was Inspector Jake Jones?"

Jake nodded.

"Oh, you remind me of a young police officer who was involved in that terrible robbery here. His name was Jake Arrow or Sparrow or something like that." He shook his head. "Terrible business - a long time ago now. That lovely young policewoman died you know. At least those responsible are behind bars."

Jake shivered as if a ghost had walked through him, and Tom and Claire exchanged glances,

Quick to change the topic, Jake asked, "What was your relationship with Lucy?"

They watched as he fiddled with his wedding ring "Purely professional, I can assure you."

"Are you aware that Lucy was pregnant?" Jake watched for any reaction.

"I was not!" The manager looked taken aback. "Oh that's so sad. Poor David; to lose his wife and baby in such tragic circumstances."

"Yes, it is," Claire agreed. "May I ask how long Lucy had worked here?"

The manager looked at Claire. "Since university. Clever girl. Worked her way up. She mostly worked here and then covered at the Gamblewood branch when needed."

"Did you know if Lucy had any enemies?"

"Lucy? Enemies?" He looked confused. "Why would you ask that? I thought Lucy had an accident at that spa. I don't understand."

"Sorry, we thought you might know. We held a press conference this morning. Lucy was murdered," Jake declared.

"Murdered?" He could hardly speak. "How?"

"Poisoned," Claire said. "Did you know if Lucy was having any problems here or at home?"

"No…I wouldn't. We didn't have that sort of a friendship. It was purely work. We talked about investments, and she had mentioned going away overseas on holiday but nothing more." He was trying to catch his breath as he spoke. "You're free to speak with any of the staff. Maybe someone at the Gamblewood branch might know more."

Jake cleared his throat. "One last thing then we'll be on our way. Lucy had several large amounts paid into her personal account. We know where one of these payments has come from, but can you shed any light on the others?"

"Deposits into her account. How much are we talking? People do buy and sell things on eBay and places like that," he suggested.

"Tens if not hundreds of thousands of pounds," Jake said with a straight face.

"Are you serious?" The Manager looked stunned. "I had no idea. I wouldn't know. Have you contacted head office? They might be able to help you more than I can."

Jake stood and thanked him for his time, telling him that if they needed anything further they would be in touch. Once outside Jake gulped in the fresh air, his throat tight and his breathing ragged.

"Sir, were you involved in that robbery here years ago? I've heard about it but..." Claire was stopped in mid-sentence by the ringing of Jake's mobile.

Jake turned away as he answered it. It was Catherine. Jake felt understandably relieved that he had been saved from answering Claire's question.

As Peter was meeting Jake, he had decided to pop home to Gaitley Manor to have a few minutes with Helen. He found her in the stables checking one of the horse's hooves.

"Hello there. Something wrong?" he asked her over the stable door.

Helen came over and kissed him. "No, she's fine. I just thought she'd lost a shoe."

"Time for a cuppa before picking up Clara?" Peter asked her.

"She's got netball practice tonight. She's not back till six - cuppa would be lovely," she said closing the stable door behind her.

Sir Henry and Mrs Wood were in the library deep in conversation surrounded by books and both jumped as Helen and Peter entered the room.

"What are you two up to? You both have a guilty look about you," Helen teased.

"Tea for everyone?" Mrs Wood asked as she quickly closed the book in front of her.

"That would be splendid." Sir Henry closed the book he held in his hand promptly and placed it back on the shelf.

As Sir Henry went to sit down, Peter went over to the bookshelf and looked out the volume Sir Henry had returned. He then picked up the book that Mrs Wood had been reading. "Toxic and exotic plants. What are you two up to?"

"Henry, we talked about this." Helen wagged her finger at him playfully.

"Did we, dear," he responded with a wink as Mrs Wood brought in the tea.

The day had proved tiring, and Dee sat with her computer on her lap, talking to her Gran about the case.

"You don't seem to have much to go on, dear," her Gran said.

"No Gran, I'm just watching the CCTV footage from Wellsdale Hall as we speak. I really need to talk to Lucy's friends. We're going to see Vicky tomorrow. We might find out more then," Dee said, feeling a little negative about their progress.

"Stay positive, dear. Something will turn up. It's not even been a week yet. Vicky? Isn't that the handsome Inspector's neighbour?" her Gran asked cautiously.

"You know full well it is, Gran!" Dee laughed down the phone. "Peter should be with Jake by now."

"Oh, Jake, is it?" her Gran teased. "Why is Peter meeting him?"

"I'm not sure. I was invited but I didn't want to go. You know I told you what happened the other day in the office…I may have imagined the whole thing. I saw him with someone - she's very attractive - at Mr Wangs." Dee could feel her heart miss a beat.

"Oh, darling. That could be anyone. His sister even." Her Gran was trying to pacify her.

Dee said, "Gran, you do not hug and kiss your sister like that!"

The landlord of the Star and Crown took the two pints he had pulled over to the table where he found Peter and Jake deep in conversation. "Nice to see you both again," he commented as he placed them down.

Jake and Peter thanked him and resumed their conversation.

"It was close, Peter. I thought he recognised me. I didn't want to explain my change of name to Claire and Tom. Fortunately just as Claire was asking me about the robbery, Catherine called. I was saved by the bell - literally."

"Yes, much water under the bridge since then. Who's Catherine?" Peter asked nonchalantly.

"She's covering for Ann," Jake explained as he took a sip of his pint.

"Oh. A Forensic Pathologist then. Don't you remember, Jake. I'm sure Cami had a friend called Catherine who was training to do forensics back then," Peter said, taking a sip of his pint and looking for a coaster to put it down on.

"It's one and the same," Jake replied.

It only then occurred to Peter that Jake and Cami's best friend had been heavily involved in a relationship - more so following Cami's death.

"Hmm, I see," Peter said.

"No, you don't see!" Jake replied. "And don't you raise those eyebrows at me!"

Peter decided to change the topic. "So why am I here? What news do you have?"

Jake took a further sip of his drink and started to explain about the contract and the payments that Lucy had received.

"Someone else is also paying her lump sums of money? What has this Lucy been up to? Do you think she was stealing it from the bank?" Peter asked him.

"We're looking into that. It's been insinuated that Lucy might have been having an affair with her boss!" Jake said in a low voice.

"I doubt that very much. Have you met the bank manager in Amberleigh, and I can assure you I know Craig Metcalfe the manager in Gamblewood very well and she certainly wasn't having an affair with him!" Peter laughed.

"How do you know?" Jake asked.

"Craig is married to Neil the cricket captain in Gamblewood. I go to watch sometimes if I get the chance," Peter said peeling the coaster from the bottom of his pint.

Jake stared into his pint for inspiration.

"Who insinuated Lucy was having an affair?" Peter asked.

"Louise Smart," Jake replied .

"Interesting!" Peter said thoughtfully.

Dee and her Gran had moved on from discussing Lucy's murder to her Gran telling her all the latest gossip from home. The pair were happily chatting and giggling away together when suddenly Dee stopped talking.

"Dee are you still there? Dee?"

"Gran, I'm still here, you won't believe what I've just seen," Dee said shocked.

"Are you alright? Are you still going through that CCTV thing while we've been talking?"

"Yes, Gran. Wait till I tell you this. I can't wait to tell Peter in the morning." Dee sounded excited.

"I told you something would turn up, dear. What is it?" her Gran asked.

"I asked Mrs Walker where she was on the seventeenth of May, the day Lucy was murdered, and she refused to answer. Now I know why," Dee told her.

"Why?" asked her Gran.

Dee replied, "She was at Wellsdale Hall!"

Chapter Twelve

To Jake it felt like the week was flying by. Although it had only been five days since Lucy's murder, he had to admit to himself and his superiors that they were getting nowhere fast!

"Damn!" he said out loud and banged his fist on the table as Claire and Tom knocked on his office door.

"Morning, Sir," Tom said a little too happily for Jake's mood.

He grunted a reply as they sat down.

Claire gave Tom a look as if to say *be careful*.

"We'll soon be into June and no further down the line with this investigation. There seems to be a lack of evidence and no clear motive as such!" Jake's tone was one of frustration.

"Sir, if I may. Maybe it's simply about the money. The husband and his mother might be in it together. We never asked when Mrs Walker found that bank statement and on reflection, I think we rather assumed it was after Lucy's death and not before." Claire looked at Jake, hoping he wasn't going to bite her head off.

"That's true Claire, but how did David and his mother poison her at Wellsdale Hall?" Jake stood and went to look out of his office window.

Claire took a deep breath. "I'm not sure, Sir. Shall we go back and talk to them."

"Yes." Jake turned and grabbed his jacket from the back of his chair. "That bloody reporter Ruth, has just pulled into the carpark. Let's leave out the back and sharpish!"

Dee woke up to a sunny May morning and chose ankle-length jeans, a white lightweight jumper, a little silver necklace with a blue pendant made of glass, and pumps. Appropriate for what she knew was going to be a long day ahead. To save time, Dee made the decision to head to Coffee Creams to fetch herself and Peter coffees and a breakfast muffin each. She sang to herself as she closed the door behind her totally unaware of the time.

"Sir, we can't go knock on Mr Walker's door. It's too early. It's only just after eight Sir," Claire said thinking David and his mother might not even be up.

"Valid point, Claire. We'll swing by Coffee Creams," Jake announced.

Tom and Claire swapped smiles. The mood seemed to have lifted.

Alison was busy setting up for the day, when she recognised the tap on the window. Dee's face was peering through the glass smiling at her. Alison went over to unlatch the door and let her in.

"You look lovely," Alison said as Dee walked in. "Usual?"

"Got a busy day, Alison. Can we have two coffees to go and two breakfast muffins, please." Dee headed towards her usual spot but turned around again. "Just popping to the loo."

Alison nodded and watched Dee disappear into the lady's toilet. The bell tinkled over the door and Alison turned to find Claire half in and half out the door.

"Haven't seen you for a while. Come in," Alison shouted over the noise of the coffee machine.

"It's all of us. Is that okay. I know you're not really open yet."

Alison nodded laughing to herself and wondering if she really should start opening at eight in the morning.

Claire beckoned Jake and Tom to come and join her and automatically went to sit in Dee's favourite spot.

"What are we having?" Alison came over to ask them as the bell tinkled once again. "What now? I think I might as well turn the sign to *Open*!"

They all turned to see a surprised Peter in the doorway.

"Hello everybody. Are we having a meeting? Did I miss something?" Peter said, joking as he joined them.

Jake spoke. "No; we needed to escape Ruth. Claire suggested here."

Peter gestured that he fully understood, surprised to realise that Ruth had not been in touch with himself yet.

"Orders please?" Alison interrupted them then looked at Peter. "Dee's already ordered yours to go."

"Dee's here. Well that's ruined that! I was going to surprise her with her favourite breakfast muffin." Peter looked disappointed. "She insisted on going through the CCTV footage last night on her own. I thought it would be a nice treat."

"We have professionals doing that, Peter. Dee doesn't have to do it," Jake remarked.

"I don't have to do what?" Dee had sneaked up on the table.

Jake turned to face Dee. He was about to say something but didn't. The pair locked eyes as if in a game of *who blinks first*.

"Sit down Dee. Here's your coffee and muffins. I take it you wouldn't want them to go now!" Alison said as she placed the tray down, pulling a face at Peter.

Dee greeted Claire with, "Hi," and gave her a hug before sitting down.

"You look amazing," Claire said to her. "Love your necklace."

"Thanks. My mum sent it from Spain. Inspector Jones, you were saying I don't have to do something?" Dee was like a dog with a bone.

Jake looked over at her. He could feel the animosity flooding from her, but he didn't know why. He knew he had felt something that day in Peter's office and hoped she had too. He must be wrong. Jake had to look away. Her anger made her cheeks flush, and she looked more beautiful than ever.

"Now, now Dee," Peter offered her the muffin. "I was saying that you were going through the CCTV footage last night, and Jake was saying that they are too. That's all."

"Have you found anything?" Dee asked Jake as Alison brought another tray laden with tea and toast for the Inspector and his colleagues.

Claire jumped straight in. "Tom and I haven't found anything significant as yet. We're still going through it."

"I have!" Dee declared looking at Peter.

Jake stopped pouring the tea, Claire stopped spreading the butter on her toast.

"Have you?" Peter asked.

"Do you know the whereabouts of David's mother on the day of the murder?" Dee asked Jake.

Tom quickly pulled out his notebook and stated, "She says she was at home most of the day."

Jake and Dee had once again locked eyes. Dee gently smiled. "That's not true."

Jake looked at Peter then back at Dee. "Is it not?" he asked her.

"No, she was at Wellsdale Hall. Mrs Walker can be seen on the CCTV footage," Dee said still smiling at the Inspector who turned to Claire and Tom.

"How did you two miss this?"

Claire looked down at her hands and Tom answered. "With all due respect, Sir, we weren't looking for her."

Jake turned to Dee. "Thank you for sharing that information. We're actually on our way to visit Mrs Walker. Seems we have more questions to ask than we first thought," he said looking at Peter before Dee.

"Great job!" Peter congratulated her.

Alison knew that Albert would be arriving at any minute and suggested they might want to be on their way but it was already too late.

Albert entered Coffee Creams carrying the local paper. "See you lot aren't getting anywhere. Why are you all sat here drinking tea when there's a killer to catch!" He passed Peter his paper. "I've not read it properly, so I want it back, but you lot better read that!"

Alison welcomed Albert as he went to sit at his usual table and looked over as the rest of them stood pouring over the news article before them.

"That bloody Ruth. I'll have to talk to her," Jake said annoyed.

"I'll do it," Peter said shaking his head. "This pretty much incriminates all Lucy's friends and anyone and everyone at Wellsdale Hall. We'll be lucky if we don't find her dead next!"

Ruth had returned to her car and sat tapping her nails on the steering wheel. That flipping Inspector was hard to track down. She wanted a quote from him, but the officer had said he was not in the building.

Her mobile rang it was Robert.

"Hi and to what do I owe the pleasure?" she tried to sound flirty.

"The pleasure is all mine, I assure you," Robert crooned back.

Ruth winced a bit. "Well, what is it?"

"His lordship wants you back here and quick!"

"Why? I saw him this morning. I don't need to come in. Tell him to phone me. It can't be anything serious." Ruth was getting impatient.

Robert's voice changed. "It is Ruth. A lawyer from Wellsdale Hall's here!"

Peter handed the paper back to Albert as Alison brought him over his tea and toasted teacake.

"Dee was a little frosty with Jake," she whispered in Peter's ear.

"I know. I suggested he take her out for a Chinese, but he hasn't yet," Peter whispered back.

"Honestly, I could knock their heads together. Suggest it again," Alison urged.

"I'm not sure. I think Catherine's back on the scene," Peter suggested.

"Who on earth is Catherine?" Alison looked surprised.

"I'll tell you some other time. We'd better get going," Peter said.

They turned to face the door; watching as Dee and Jake went to open the door at the same time.

"After you." Jake smiled at her.

Dee replied, "No I insist; after you!"

Tom barged through the middle of them both. "If you two are going to argue about who's going first then I will!"

Dee fell into Jake who caught her and held her for just a moment longer than he needed to. Dee could feel herself relaxing into his arms but Jake, suddenly aware of his surroundings, promptly let her go. Dee took a step back to steady herself, then excused herself and practically ran to the toilet.

Jake waved at Peter and Alison and made a hasty retreat closely followed by Claire.

Peter and Alison stared at each other smiling, thinking themselves alone in knowing what they had witnessed but Albert interrupted their thoughts. "Love is a funny carry on!" he declared.

Louise Smart tapped away at her laptop, reflecting on the wonderful day she'd had before. She was revising the contract for the house she'd just sold to a wealthy couple eager for a weekend retreat from London. Once she printed the document and tossed it onto her desk, she glanced at her watch - it was just after ten - before making her way to the stylish coffee machine. Unexpectedly, the door to Blacks opened and Louise turned to welcome the couple as they entered.

"How can I help you?" Louise offered them the chairs on the other side of her desk as she sat down. She thought to herself she needed to be careful Either the man was dating a much younger woman, or he was buying a place for his daughter.

"We're looking into the murder of Lucy on behalf of David and his mother. We would like to ask you a few questions if possible?" Peter asked her.

Louise was caught off guard. "I've given a statement to the police. Why would I talk to you?"

"I was the one who found Lucy in the Cave Pool. I still have sleepless nights about it." Dee put on a sad face. "They've asked us to help them find out who did this to Lucy, and I personally would like to." Dee handed her their card.

"Yes, I thought I vaguely recognised you from Wellsdale Hall," Louise lied.

"That was me," Dee smiled pitifully then brightened. "Can I say your hair and skin are gorgeous and that's a fabulous cut!"

"Thank you." Louise touched the elegant bob. "All Jett and Sofia's work; marvels the pair of them!"

"I've heard they're quite expensive, probably out of my budget!" Dee looked downcast.

"Worth every penny. How can I help you both regarding Lucy?" she asked them and moved the newly printed agreement to the edge of her desk.

"We understand you were all good friends, but it has been inferred that Sofia and Lucy were heard having an argument in one of the saunas. Do you know anything about that?" Peter asked.

Louise screwed up her face. "Sofia and Lucy arguing? Well if they did, they hid it well. I don't know of any falling out. If anything they seemed closer than ever."

"We understand you knew about Lucy's pregnancy?" Dee enquired.

"Only when the police told me. Lucy hadn't mentioned a word!" Louise looked put out.

"We work closely with the police," Peter told her. "We understand that you thought Lucy might be having an affair?"

"What other explanation is there. We know it's not David's. He's been away for weeks!" Louise stood up "Would you like some water?"

"No ta," Dee answered. "How close are you and Sofia? Do you tell each other everything?"

Louise returned and sat back down knocking the agreement to the floor. Dee bent down to pick it up.

"Not as close as we used to be in the early days, but we still see each other and chat most days," Louise said taking the document back from Dee.

Dee looked at Peter. He read her mind and nodded. "Louise, Lucy wasn't having an affair. She was being a surrogate mother for Sofia and Jett."

"What?" Louise looked upset. "In that case, I guess I'm not as close to either of them as I thought. Gosh I bet that cost them!"

"Sorry, why did you say that?" Dee asked.

They watched as Louise started fiddling with things on her desk and checked the time on her watch. "Nothing really. I do need to get on. Is there anything else? Anything at all?"

"Just one more thing. Did Lucy have any enemies that you know of?" Peter questioned.

"Lucy enemies? What a ridiculous question!" Louise said standing up to make it obvious she wanted them to leave.

"Someone wanted her dead," Dee said flatly.

"Well, it wasn't me and, if she was carrying Sofia and Jett's baby, it won't be them either, so I suggest you look elsewhere!" Louise was almost shouting at them.

"We will," Dee replied. Then as she made her way to leave she asked, "This is nice. What is it?"

Peter looked at Dee. She was pointing at a plant in the window.

Louise looked at them both. "How should I know? I can't tell a plant from a weed!"

At Gaitley Manor, Sir Henry had asked Helen if she had managed to secure a reservation at Wellsdale Hall as Mrs Wood poured them fresh coffee.

"Henry, are we really going through with this?" Helen sighed.

"Yes, of course, dear!" Sir Henry was enthusiastic about his idea.

"We couldn't get in till Sunday, are you still alright to join me, Mrs Wood? After all that's your day off?" Helen asked her.

"Of course. I will look forward to it!" Mrs Wood smiled at Sir Henry.

"Peter is fishing all day on Sunday and he's leaving early. Who's going to look after Clara?" Helen asked them.

"Me" said Sir Henry. "I will have a full day of activities planned!"

Helen decided to say nothing more and settled back to drink her coffee.

Ruth walked into her editor's office to be met by a young man in a grey suit who could be nothing else but a lawyer.

"Hello," Ruth said as she sat down, subtly adjusting her skirt to show more leg.

Her editor introduced them. He was being more than pleasant with them both, which unnerved her.

"About this article; we would like a full apology from you personally and the newspaper."

Ruth sat up straight. "Why do you need an apology?"

"You're inferring that a member of staff or management could be involved in the murder of Lucy Walker. You have no evidence to support this, only gossip and hearsay." He looked her straight in the eye. "This could be damaging to the reputation of Wellsdale Hall."

Ruth smiled to herself. Her editor had seen that look in her eye before and grabbed the edge of his desk.

"I don't give a monkey's arse about the reputation of Wellsdale Hall. A girl has been murdered on said premises. How do you know it wasn't a member of staff?

You don't." Ruth stood and walked behind her editors desk to stand at his side. "I suggest you leave here immediately or my next article will be about you and your company's intimidating behaviour. I feel sure if you're here acting on behalf of Wellsdale Hall, they wouldn't want it said publicly that they're more interested in looking after themselves than a dead girl's family!"

The lawyer stood. "I can assure you, we're doing everything to help the police with their enquiries. Print anything like that again and we'll see you in court!" He bid them farewell and left immediately.

"You were close to the bone there, but nicely put. Watch yourself Ruth. One day you might go too far!" her editor warned her.

Ruth smiled as she left his office to a round of applause from her eavesdropping colleagues.

Mrs Walker had returned with glasses of water and a cup of tea for herself. She patted David on the leg as she sat down.

"We have instructed the Gill agency to look into Lucy's death, just in case you didn't know," Mrs Walker said politely.

"We do know, Mrs Walker, but what we don't know is why you were at Wellsdale Hall on the day of Lucy's death?" Jake asked just as graciously.

"I wasn't, I was at home," she insisted.

"We have identified you on the CCTV," Tom chipped in.

"Have you indeed? Then I must have been there. Let me fetch my diary." With that Mrs Walker left the room and didn't return for several minutes.

"David, although we're having the deposits traced, it does look like other payments were made from elsewhere.

It wasn't all from the Baileys. Would you be able to shed any light on that?" Jake asked.

"No, no I can't. Lucy looked after all our finances, especially once I'd started gambling again." He looked upset. "All she said was that she was sorting it all out and I didn't need to worry. We were looking to move overseas away from my mother!"

"Yes, yes I see," Jake said in an understanding voice. "If you had to guess who would want to kill your wife, who would it be?"

Unfortunately Mrs Walker re-entered the room at that point. "Don't you ask my son a question like that. That's your job!"

"Sorry, David, that was insensitive of me but if you do have any thoughts, please let us know. Sometimes it's just a little thing that helps us to solve a murder," Jake appealed directly to him.

"Mrs Walker, I see you have your diary?" Claire tried to be as nice as possible.

"Yes, I was at Wellsdale Hall that day. You are correct?" she said.

"I'm surprised you would have forgotten that fact Mrs Walker," Jake said to her.

"Who said I had forgotten? I just didn't think it was important. After all I am a member." Mrs Walker glowered at them all. "I didn't know Lucy and her cronies were there."

Tom was busily writing away in his notebook.

"We can easily check that out. Don't worry, Mrs Walker. I think you must have had so much on your mind that day." Claire spoke soothingly.

"Yes, indeed I did," she said looking directly at Jake and then at David.

"Just to clarify something. When did you find Lucy's bank statement and where? The one you gave to Peter Gill," Jake pressed her.

"Like I have already told them, it was behind the microwave. I found it while I was cleaning after Lucy died. David wasn't up to it, were you, love?"

David nodded and changed the subject. "When can we have Lucy's funeral?"

The question took Jake by surprise. "I will speak to Catherine…sorry, Forensics, and see what can be done. I will let you know, David." Jake looked over at Claire. "Do we have any further questions? If not we'll leave you good people in peace."

"Just one if I may. I see you have a greenhouse. Who's the one with the green fingers?" Claire asked, pointing out of the window.

David responded before his mother could. "That's all Lucy. She was always growing things for her hobby. She made lotions and potions. She was always looking for ways to help her psoriasis."

"Thank you. Is it alright if we take a look on our way out?" Jake asked.

"Please do. Do you want me to come with you?" David asked.

"No, we'll only be two minutes," Jake said and then nodded to Tom and Claire to go look in the greenhouse. "Thank you once again," he said. "We'll see ourselves out."

As soon as they were gone, David turned to his mother. "Why would they want to look in the greenhouse?"

Mrs Walker scowled at him. "Why do you think? They will be looking for Poison Ivy you nit wit!"

Chapter Thirteen

"Any plans for the weekend?" Peter asked Dee as they walked back to the car after leaving Blacks Estate Agency.

"No, you?" she asked.

"I'm fishing all day Sunday in one of the local competitions. Mind you it's an early start!" Peter tutted to himself.

"Best of luck with that. What will Helen and Clara be up to?" Dee asked him.

"Something horsey, I imagine!" he laughed.

"Peter, I can't help thinking that Louise was hiding something. Did you?"

"Not so much that she was hiding something, but I think she was jealous of Lucy and Sofia's friendship," he replied.

"I'm not sure about that. I just feel maybe she wasn't as keen on Lucy as she's leading us to believe. It's just a feeling." Dee shrugged.

"Well, someone didn't like Lucy that's for sure!" Peter stated as they reached the car.

Back at the Walker's there was nothing to be found in the greenhouse.

"You wouldn't leave it lying around would you? They could have disposed of it," Claire suggested.

"They could have, but how would they do it? How's anyone done it? That's the question!" Jake sounded frustrated.

"Where are we going, Sir?" Tom asked the Inspector.

"Back to the office. I need you both to go through that CCTV again and chase up where these deposits have come from. I'm nipping home and I'll call on Vicky at the same time," said Jake.

"Is that wise, Sir, going on your own. She'll try to eat you alive!" Claire said giggling.

"She can try!" was the reply.

The morning of the twenty first of May had turned into the afternoon and Dee and Peter were making their way towards Vicky's front door when they heard Jake shouting at them from his car.

"Hang on, I'll come with you!"

Dee and Peter walked back to the gate to meet him.

"I was just nipping back with some paint samples; I have a decorator coming round tomorrow to give me a quote," Jake explained.

"Dee could help you with that. She's done all her own decorating, and you've seen what a great job she's done with the office," Peter said nudging her.

"Yeah sure, if you want any help let me know." She glared at Peter.

"Thanks, maybe after this you could both nip in and let me know your thoughts on paint colour. I'm not very good at that sort of thing," Jake had joined them in Vicky's front garden.

Dee wanted to say, "Ask your girlfriend then," but didn't.

"I know why I'm here to see Vicky, but could you tell me why both of you are here?" Jake asked as they approached the door.

"Same as you. Hoping she'll be more helpful than Lucy's friends," Peter said as he knocked on the door.

"Have you spoke to the Baileys yet?" Jake asked the pair.

"No, just Louise Smart and we didn't get far there!" Peter replied as Vicky opened the door.

"Jake come in. Oh and you two. I'm pleased you're here I haven't got long. I'm dreading the school run. I wish someone else could pick them up for me." Vicky grabbed the Inspector by the arm.

Jake shrugged her off and avoided sitting on the sofa as did Peter, leaving Dee to sit down next to Vicky.

"Have you seen that horrible newspaper article. I come out of it lightly, but they'll all be asking me questions at the school gate. Honestly, it does imply that Sofia and Lucy had been arguing, and she was poisoned with Poison Ivy. How did they do that?" Vicky finally stopped to take a breath.

"Vicky, at any point did any of you leave the dining room. Did anyone of you fetch food for Lucy?" Jake looked across at Peter.

"No, we all sat together, and we went to the buffet at the same time. I was the only one who went back on my own for more; the chicken pasta was out of this world!"

Dee stifled a giggle.

"Did anyone order from the kitchen and not have the buffet?" Peter asked.

"No, we didn't. We all ate from the buffet; it's award-winning." She smiled and reached forward to pat Jake's knee.

Dee looked away as Jake shifted in the chair so Vicky could not reach him as easily.

"At any point was Lucy's plate left unattended?" Jake asked.

Vicky looked confused. "Unattended? What do you mean?"

Dee explained. "Vicky, did anyone at that table have the opportunity to put poison in Lucy's food?"

"No!" Vicky looked horrified. "We went into the dining room together and left together. Then we went to have our treatments after lunch. No one could have put anything in anyone's food I can assure you!"

"Do you know if Lucy had a falling out with Sofia or Louise at all?" Jake asked.

"I met Sofia for the first time that day, but Louise and Lucy have never mentioned any falling out. I've told you this before. However, there was something." Vicky looked thoughtful.

"Yes?" Jake urged her to go on.

"I'm not sure. Louise was asking why Lucy wasn't having a drink and Sofia told her to leave her alone." Vicky shrugged. "If she didn't want to drink, she didn't have to, it's not as if she was pregnant."

The three swapped glances. Jake spoke into the abrupt silence. "Vicky, Lucy was pregnant."

"Was she? Oh poor David. How awful." Vicky stood up and walked over to the patio doors, starting to cry.

Dee and Jake went towards her at the same time, but she launched herself at Jake. "How far along was she? David and his mother will be devasted. Why didn't anyone tell me?" She buried her head in Jake's chest.

Dee went to sit back down, and Peter calmly interrupted the scene. "Vicky if you can take a seat, we can explain."

Dee watched as Jake peeled Vicky off him and escorted her back to the sofa.

"Lucy was six weeks pregnant and no it wasn't David's. She was being a surrogate mother for Jett and Sofia" Dee said grabbing her hand.

Vicky looked visibly shocked.

"We presume that's why she wasn't drinking," Peter said.

"No, Lucy said she had bad stomach-ache, with cramps and had taken a strong painkiller and she didn't think she should drink. I presumed like the rest of us to be honest that she was having her period. Her being pregnant never crossed my mind!" Vicky pulled her hand away from Dee's.

"I'm aware of the time," Jake said. "We'll be on our way, but Vicky do you have any idea or reason who and why someone would want to kill Lucy?"

"I don't. I wish I did," Vicky said drying a tear with a tissue from her jeans pocket.

Once outside Jake sighed. "This is getting ridiculous. Lucy has upset someone somewhere and all that money... I wish we could catch a break!".

"We will," Peter said putting an arm around him. "Show us these paint colours then."

Sofia and Louise sat having a glass of champagne in Sofia's kitchen.

"Why didn't you tell me about Lucy and the surrogacy Sofia?" Louise looked genuinely upset.

"We couldn't tell anyone. I didn't even know it had worked. Jett did but I didn't!" Sofia took a gulp of champagne.

"Jett did? How did he know and you not?" Louise looked bewildered.

"They were going to tell me on my birthday next week. Not that it matters now; my baby died with her." Sofia started to cry.

Louise put an arm around her, "Sofia was it your egg and Jett's sperm?"

"Yes of course it was. We did it properly and we paid her for it." Sofia wiped away a tear. "I don't care about the money!"

"You don't have to!" Louise said sardonically as Jett walked in carrying the local newspaper.

"Are you alright" he said hugging his wife. "You two need to read this!" There printed in black and white was a picture of Sofia and the salon, plus a picture of Louise and the outside of Blacks Estate Agency.

"What the fuck is this!" Louise was reading the article intently as was Sofia. "Who is this Ruth woman? She's inferring we could have poisoned Lucy, the cheeky cow. I'll have the lawyers onto this in the morning!"

"Don't bother!" Jett said. "It'll be chip paper tomorrow as they say."

"Jett, this could impact my business," Louise stammered.

"And ours!" Sofia spat out.

"Sofia, on the back of this, we've had more new clients and bookings in one day than ever. If anything this woman has given us free advertising!" Jett laughed as he poured himself a glass of champagne.

Louise put her drink down and said she had to leave.

"Don't rush off!" Sofia said to her.

"I've Charles Black to deal with, my business partner!" Louise said already dialling his number as she closed the front door behind her.

As her mobile tried to connect, she turned back to look at the house that stood before her. "Those two always come out smelling of fucking roses!" she muttered angrily to herself.

Dee felt a flutter of nerves as she stepped into Jake's home for the first time. She vividly remembered how it had looked when Muttering Margo owned it - the floral chintz curtains that once framed the windows had been replaced, yet the familiar sense of comfort lingered. Thankfully Jake hadn't changed it too much since moving in. The house retained a homely feel, with its neutral palette: soft beige walls and cream-coloured rugs gave the space a gentle warmth. Green checked throws were draped over the arms of the sofa and a matching armchair, adding a cosy touch. A mirror now hung above the fireplace, and a framed photograph of Jake with, Dee presumed, his parents was proudly displayed on a pine side table.

Jake shouted to them to come through to the kitchen. He was holding up two different shades of white.

"You've done all this yourself?" Peter said impressed.

The kitchen was unrecognisable from when Deehad last seen it. All the dark wood was gone. Cream wooden cabinets now lined the walls, giving the space a bright, airy feel. Below, sage green cabinets provided a gentle contrast. A matching countertop tied the two colours together seamlessly. At the far end, Jake had even built a small breakfast bar, complete with sage green stools to match. Each detail, from the soft cream to the cool green, created a welcoming and inviting atmosphere.

"Any ideas which one?" Jake said holding the paint samples against the wall.

"You've done a great job with the kitchen; modern but suit's the house's character perfectly," Dee praised him "Now if you look closely that white one has a pink undertone and that one a green one. I'd go for the green, given the cabinets and the throws."

"Then this is the one! "Jake held the sample up in the air. "Thanks - it took a while, but..." Jake was interrupted.

"I have work to do. If you two want to talk decorating why don't you go out for that meal you owe Dee and discuss it then." Peter crossed his fingers behind his back.

"I'd like to, but I can't tonight," Jake said looking questioningly at Peter.

"It's fine. I already have my tea in the slow cooker," Dee lied, feeling embarrassed. "Actually, I need to get back and rescue it!"

They watched as Dee picked up her things and made her exit.

"I'm meeting Catherine later," Jake said to Peter as he showed him out.

"I see!" Peter said with raised eyebrows,

"No, you don't. Let me explain," Jake said exasperated.

"It's all good, Jake. I have to get Dee back. See you soon!" he shouted from halfway down the garden path.

Jake closed his front door behind them with a slam.

Louise sat in her car a little further down the lane from Sofia's house. Her call with Charles Black hadn't been as bad as she'd expected. Fortunately for Louise, he'd also chosen to ignore the insinuations and treat them as free advertising. Louise let out a slow breath she hadn't realised she was holding, her hands still trembling slightly on the steering wheel. As the adrenaline faded, she stared through the windscreen, collecting her thoughts.

After a moment or two, Louise reached across to her handbag on the passenger seat for her mobile. She scrolled through her contacts, finally finding the number she was searching for. The person on the end of the line answered, "Angela Myers here. How can I help?"

"Angela, this is Louise Smart. We need to talk!"

Chapter Fourteen

A sunny Saturday morning had arrived. "Good morning!" Dee's Gran voice boomed cheerily from the speaker on her mobile.

"Morning, Gran. I was going to call you to update you yesterday, but nothing's really happened. Everyone seems to know nothing!" Dee answered, spooning yoghurt into her mouth.

"There has to be something, dear. Try looking elsewhere. Have you spoken to the fancy hairdressers yet?" she asked.

"No, Gran. That's on the agenda for Monday, but I know Jake's been to see her; upset her from what Claire told me."

"How are Claire and the other ladies?"

"They're all good, but Claire's a bit off. Jake seems to be on her case a lot. Ooh I've just remembered, I haven't told you about the CCTV!" Dee grabbed her coffee and plonked herself down on the sofa.

"Go on!" her Gran encouraged.

Dee explained that Jake was not impressed that Claire and Tom had missed picking up Mrs Walker on the footage.

"You know, dear, why don't you have a spa day yourself; see what you can find out there. Incognito as such!"

"I've been thinking about that. If I can talk to the staff, I'm sure I could find out much more. That manager isn't squeaky clean, Gran, I'm sure of it." Dee's voice dropped "But it's expensive and I don't want to go on my own."

"You don't have to. I'll come with you. I've always wanted to go to one of those fancy spas!" Her Gran continued, "Don't you worry about the money. They've cancelled the bingo trip to Filey, and I've had a full refund. That will pay for it."

"Really Gran are you sure?" Dee knew there was no changing her Gran's mind once it was made up.

"Absolutely. Try and get us in as soon as you can. I'll look forward to it!" she replied.

Dee hung up and phoned Wellsdale Hall followed by a quick check of the train times. Twenty minutes later she was back on the phone to her Gran.

"How about tomorrow? There's a train at three this afternoon from Leeds to here. I can meet you at the station. Fancy Mr Wangs tonight, Gran?" Dee could feel the excitement welling up in her.

"That all sounds wonderful, dear. I will be at Leeds train station for three o'clock. Now, I'd best be off to find my bathing suit!"

Dee was still laughing to herself as she phoned Wellsdale Hall to confirm the reservation she had on hold. While booking the train ticket for her Gran, Dee realised she had no food at home and would finally have to face a supermarket shop. She usually avoided it at all costs, but today there was no escaping it.

At Gaitley Manor, Sir Henry was sitting in the orangery playing a game of snap with Clara.

"I wondered where you two had got to?" Helen smiled as she and Peter came in to join them. "Such a lovely day Clara. Fancy a quick ride through the grounds?"

"Wonderful idea!" Sir Henry agreed "Are you sleuthing today, Peter?"

"No, Dee and I need to take a step back and start again. We need to speak to the Baileys and I'm hoping by Monday Jake will have something on where those payments have come from." Peter's frustration was obvious.

"You and Dee will get to the bottom of it. From what you were saying last night, do you think the husband's mother could be involved?" Sir Henry asked Peter as Helen was ushering Clara out of the door.

"What - for the money? Maybe, but how did she do it?" Peter shrugged. "I'm thinking I might not go fishing tomorrow. I think I'll stay here instead. I need to clear my head!"

Helen turned quickly in the doorway and looked to Sir Henry for help.

"No, no Peter you don't want to do that," Sir Henry was on his feet. "Fishing is good for the mind. The fresh air will help you think more clearly!"

"I suppose you're right. Is it still alright with you Helen? I'll be away most of the day?"

"Of course. There's plenty to keep us two busy isn't there?" she said smiling at Clara.

"Mummy, can we go now?" Clara asked pulling her out the door.

As Clara left and Peter followed her out, Mrs Wood came into the Orangery.

"Hear any of that?" Sir Henry asked her.

Mrs Wood answered, putting her hand on his arm. "All of it. That was a close shave!"

Ruth was laid in bed. Robert walked in bringing them both a mug of coffee. "See you have caused another sensation!" he said passing over her mug.

"Hopefully it will stir up a little trouble!" Ruth laughed as she threw the paper down on the bed.

"From what I heard in the office yesterday you've already got the lawyers hunting for blood." He sidled in next to her.

"It's not the first time and it won't be the last!" she said throwing her head back.

"Who do you think did it?" Robert asked taking a sip of his coffee.

"I wouldn't tell you or anyone for love nor money where my bets are placed!" she teased him.

"Then in that case, I'll try another method!" he said. He took the mug from her hand and pulled her under the covers.

Jake had wanted to get to work early, but things hadn't quite gone to plan the night before. "Good morning you two, I can't offer you much in the way of breakfast, but I can make a tea or a coffee," he offered.

"Coffee for two please." Catherine laughed, then patted her tummy. "I meant three."

Ben came and wrapped his arms around her. "Thanks for last night, Jake. It was great to catch up."

"Feeling better?" Jake asked Catherine.

"Much. Just a bit of a scare. I've been overdoing it a little." She kissed Ben on his cheek.

"That you have," Ben agreed. "This case has got her working all hours!"

"I know Ben, but that's what I do. It's intriguing. You don't get cases like this every day!" Catherine smiled at Jake.

Jake smiled back at the couple. "It's a good job we don't!"

"I'm sorry about last night. One minute I was fine and the next…I feel awful that you had to sit in hospital with me till Ben came." Catherine went over to the fridge to fetch the milk.

"Catherine, I was not leaving you. You had a proper turn. We shouldn't have been at the lab that late." Jake took the milk from her. "At least you're both okay and that's all that matters!"

"Yes, it is!" Ben came over to Jake and put his hand on his shoulder. "Thank you for looking after them till I could get there and for putting us both up at short notice."

"You're welcome anytime. You weren't booking into a hotel at that time in the morning!" Jake said firmly, handing out the coffees.

"Jake, do you mind if I mention something?" Catherine was opening cupboards one after another.

Ben and Jake exchanged glances.

Catherine stood with her hands on her hips. "Jake Jones there is no food in this house!"

Dee was about to jump in the car to head off to the large supermarket on the outskirts of Gamblewood but decided to call in at Coffee Creams to tell Alison all about her Gran coming to visit and the spa day they had planned.

"That's fabulous, I wish I was coming with you," Alison said taking a seat opposite her.

"Quiet in here for a Saturday, isn't it?" Dee asked looking round the café.

"You know it is today," Alison agreed. "We haven't had the usual cyclists in this morning or the gym bunnies from the park."

"That yoga lot weren't in the park this morning and there's a cycle race in Amberleigh," Albert spoke from behind his newspaper.

Dee laughed "Is there anything you don't know Albert?"

"Not much, and I do know a little more than you!" Albert said putting his paper down.

"Give over, Albert!" Alison giggled.

"What about, Albert?" Dee asked, playing along.

Albert beckoned for them to come over to his table. "The manager at that spa place."

Dee was suddenly interested.

Alison chipped in, "Albert you know nothing about Wellsdale Hall. I bet you've never been!"

"Okay I haven't but my Annie went a couple of times, and she saw something once. Very observant my Annie," Albert said looking pleased with himself. "She said she'd heard the rumours."

Dee could hardly contain herself. "Rumours? Albert what did Annie see?"

"It's a fair while ago now. As you know Annie has been gone for some time, but there was a rumour about the new manager back then, swapping labels on products and a woman had a reaction because the label said it didn't contain nuts, but it did. It had coconut in it."

"What happened? Did she sue them?" Alison asked before Dee could.

"Nah, she only had a mild reaction, and the manager gave her a free membership."

"How do you know that?" Dee asked not really believing him.

"Annie talked to the woman herself, so the rumour was true and Annie said she saw one of those spa girls refilling the shampoo dispenser things in the changing rooms." Albert paused for a breath. "Supposed to be posh stuff if you look at the label, but Annie said it was cheap rubbish they put in!"

"I bet lots of hotels do that," Alison said. "Cost cutting!"

"Cost cutting or not, that's not a good reputation for a place like Wellsdale Hall to have." Dee looked lost in thought as she gathered her things to leave.

"Penny for them?" Alison asked nudging her.

"Mushrooms!" Dee replied as she walked out the door.

Vicky, Jake's neighbour, called out to her children, telling them to stop running across the supermarket car park for what felt like the hundredth time. She paused, recalling the awkward conversation she'd had earlier while fastening the boys into their car seats. She had exchanged polite words with the attractive brunette Jake was helping into her car, making small talk about the trials of learning how to use child seats - her hand resting on her growing baby bump as she spoke. Vicky hadn't noticed the man standing in Jake's doorway chatting into his mobile; her attention was on Jake and the woman.

She pushed her trolley into the supermarket, her frustration simmering beneath the surface. The idea of Jake having a girlfriend, let alone a pregnant one, was unsettling as was the prospect of an attractive woman living next door.

With a final shout to her boys, she entered the shop, not truly caring whether they listened or not!

Dee was already halfway through her shopping when she spotted Vicky and her struggle with the boys.

"Okay there?" Dee said.

"Oh, it's you. These two are so unruly today. If my husband doesn't come home this afternoon, I swear there will be hell to pay!"

She plonked the younger one of the two in the seat of the trolley.

"You do have your hands full. How are you doing since Lucy's death?" Dee asked.

"I'm okay, it's just the baby thing that shocked me. Talking of the baby thing, our lovely Inspector kept that quiet, but I guess you knew?" Vicky was now wrestling with the elder child.

"Knew what?" Dee looked puzzled.

Vicky, noticing Dee's expression, chose to stay silent. "It's not my concern; I should go before these two-cause total havoc!"

Dee watched as Vicky and the boys went down the next aisle, but she could still hear her shouting at them as she went to the till to pay.

Then as she made her way out, Jake entered the supermarket.

"Dee, Hi, I was going to see if…" Jake stopped as Dee interrupted him.

"Congratulations!" she said solemnly and walked away pushing her trolley as fast as she could.

Sunday morning had arrived. Dee and her Gran had enjoyed a wonderful evening at Mr Wangs, who had spoilt her and Gran with extra free dishes to try.

Dee's Gran clutched her stomach and said, "I'm still stuffed from last night. Mr and Mrs Wang really are so kind and generous."

"I know, lovely people. Are you nearly ready Gran? We need to get a move on!"

"That I am!" her Gran replied.

Over at Gaitley Manor, Mrs Wood was in the car and waiting for Helen to join her. She checked the list of instructions Sir Henry had given her. It was quite a list.

"What have you got there?" Helen said as she climbed into the passenger seat.

Mrs Wood decided to come clean and handed Helen the piece of paper.

"Henry, seriously wants us to sneak around Wellsdale Hall and if we get caught, we're to pretend we're lost!" Helen looked bewildered.

"He's full of ideas. Read the rest of the list," Mrs Wood instructed as they negotiated the long drive.

"Why would we ask this?" Helen pointed at one of the questions on the list as Mrs Wood came to a stop waiting for the electric gates to fully open.

"Your guess is as good as mine!" She shrugged as they pulled away.

Dee and her Gran were sitting in the conservatory swaddled in the luxurious white robes of Wellsdale Hall looking out onto the courtyard garden.

"You can't imagine anything such as a murder happening here," Dee's Gran remarked.

Dee didn't answer. She sipped the herbal tea they had been given on arrival and was deep in thought.

"Dee after this can we go to that pool area. I would like to take a dip in the Cave Pool if you're alright to go back in there after you know what last week?"

"Course we can. I'll be fine," Dee said putting her cup down on the glass coffee table. "As long as there's no dead bodies floating in it!"

Meanwhile Helen and Mrs Wood were upstairs being shown the bedrooms by the hotel manager.

"Your guest hens…" she giggled "Can all be accommodated. As you can see, we have a number of deluxe rooms. Breakfast is served in bed every morning and we also have a private room available for your evening meals if required."

"This is all very acceptable, Ms Myers." Mrs Wood smiled at her.

"I don't want to take up too much of your time, so please enjoy everything that Wellsdale Hall has to offer and if you have any further questions, please call me any time." Angela handed her card to Mrs Wood. "All staff have been instructed to look after you, so if you require anything, anything at all, please ask."

They thanked her and said they would see if she was available before they left.

Angela was thrilled that Lord Gaitley's daughter was considering hosting her hen party at Wellsdale Hall. It would bring much-needed positive publicity after recent events. She sang to herself on the way to her office.

"Ooh, it's creepy, Dee. I'm not sure about this. I don't like it." Dee's Gran was struggling to settle in the Cave Pool.

"Me neither. I think the hot tub would be a far better option," Dee said already making her way towards the steps. "Too many ghosts in here for me!"

"This is very relaxing Helen, but we haven't asked any questions yet." Mrs Wood seemed agitated sitting in the hot tub.

"I know, Mrs Wood. I have no idea where to start!" Helen exclaimed.

"You have got to be kidding me, Helen, Mrs Wood!"

Dee launched herself into the hot tub and greeted them both with a hug.

Dee's Gran was struggling to climb in to join them.

"Sorry, Gran." Dee grabbed her hand and helped her in. "This is my Gran. Gran this is Helen, Sir Henry's daughter and this is Mrs Wood, their housekeeper."

They exchanged pleasantries and idle chit chat until Dee asked, "You're here about your hen do, I assume. Does that mean we have a date?"

Mrs Wood went quiet. Helen looked across at her and then said quietly, "No Dee, we haven't. It's a bit of a pretence. Sir Henry thought we might be able to do a little investigating to help you and Peter, but the truth is we really don't know what we're doing or where to start."

Dee let out a laugh. "I don't believe it. So are we."

"What have you found out?" Helen asked her.

"Nothing so far. We've drank tea and used the spa! Shall we have an early lunch and hatch a plan?"

All four agreed and went to the changing room to get changed into dry swim wear.

Over lunch they decided Helen and Dee would have a treatment each and Dee's Gran and Mrs Wood would have a walk around the gardens and ask a few questions.

Dee came back to the table with her plate. "That doesn't work; you could choose anything. Any of the guests could have been poisoned," Dee explained.

Mrs Wood had an idea and beckoned a waiter to come over. "Excuse me, if I had an allergy would I need to order from the kitchen?"

"No, madam." The young waiter looked surprised. "We don't tend to serve from the kitchen at lunch time unless it's by special request. If you look at all the labels attached to each dish - even the lettuce on the buffet -

they're clearly marked for all allergies: dairy, gluten free, nuts, and so on."

"Thank you," Mrs Wood said politely.

"We're here to help," the waiter continued "Would you need anything else?"

"Could the dishes be labelled incorrectly?" Helen asked him.

"No, not at all. Allergies are taken very seriously here and in the treatment rooms. "He smiled at them "If you need anything else, please ask."

They watched him walk to another table and out of ear shot.

"I have a thought," Dee announced.

"What is it?" her Gran asked.

"I'll let you know later. It's just a thought for now." Dee smiled tucking into her lunch.

Lunch finished, Dee's Gran and Mrs Wood were enjoying a pleasant stroll round the extensive gardens.

"By the way my name is Pat," Dee's Gran introduced herself to Mrs Wood properly.

"I'm Doris. Pleased to make you acquaintance!" Mrs Wood chuckled.

"It's a little cold, to say we'll be heading into June soon. It's not as warm as usual." Pat shivered.

"I agree. Do you like doing jigsaws, Pat?" Mrs Wood enquired.

"That I do Doris, along with a nice pot of tea!" Pat enthused.

"I saw a jigsaw room. Shall we go and hide in there?" Mrs Wood suggested.

They giggled like a pair of schoolgirls and made their way back towards Wellsdale Hall.

"Gosh this is an extensive form to fill in," Helen said to Dee. They were sitting in the waiting area for treatments.

"That answers my question about allergies. They ask you anything and everything. By the time I've filled this in, I'll need my massage," Dee said.

"Are we done, ladies?" The young therapist stood in front of them. "We're nearly ready for you both."

Helen handed her form to the girl and Dee said she wouldn't be much longer. The therapist smiled and said she would return in a minute or two.

A few minutes later Dee handed her form to the girl. "Can you ask for a certain therapist to do a particular treatment?" Dee asked her.

The girl smiled sweetly. "All girls are allocated their treatment rooms for the day in the morning; with the exception of reiki we are all fully trained to the highest standard to do all treatments available."

Dee and Helen thanked her. As she left them a therapist of more mature years stood at the top of the room calling Dee and Helen's names.

They made their way towards her and were greeted warmly. She introduced herself as Laura and explained that she would be Helen's therapist for her facial and that Lori was adding the final touches to Dee's treatment room for her massage.

They parted company when Dee was greeted by a very attractive girl in her late twenties. "I'm Lori. Sorry I wasn't at reception to meet you. I was just lighting all the candles," she proudly.

"It's beautiful. They smell amazing!" Dee was astonished at the number of candles in the room.

I'll be outside, please get undressed and lay under the blanket for me. You may keep your knickers on!" She giggled.

Dee laughed, "I take it that's happened before."

"More than once!" Lori smiled as she closed the door behind her.

Dee did as instructed. Her completed questionnaire lay on the side surrounded by lotions, oils and equipment she had never seen before.

When Lori re-entered the room, she asked if Dee was comfortable. "I've read your form, and you have no allergies. Do you like a particular scent of oil for your massage?"

"I've no idea. Do you have a preference." Dee asked her.

"It states on your form that you're not pregnant or trying to get pregnant and I love the lavender oil. Is that okay?" she asked washing her hands in the tiniest basin Dee had ever seen.

"That's great!" Dee said. She had winced at the word *pregnant*.

In the other treatment room, Helen was having a chat with Laura asking her how long she had worked as a therapist, and which was her favourite treatment to do.

"The facial you're having is one of my favourites. I love all the Bailey skin care range. That's what I'm going to use on your skin today. You'll be glowing by the end of this treatment," she said assessing Helen's skin. "Shall we begin?"

Helen nodded but asked, "What's behind that door?"

"It goes into the treatment room next door. These are the only two connecting treatment rooms. We use them for couples sometimes if requested," Laura explained as she applied a cold cleansing cream to Helen's face.

"Is it locked?"

"Yes. No one is coming in here. Only the manager has the key," Laura said. "Please close your eyes for me and relax."

Dee was halfway through her massage.

"Is this pressure okay for you?" Lori asked her.

"It's great, are the oils and the candles made by the same company? I'd like to buy one," she asked.

Lori answered enthusiastically. "This oil and the candles are from the new Bailey collection; they're available in the shop. Jett and Sofia live here in Amberleigh. They have an amazing salon. You must try it."

"I will. You say Jett and Sofia; do you know them well?" Dee probed.

"We all do. They do the training here on how to use and apply Bailey products. Sofia is great and Jett, he's a whizz with hair. I modelled for him once."

"Oh, so they're here a lot," Dee asked.

"Jett more than Sofia, but we all know why," Lori said with a sarcastic edge as she dug her fingers into Dee's calf.

"What do you mean?" Dee enquired pensively.

Lori clammed up. "I meant nothing. Jett delivers here most weeks. Now, please relax."

Helen had no idea what was happening. She'd had a face mask applied and the therapist explained that she would leave her to enjoy the tranquil music and to relax while the mask set and she felt her pop a cooling pad over each eye.

Once Laura had left, Helen jumped off the bed and scoured the room looking at all the different bottles on display. There were others by larger companies, but the Baileys' skin and hair care range held the majority. She wasn't sure what she was looking for, but none had Poison Ivy written on them, not that she thought for one minute they would. She heard voices outside the door, and recognising the managers voice from earlier quickly jumped back on the bed and replaced the eye pads.

Laura re-entered the room, removed the eye pads and started to remove the mask. "I've just been informed you're a VIP guest, so as an extra treat I am going to give you a hand massage."

Helen couldn't answer, her face was rigid under the mask.

Mrs Wood and Dee's Gran were sitting enjoying the view out onto the tennis courts from the jigsaw room.

This is such a beautiful building. You can imagine how it used to be years ago can't you?" Mrs Wood said.

"Oh yes, ladies in long dresses courting young gentlemen." Dee's Gran smiled dreamily. "Top up of tea Doris?"

"Yes please." Mrs Wood moved her cup and saucer towards Dee's Gran. A couple of puzzle pieces had stuck to the bottom and they watched as they fell to the floor. Both ladies were bending to pick them up when the door to the jigsaw room opened.

"There's no one in here," Angela declared. "How can I help you. You did seem a little cryptic the other day on the phone."

Mrs Wood mouthed at Dee's Gran to stay down.

"I'm a friend of Lucy Walker," Louise said calmly.

"I thought I recognised you. You're the estate agent. I'm so sorry for what happened to your friend," Angela said offering her a seat by the door.

"Are you?" Louise's voice had changed "Are you really?"

"I'm sorry Ms Smart, but Wellsdale Hall isn't accountable in any way for what happened to your friend." Angela sounded pleasant but stern.

"Wellsdale Hall might not be held accountable, but you could be." Louise's voice held a flutter of anger.

"I don't appreciate what you're saying or why you're saying it. What do you mean I could be held accountable? Accountable for what?" Angela was becoming angry at the accusation.

"Lucy knew you were having an affair with Jett; easier if she was out of the way?" Louise asked her sarcastically.

"The only person I need out of the way is you and I'll have security here if you don't leave immediately."

The hidden snoops could hear Angela rising from her seat and heading to the door.

"You're not denying it then!" Louise spat at her.

"What I do is none of your business. Do not contact me again. Do you hear?" Angela held the door open for Louise to leave. "You have one minute to be off these premises, and you can remove me from the Blacks mailing list!"

The door slammed shut.

Mrs Wood and Dee's Grandmother cautiously peered over the back of the sofa, silently sharing a look of shock.

Chapter Fifteen

Dee was sitting back in the treatment waiting area sipping a glass of water while waiting for Helen.

"Dee, you won't believe what we've found out!" her Gran whispered into her ear from behind her.

Dee jumped so hard that her water spilt over her dressing gown.

"Gran, what are you doing? You made me jump a mile!"

"Sorry love, but we've something to tell you," her Gran apologised.

"It's really important!" Mrs Wood chipped in.

"Oh Helen, here you are, you've been a while," Dee said realising her dressing gown was drenched.

"That took forever, and I really didn't like it," Helen rolled her eyes. "Laura insisted as a VIP on giving me a hand massage as well as the facial."

"Why didn't you enjoy it?" Mrs Wood asked her.

"The whole thing is suffocating. You can't move. That mask sets your face rigid." Helen paused and pulled a face. "I felt totally claustrophobic, the room was so dark, and on top of that, I'm sorry, but I found out nothing!"

"Well, your skin is glowing!" Mrs Wood said, and they all agreed. "Helen, we've found out something!"

"Have you, Mrs Wood. What?" Helen looked surprised.

"Not here," Dee's Gran said. "We need somewhere quiet away from prying eyes and ears!"

"Gosh it must be serious," Dee said uncomfortable in her wet dressing gown. "I wonder if I can change this. I'll come and find you."

Dee made her way over to the treatment reception desk.

"Excuse me, is it possible to change my robe?" Dee hoped the woman wouldn't say no.

"Of course, robes and towels are in the spa. Just go and ask. They have trolleys full of them." The lady smiled and then returned to her computer screen.

Dee managed to catch the others up and they agreed to meet in the jigsaw room; Mrs Wood thought it would be best so they could explain exactly what had happened. Dee made her way quickly to the spa area.

"Hello," the attendant greeted her.

"Hi, can I change my robe please. I spilt a whole glass of water on it!" Dee told her.

"Yes, we've loads. Just pop that one in there and then collect a clean one from the pile here."

Dee went over to where the girl had pointed. There was a large unit with two holes in the top. One was labelled *towels* and the other *robes*. Dee removed her robe and tried to push it thought the hole.

"Excuse me!" came a voice from behind her. "I'll just change the trolley."

Dee stepped back. The girl opened the cupboard underneath and removed a full container of used robes and replaced it with an empty one. Dee smiled and thanked her as she took the damp robe from her and placed it on top of the others.

"Can I ask how often does that get changed?" Dee said following her.

"Depends how busy we are. Towels are the worst! We seem to constantly be changing that trolley or restocking the spa area. I don't know why people must use so many!"

Dee agreed and then realised something. "Do you wash them all here?"

"Yep, there's a laundry through there, glad I don't have to do that!"

The girl then disappeared through some double doors and Dee went to join the others in the jigsaw room.

"Do you know they wash all the towels and robes here at Wellsdale Hall. Can you imagine that?" Dee said to them as she sat down on the sofa next to Helen.

"That would be a lot of washing powder," Dee's Gran stated. "Hold on to your hat, dear. Wait till you hear this!"

"I'm not wearing a hat!" Dee said, laughing. Mrs Wood and her Gran rolled their eyes.

Mrs Wood explained in detail where they had been sitting and what they had heard.

"Did you say that you're going to see Angela before you leave?" Dee asked.

"If she's available yes, but I don't have to," Helen answered her.

"Yes, you do!" Dee's mind was whirling. "…and I'll come with you."

They all decided to get changed ready to go home and were heading towards the changing rooms when Angela caught up with them anyway.

"Hello there. Have you had a lovely day?" she asked.

"Yes, very much," Helen answered blushing a little.

"Angela, lovely to see you again." Dee stepped forward.

"Oh, it's you. You should have let me know you were coming here today." Angela looked a little taken aback.

"It was a last-minute treat from my Gran." Dee smiled.

"How lovely, are you heading off now?" Angela asked, hoping they were.

"Angela, can Helen and I have a minute with you in your office please," Dee asked her.

Angela wobbled thinking about it. "If it's quick, I should have left half an hour ago."

Dee's Gran and Mrs Wood continued to the changing rooms as Helen and Dee followed Angela to her office.

Dee joked "I don't know how you walk around here all day in those heels."

Angela didn't turn round. As she opened her office door she simply replied, "You get used to it. Take a seat. Now what can I help you with?"

"I would like to enquire which dates you have available for my hen do?" Helen smiled.

"Oh, how fabulous. Can I ask how do you two know each other?" Angela looked at them both.

"Dee is a good friend of Sir Henry," Helen said realising how ridiculous that sounded as soon as she said it.

Angela merely nodded and tapped away on the screen. "How many would it be for and would you all be staying over?"

"There might be ten of us," Helen stuttered making it up.

"Yes, we have availability in a month's time. Does that fit in with your plans?"

"I would need to check," Helen smiled. "Could you write the dates down for me please."

"Would we be able to all have our treatments at the same time and near each other?" Dee asked.

Angela handed Helen the dates that were available before answering. "We can try. It's not guaranteed. We only have set of connecting rooms. I believe you were in there today Helen with Laura, but we can try and put you all as close as possible."

"Do you see anything of Jett and Sofia out of work or just here?" Dee asked. Helen shifted in her chair.

"Purely work. Jett is my hairdresser, and he comes and goes when we need more stock and Sofia trains the girls on how to use the Bailey products on clients." Angela looked directly at Helen. "I can tell from your skin that Laura gave you the Bailey Golden Glow facial."

Helen smiled.

Dee continued. "Who did Sofia and Lucy's treatments on the seventeenth May?"

Angela became defensive. "I thought you were here about booking a hen party?"

"I'd like Laura again, if that's possible?" Helen jumped in.

"Sofia always has Laura. She's one of our top therapists." Angela turned to Dee and said with a touch of sarcasm, "Would you like to request a certain therapist?"

Ignoring Angela's tone, Dee asked, "Do the same therapists always work in the same treatment room?"

Angela was becoming irritated. "Not always, but on the whole yes."

Helen was now feeling thoroughly uncomfortable. "Thank you for your time, Ms Myers. I'll be in touch to confirm the hen party date and numbers as soon as possible."

Angela stood and shook Helen's hand. Dee offered her hand too, but Angela ignored it.

Once outside the manager's office, Dee turned to Helen. "You didn't mention your treatment room had a connecting door."

"I checked it was locked. Laura told me Angela keeps the key in her office." Helen looked confused. "I thought we were about to be kicked out then!"

"She doesn't like talking about Jett and Sofia Bailey that's for sure!" Dee turned to face Helen. "You know I'm going to have to spend tomorrow morning telling Peter all about today."

"No, you're not. I was thinking earlier, I'd like to invite you and your Gran to dinner at Gaitley Manor tonight." Helen smiled at her. "You know a certain person will want to know everything!"

"Sir Henry?" Dee laughed.

As they made their way to join Mrs Wood and Dee's Gran in the changing room, they were met by Laura going the other way.

"Hello again .I must say your skin looks amazing!" Laura beamed at her.

Helen smiled back. "Dee, this is Laura who did my facial."

"We've just been talking about you. Ms Myers was singing your praises. She said you're one of her top therapists. I understand you do all Sofia Bailey's facials too!" Dee was being overtly nice.

"Yes, I do. I love her products. Sofia is wonderful" Laura replied.

"It was awful what happened to her friend. Lucy." Dee looked at Laura. "Did you do Sofia's treatments that day?"

"Yes of course..." Laura stopped midsentence. "No, actually they swapped treatments. Sofia had a massage, and I gave Lucy a facial."

"I didn't know you were allowed to do that," Dee said.

"You're not really but Sofia went and checked with Angela – sorry, Ms Myers," Laura corrected herself. "She said it was fine."

"Did Lucy enjoy her facial?" Helen interrupted.

"I believe so, I got called away and another therapist took over, but I hope she did." Laura looked sad.

"Who took over from you?" Dee asked, a little too eagerly.

"I don't know. You'd have to check with Ms Myers," Laura said more brightly.

"Do you see Jett and Sofia here often?" Dee asked trying to change tack.

"I only see Sofia for her treatments or training, but Jett is here quite a bit. I'm sure he was here the day Sofia's friend died."

"Was he?" Helen was finally enjoying this. "What was he doing?"

"Ms Myers probably!" she laughed. "Only joking. I've got to go. I have another client."

"This gets more intriguing by the second!" Helen said and linked arms with Dee.

"You're not wrong. It definitely raises more questions than answers!" Dee said thoughtfully as they entered the changing room.

Outside in the carpark of Wellsdale Hall the ladies had said their goodbyes and Helen had arranged with Mrs Wood for them to arrive at six thirty for pre-dinner drinks.

Dee and her Gran left the carpark and started to make their way back to Dee's flat.

"Are there any shops open. I don't have anything to wear tonight." Her Gran sounded perplexed.

"Gran, you'll be fine in whatever you have with you."

"No Dee, I'd like to make an effort. It's not everyday someone like me receives an invitation like this." There was concern in her voice.

"Tell you what, we can go through Amberleigh and see if anything is open but at this time on a Sunday, it's highly unlikely!"

Her Gran smiled, looking much happier.

Tom and Claire had nipped into Amberleigh after work. They had spent Sunday morning and most of the afternoon going over the CCTV footage once again.

"There's just nothing much on there," Tom stated

"I know, but we did miss Mrs Walker," Claire said playing with her glass. "That was a mistake!"

"Stop being so hard on yourself." Tom tried to get her attention. "Are you okay?"

"I'm alright," she replied unconvincingly and turned to look out of the window. "Is that Dee?"

Dee and her Gran had pulled up outside the only dress shop in Amberleigh. The light was on, and Dee could see the owner inside. She got out of the car and knocked on the door.

"I'm closed," the owner mouthed through the glass before recognising Dee and opening the door. "I remember you. You bought the blue scarf, and your friend bought a dress. Is everything alright?"

Dee smiled hoping it would be and explained they had been invited to Gailey Manor, and her Gran needed something suitable to wear.

"Well bring her in. I'm in a bit of a mess as the autumn stock has just arrived but please feel free to try anything on," she said, opening another box.

Dee went outside to tell her Gran to come in when she saw Claire waving at her from the cocktail bar across the street. "Gran you go in. I've just seen Claire. I'll be two ticks?" Dee announced locking the car.

Claire and Dee greeted each other with a big hug while Tom stood awkwardly by.

"How's the investigation going?" Dee asked.

"Very slow," Tom answered. "We've been going through the CCTV footage again!"

Claire smiled at her as she sat back down "How's your investigation going?"

Dee had planned to tell Peter everything they had learnt first before saying anything to the police. She replied with a shrug and Tom excused himself and went to the gents.

Dee noticed that Claire was not her normal bubbly self. "Are you feeling alright, Claire?"

"Yeah. I just can't seem to do anything right at the moment. I think Jake's unhappy with me," she replied, playing with her glass.

"Don't take any notice of him, From what I've heard he's going to be too busy and too tired to notice anything!" Dee said smartly.

"What do you mean?" Claire looked up at her.

"Nothing." Dee shook her head. "Claire when you were going through the CCTV footage did you see Jett Bailey?"

"No, should I have?" Claire asked, worried she'd missed something else.

"I'm going to go through it and look again. Will you?" Dee winked at her as Tom returned. "I've got to go!"

Claire mouthed a silent *thank you*. After all, two pairs of eyes are better than one.

Dee's Gran was admiring her reflection in the long gold mirror.

"What do you think?" she asked her as Dee entered the shop. "Natalie has been so helpful."

"Gran that's lovely." Dee smiled lovingly at her.

"I'll take it, thank you."

Her Gran was grinning from ear to ear.

Dee waited for her Gran to go into the changing room before mentioning to Natalie that she had been talking to her friend who ran the shop at Wellsdale Hall.

"Chrissy? Yes she's had her shop based at Wellsdale hall for years now!" Natalie told her. She watched as Dee looked through the swimwear rail. "Are we going away?" she asked Dee.

"No, I thought I saw this in the shop at Wellsdale Hall. I'm sure it was more expensive," Dee said, acting the innocent. "I must be wrong!"

"No, Chrissy and I can have the same stock, but we always differ slightly in colour and of course I don't have to pay the overheads that Angela demands. Which explains the price differential," Natalie said.

"Yeah, I see." Dee smiled back at her.

Dee's Gran paid for her new dress, and they thanked Natalie for helping them.

"Anytime!" Natalie smiled at them as she closed the door and locked it, pleased to have made a hundred and twenty-five pounds more than she'd expected on a Sunday.

Mrs Wood was fussing around in the kitchen getting canapes ready for Dee and Pat's arrival when Helen entered the kitchen and said it was time she got changed.

"Changed dear, me?" Mrs Wood said as she heard the kitchen door open.

"Yes, Mrs Wood. You're joining us this evening. After all this is supposed to be your day off!" Helen said curling her nose up. "What is that smell?"

Then Peter was standing in the doorway holding three trout proudly aloft. "Here you are, Mrs Wood, for tomorrow."

"Well done, Peter, nice looking fish," she praised.

Peter was beaming like a schoolchild who had won an award, and came towards Helen for a kiss.

"No, you don't. You stink!" she laughed.

"You see, Mrs Wood, how my future wife adores me!"

"Not right now, I don't. Please get changed and be quick. Dee and her Gran will be here shortly and that goes for you too, Mrs Wood." Helen made shooing gestures.

"Dee coming for dinner. That's nice," Peter said, then asked, "Why?"

"All will become clear," Helen replied.

Mrs Wood greeted them at the door ushering them into the drawing room where Dee's Gran was overwhelmed with the opulence of Gaitley Manor.

"Dee, wonderful to see you," Sir Henry said as he gave her a hug and kissed her on both cheeks.

Her Gran put her hand out to shake Sir Henry's, but he pretended not to notice and gave her big kiss on the cheek instead. He then invited her to sit next to him. Dee noticed her Gran was blushing.

"It's a pleasure to finally meet you," Sir Henry said to her Gran warmly as they sat down. "Fine Yorkshire stock, that you are."

Dee's Gran looked lost for words and burst out laughing as Mrs Wood entered with canapes and a tray of drinks.

Peter went to help her.

"Henry please behave!" Helen winked at him "I'm sorry Pat, he refers to us all in some form of farming jargon!"

"It's a compliment," Sir Henry said and here's another. "Mrs Wood these are fine canapes!"

They all agreed as Peter poured the wine.

"Who is going to begin? My instincts tell me while I've been fishing you lot have been doing some fishing of your own!" Peter said handing out the glasses of wine.

Helen was about to say something when Clara came bounding through the door. "Auntie Dee, Auntie Dee!" The child launched herself at her.

Dee caught her and sat her on her lap. "How's my favourite girl in the whole wide world?"

Clara giggled as Dee tickled her.

"Let me introduce you to a special person Clara. This is my Gran." Dee pointed her out.

"Hello, dear. Nice to meet you." Dee's Gran smiled.

"Hello," Clara said sheepishly and then, "That's a pretty dress."

"Thank you, Clara, and your pyjamas are cute too."

"Do you like unicorns too?" Clara asked.

"Don't tell anyone, Clara, but I do," Dee's Gran teased.

"Clara, time for bed. You have your schoolbook to read," Helen reminded her.

Clara pulled a sad face, and they all laughed.

Peter picked her up and threw her over his shoulder "C'mon you. We'll have you tucked up, in a jiffy!"

They could still hear Clara giggling as Peter took her upstairs to bed.

Everyone had now moved into the dining room and Peter had returned to join them. Dee, Helen, and Sir Henry were happily chatting as they waited for Dee's Gran and Mrs Wood to join them.

"You're Gran is lovely Dee. I can't believe we haven't met before today," Peter said interrupting their conversation. "I hope there's been no vital chat while I was out of the room."

"No," Helen said nudging him in the ribs. "We wouldn't do that!"

Mrs Wood and Pat came into the dining room carrying a tray each laden with plates.

"Mrs Wood!" Sir Henry exclaimed. "...And Pat you're my guest!"

"I tried stopping her, but she wouldn't have any of it!" Mrs Wood explained.

"No, I wouldn't!" Dee's Gran was smiling at Sir Henry. "Sit yourselves down before this wonderful food my friend has cooked goes cold!"

Sir Henry laughed, as did everyone else. As they took their seats Sir Henry patted Pat on her knee under the table and whispered, "That is a pretty dress. You look lovely this evening."

Dee's Gran blushed and replied, "You're as daft as a brush!"

Peter coughed to get everyone's attention. "Who is going to enlighten me on today's events?"

The others all looked to Dee. "Seems like it's me, but please jump in if I miss something or don't say it quite right." She went on to explain in detail how they had bumped into each other at the spa and what had happened after lunch.

"That's a lot of information to wade through, Dee. You'll have to get this all typed up tomorrow!" Peter said, "We can arrange to meet Jake tomorrow night if he's free."

"I doubt he's going to be free for years to come!" Dee said under her breath.

"What's that, dear?" her Gran asked her.

"Nothing, just talking to myself!" she answered.

"Dee, we're definitely going to the Bailey's salon tomorrow," Peter said thinking out loud.

Dee nodded. "What I don't understand is Laura and the other therapist must have given statements. Why hasn't anyone thought it's odd that Sofia and Lucy swapped treatments and rooms."

Helen said, "Like Laura said it was a last-minute thing. It might have been Lucy who changed her mind and Sofia did ask Angela if it was okay to swap."

Mrs Wood chipped in. "It reminds me of a friend in Scotland who picked up the wrong dog from the kennels!"

They all turned to look at her.

"Go on, Mrs Wood," Sir Henry urged.

"Same type of dog, identical in colour but very different names. However, after one of the walks they had been put back in the wrong kennel so on collection my friend took the wrong dog home."

"When did she notice?" Dee's Gran asked her.

"Oh, very quickly. The dog wouldn't respond when she shouted him and he wasn't of the same nature. He was returned the next day."

"Dee, are you thinking what I think you are?" Peter asked her.

Dee nodded, and the table went quiet.

"Maybe Lucy wasn't the intended victim after all!"

Chapter Sixteen

Ruth was lying on the bed swaddled in purple velvet blankets in one of the treatment rooms at Bailey's Hair and Beauty salon.

"Good morning, Ms Watkins," Sofia greeted her.

"Please call me Ruth." Ruth smiled at her.

"Ruth it is. I understand we're having a full facial, makeup and to finish you're having your hair styled by Jett," Sofia stated, moving around the treatment room.

"I am. It's a full day." Ruth watched her constantly as she opened and closed drawers.

"Excellent, are we going anywhere special?" Sofia asked as she came to sit behind her at the head of the bed.

"I'm going out for dinner tonight with my boyfriend." It was a half-truth.

"Is it an anniversary or something special?" Sofia was looking at Ruth's skin through a magnifying glass with a bright light that was attached to the table next to her.

"I think he's going to propose!" Ruth lied.

"How wonderful. By the time Jett and myself have worked our magic, he'll be proposing as soon as he walks through the door!" Sofia said starting to massage a cleansing cream into Ruth's face.

Ruth closed her eyes thinking, 'I hope not. The last thing I would ever do is get married!'

Dee was up early as her Gran had to catch the first train back to Leeds and they said their goodbyes as Dee's Gran had jumped into a taxi to take her to the station.

By the time Peter arrived at the office, Dee was making good headway typing up her report.

"Has your Gran already left?" was the first thing Peter asked.

"Yes," Dee replied, still typing away. "Her train was at eight thirty, so we had an early start."

"Shall I go and fetch us both a coffee and maybe one of Alison's breakfast muffins? I don't want to break you off from typing your report."

Dee merely nodded and smiled which Peter rightly interpreted as a 'Yes' and strolled down Gamblewood's High Street to Alison's café.

"Good morning, Peter." Alison smiled as he walked through the door of Coffee Creams.

"Morning. Morning Albert!" Peter greeted them both.

"Have you found out who killed that girl yet?" Albert was nothing if not blunt.

"Not yet, but we're getting closer by the day!" Peter answered.

"Not according to this you're not. Mrs Walker is saying the police are useless and that the private detective agency she hired is doing no better!" Albert turned his newspaper to show Peter a photograph of Mrs Walker, holding a framed picture of her daughter-in-law.

"May I read that Albert," Peter asked him as Alison took his order.

"Why don't you buy your own!" Albert grumbled as he passed his newspaper to him.

Peter scanned the article quickly and tutted.

"Here you are, Peter! "Alison shouted across the café raising the two takeaway cups in the air.

Peter handed Albert his paper back and went over to the counter to collect his order.

"Seems like Mrs Walker has a lot to say!" Alison whispered so Albert could not hear.

"Yes, she does, but most of that has Ruth's bloody spin on it!" Peter paused as he picked up the takeaway cups. "Funny how she doesn't mention that she was at

Wellsdale Hall on the day her daughter-in-law was murdered!"

Alison looked shocked. "She was there?"

Peter nodded. "She sure was!"

After taking Clara to school, Helen returned to Gaitley Manor and was chatting with Mrs Wood in the kitchen when Sir Henry joined them.

"Fine meal last night, Mrs Wood. You are a very accomplished cook!" Sir Henry said.

"Thank you." Mrs Wood smiled back at him.

Sir Henry kissed Helen on the cheek.

"Why are you two in my kitchen? I'm sure there are plenty of things you should be doing!" Mrs Wood said starting to dry the dishes on the side.

"Mrs Wood, you seem to have a lot of friends in Scotland. We were wondering what the connection is?" Helen asked her.

"I do and I also have friends all over the world," Mrs Wood laughed. "Now shoo out of my kitchen. I've promised Clara jam tarts for supper this evening!"

Sir Henry and Helen left the kitchen feeling like scolded children. "We didn't get a straight answer there did we!" Helen said to Sir Henry.

"No, my dear, we didn't!" Sir Henry replied.

Back in their agency's office, Dee had finished typing her report and Peter was telling her about Ruth's latest news article as they finished their coffee and muffins.

"Ruth has it in for us all, doesn't she?" Dee said, clearly annoyed.

"So, it seems. We'll pick up a paper on our way to see the Baileys so you can read it properly," Peter said scanning Dee's report.

"One day I will give that Ruth a piece of my mind. It's not good for business, Peter!" Dee said her cheeks beginning to redden.

Peter could see Dee's annoyance in her flushed cheeks "We'd all like to give Ruth a piece of our mind, but I'm afraid it would be like water off a duck's back!"

Peter's mobile began to ring. It was Jake.

"Yes sure. Is this afternoon okay? We're heading to the Baileys this morning," Peter said.

After that Dee could hear Peter chatting away in general with Jake. She left him to it as she went into her flat to grab a lightweight jacket. On returning he was by the door waiting for her.

"Is Jake coming here this afternoon?" Dee enquired.

"No, he'd like us to go to the Police station. Something's come up regarding the deposits into Lucy's bank account. Turns out she was not only receiving money from the Baileys!" Peter explained on their way to his car.

The Baileys' salon seemed busy for a Monday. Ruth had managed to ask a few questions during her facial, but Sofia was very guarded. She was hoping to get more out of the manicurist she was seeing next once she'd been ushered into a conservatory area off the main salon.

"Would you like a cup of tea, coffee or a water?" the manicurist asked her.

"A coffee would be lovely. I've drunk so much water already!" While answering Ruth was straining to see who Sofia and Jett were talking to.

"Is everything alright?" Ruth was asked as the manicurist turned round to see what she was looking at.

"It's fine. I thought that was someone I know!" Ruth replied. She had thought she recognised the voices.

"They've never been in here before. Jett will be desperate to get his hands on her gorgeous red hair!" she explained taking a file to Ruth's nails.

Ruth now knew exactly who it was.

The police station, in comparison to Bailey's Hair and Beauty Salon was unusually quiet. Jake had summoned Claire and Tom into his office and was explaining the latest report on his desk in front of him.

"Why would Louise Smart be sending money to Lucy too?" Tom looked puzzled.

"That's what we're going to find out!" Jake said to them both.

Dee and Peter were sitting comfortably in the Bailey's office and Dee commented on how beautifully decorated it was. They thanked her and offered them cups of coffee from the fancy machine sitting in the corner on top of a grey sideboard. Peter and Dee accepted their offer.

Peter started as he wanted to be as sensitive as he could. "I know you must have and will still be having a difficult time coming to terms with Lucy's murder."

Sofia and Jett looked at each other and Jett made to hold her hand, but she pulled it away.

"We work closely with the police, but we're here under Mrs Walker's instructions. She's hired us to investigate Lucy's death."

"Mrs Walker!" Sofia spoke first. "That dragon made Lucy's life hell. Wouldn't be surprised if she did it!"

Jett intervened. "You can't say things like that, Sofia. Sorry - she doesn't mean it!"

Dee asked before Peter could say anything, "Did they not get on? Why did she make life difficult for Lucy?"

"Lucy said she was always there at the house, meddling, interfering, telling them where they should live, when to have kids!" Sofia stopped talking as she started to well up.

"That doesn't sound a reason to kill her." Dee said. "Maybe it was her way of looking out for them."

"Only if it suited her. She never felt Lucy was good enough for her David and honestly he's no angel. He gambles you know!" Sofia put her hand in her pocket and pulled out a tissue.

"Sofia, stop now. I'm so sorry about this. You see it's more personal for us," Jett said looking at Sofia.

"If you work closely with the police, I guess you will know about the…" Jett didn't finish his sentence.

"The baby." Peter said it for him.

Sofia finally took Jett's hand as he said, "Yes, not only did they murder out best friend, but they murdered our baby too!"

"And you think Mrs Walker could be involved in that?" Dee pressed them. Peter pulled a face to tell her to be gentler.

"She wouldn't be happy if Lucy had told her she was carrying our baby and not David's. She'd been nagging Lucy for years to have children!" Sofia spoke quietly.

"Even though that's true, David and his Mum would never hurt Lucy!" Jett interjected.

Peter jumped in before Dee could. "Do you know anyone else who'd wish to harm Lucy?"

"No, we don't and we've talked of little else. We knew Louise and Lucy had been having words but nothing serious. Louise could say things without thinking; that was all!" Jett said.

"How do you feel about what was happening with Lucy and Louise, Sofia?" Dee asked

She looked over at Peter seeking his approval.

"Louise can be insensitive, that's all, she was probably a little jealous of Lucy and I. She would take the micky out of Lucy sometimes," Sofia said trying to reach her coffee.

Jett passed her the cup and said, "Louise knew Lucy wasn't in the same financial bracket as ourselves or her. She would just have a few digs; that's all."

"Lucy was overheard arguing in the sauna on the day of her death. We've been led to believe that was with you, Sofia," Peter said watching her reaction.

"As I told the police, it wasn't me," Sofia stated firmly.

"Talking about that day, I believe you might have swapped treatments and rooms with Lucy. Is that correct?" Dee pried.

"I'd forgotten all about that. Yes we did. Lucy didn't want a massage. She wouldn't say why but she was adamant, so we swapped," Sofia looked at Jett. "I suppose we now know it was because she was pregnant!"

Peter asked, "Did you not know Lucy was expecting?"

Jett answered. "No, we were going to surprise Sofia on her birthday with a scan of the baby."

The room went quiet for a moment or two as they all thought about the implications of that.

It was Dee who interrupted the silence. "Jett, on the day of Lucy's murder, did you go to Wellsdale Hall at all? Making a delivery or anything like that?"

"Me no, definitely not. Let me check the diary." Jett went over to the grey sideboard, pulled out a drawer and opened a leather-bound diary. "I was in the salon all day,"

"Oh, I'm sorry. Someone said they thought they had seen you there. Do you open the salon on a Sunday?"

"No, we don't. Unfortunately for me, I was stocktaking and definitely in the salon all day," he said.

Sofia had been quiet for some time but finally spoke up. "I want to go back to something you said earlier, about the rooms."

"Yes," Peter said.

"Because we swapped rooms do you think they meant to kill me and not Lucy!" Sofia looked terrified.

"Don't be so ridiculous!" Jett said, putting an arm around her shoulders.

"It's not ridiculous," Peter said very matter of factly. "It's a distinct possibility!"

Opposite Bailey's Hair and Beauty Salon, Louise Smart was having a difficult morning. Some of her clients had not paid their rent and she was having to chase on behalf of the landlords. She slammed her mobile on her desk a little too hard and it forced her to check to see if she had cracked the screen just as Jake, with Tom and Claire in his wake, entered the Blacks Estate Agency.

"How can we help?" A smiling Louise said sarcastically, "I guess you're here about Lucy and not to buy a house?"

"Yes, Ms Smart," Jake replied. "Can we ask you some questions please?"

"You can, but do I need a lawyer? All this is getting very tiresome!" She rolled her eyes as she spoke.

"Not unless you've done something wrong!" Jake said.

Louise Smart took a deep breath. "Go on then. What do you want to know?"

Jake stared at her wanting a reaction. "Why are you paying Lucy Walker lump sums of money?"

Louise looked shocked at the question. She rose from behind her desk and grabbed her phone. "I am calling my lawyer!" she said loudly.

Jett had to go to the drink's cabinet to fetch Sofia something stronger to calm her nerves. She was visibly shaken and upset.

"Why would someone want to kill me? I've not done anything to anyone!"

Jett was aware that clients and staff in the salon could possibly hear her and told her to keep her voice down.

"I'm going home!" Sofia said. "You'll have to finish my client and ask Becky to do her make-up."

"Okay I will. Which client are we talking about?" Jett asked her.

"Ruth; Ruth Watkins. Her boyfriend is proposing to her tonight," Sofia said as she picked up a set of keys from one of the desks.

Dee and Peter exchanged a look of surprise.

"I'll follow you out," Peter said to Sofia.

"Can I use the bathroom please, before we leave?" Dee asked Jett.

"Yes, you can use the staff one." He signalled where to go and she followed Sofia and Peter towards the back of the building.

Dee had finished in the bathroom and was heading out of the door at the back when she heard someone crying from behind a closed door opposite the bathroom. She knocked gently and went in.

"Hi, are you okay?" Dee asked.

In front of her sat a young girl holding a comb and a pair of scissors. She had what looked like the head of a mannequin in front of her.

"Oh, who are you?" she asked Dee, wiping away a tear.

"I'm here seeing Jett and Sofia. Wow these are impressive! "Dee said touching one of the different wigs on display.

"Yes, we train on some of them but I can't get Jett's signature bob right. He'll let me go if I don't master it soon!" She started to weep again.

"Don't cry. I'm sure Jett's not like that," Dee tried to comfort her.

"Yes, he is. He's let two girls go in the last three months!"

"I think that looks remarkable. Look at that cut. It's amazing!" Dee put a hand on her shoulder.

"Thank you, but I know it's not perfect," the girl replied.

Dee turned to her and said, "Life never is!"

Ruth was now having a pedicure. The girl attending to her talked more openly than Sofia, but said nothing of any importance.

"Did you hear that?" Ruth asked her.

"Yes, it sounded like Sofia shouting," answered the girl "I wonder what's going on?"

"I'm ok for a minute or two. Why don't you go find out!" Ruth urged her.

The girl was of a nosey nature and waved one of her salon colleagues over. "What was all that about Becky?" she asked her.

The girl bent down and whispered in her ear. "Sofia thinks someone is trying to kill her!"

Ruth watched the other girl walk away and asked, "What did she say?"

"Nothing. She's upset and has left for the day!" The girl smiled at Ruth as she continued massaging her feet.

Ruth was not exactly hard of hearing and had heard and noted carefully exactly what had been said.

Jake was sitting back in his office contemplating his next move. He'd had a minor rollocking from above about Ruth's newspaper article.

Claire knocked on his door and came in. "Sir, I've checked the timings for Mrs Walker. We can see her enter Wellsdale Hall but, on the CCTV, we don't see her leave."

"Are there other exits she could have used," Jake asked her.

"Yes, but they're for staff, and those doors have a keypad on them. I checked that when we were there," Claire said.

"Hm, I see. Check again. What about her car? She must have driven there. Does the carpark log number plates going in and out," Jake asked.

"I'll check?" Claire said, looking at her feet.

"You surprise me, Claire. I would have thought you would have already done that!" Jake moved from behind his desk to look out of his office window and into the station carpark.

Claire put her head down. "Yes, Sir," she replied and left his office. As she closed the door behind her a tear fell onto her cheek, which she wiped away quickly as Jake opened his door to say to her, "Peter and Dee are here!"

Neatly nestled in Jake's office the five of them swapped pleasantries as a PC came in carrying cups of tea for them all. Jake thanked the young man and waited till he had closed the door.

Dee noticed that Claire had positioned herself at the back of the office. She turned to catch her eye and Claire looked away. Dee knew her friend was upset about something.

Jake spoke first about Lucy's bank statement and the traces that had been done.

"To clarify," Peter said, "...Lucy was receiving money from Sofia and Jett not only for the surrogacy but other payments from a different bank account that you've traced back to them too as well as money from Louise Smart."

Jake nodded.

"Lucy was coining it in!" Tom announced.

Dee didn't look at Jake as she took the report from his desk. "None of these are regular payments, they're quite intermittent," she said.

"Yes, and irregular in their amounts. It's not like a salary going in or anything like that," Claire offered.

"Have you spoken to Louise Smart about this?" Peter asked Jake.

"Yes, but we have to formally bring her in later. She's insisting on being interviewed with her lawyer present." Jake sat back in his chair.

"We do have something for you." Peter passed over the report Dee had typed up that morning.

"You're kidding me, you two. Read that!" Jake passed it over to Tom first.

They calmly waited until both Tom and Claire had finished reading.

"I'll fetch their statements!" Claire said jumping up.

"I'll help you; it'll be quicker," Tom said following her out.

"There's a chance they meant to kill Sofia Bailey and not Lucy then," Jake said.

Dee looked away. She didn't want to look into Jake's cool blue eyes.

"It's got to be a possibility, Jake," Peter answered him.

"Have either of you any idea why someone would want to kill her?" Jake asked thoughtfully.

"No but Mrs Walker's name keeps cropping up, and she really doesn't like Sofia Bailey," Dee said.

Jake looked at her. The sun shone on her hair, and she was watching him, waiting for an answer.

"Interesting. There's something else. We've just realised that on the CCTV we see Mrs Walker entering Wellsdale Hall, but we don't see her leave."

Peter asked, "Dee, did you notice that when you checked it?"

"No Peter, I didn't." Dee felt rather stupid. She flushed with embarrassment. "I'll go through it again tonight."

Jake could feel himself staring; her cheeks were dotted with red circles, and she was struggling to look at him. And he hated it.

Claire and Tom returned with Laura's statement and those given by couple of the other therapists.

"We've been through them, Sir. There is nothing about Laura being called away and no mention of Lucy and Sofia swapping rooms," Claire said as she handed the statements over to him.

"Maybe we didn't ask the right questions!" Jake said.

Claire said nothing as she she returned to where she had been sitting. Tom and Dee swapped glances.

"Does Angela's statement mention that she knew they had swapped rooms, and which therapist took over when Laura was called away?" Peter asked Jake.

"I'll go and fetch it," Claire said as she made her way towards the door.

Tom wanted to check on her. "I know where it is. We won't be a moment."

Jake started to pace up and down behind his desk until Claire and Tom returned with the statement. He read it and passed it to Peter who then passed it to Dee for her to read.

"Seems no one's being totally honest!" Peter said.

"Or she didn't know!" Dee chipped in. "But if she's having an affair with Jett then maybe…" Dee trailed off, deep in thought.

Before anyone could make further suggestions, Jake's mobile rang. Dee could see the face of the mobile clearly. It was someone called Catherine and Jake immediately excused himself and took the call outside his office.

"With the exception of David, it looks like they were all there on the day Lucy was murdered; Sofia, Jett, Vicky, Louise, Angela and Mrs Walker," Peter said tapping his chin.

"Jett said he wasn't at Wellsdale Hall, Peter. He was at the salon stocktaking," Dee corrected him.

"Jett isn't on any of the CCTV." Claire looked at Dee. "I went through it this morning. He's not on any of the footage."

"Claire, do you fancy popping round for a glass of wine tonight and a chat and we can go over it again together?" Dee asked her.

"You're honoured. I thought we had to wait for the grand opening! None of us can get a foot through that flat door since this one's redecorated!"

Claire smiled and accepted Dee's invitation but declined the wine as she would be driving. Peter was still laughing as Jake rejoined them

"I think we need to pay Angela Myers another visit," Jake said. "Claire can you see if she's still there. If she is we'll go straight away!"

Peter and Dee took that as their cue to leave.

"Drink at the Star and Crown tonight?" Peter asked Jake as he left.

"Can't. Something's just cropped up!" Jake explained. Peter nodded.

Once out in the carpark Dee turned to Peter and said, "I think the thing that's just cropped up is called Catherine!"

At Wellsdale Hall, Angela Myers was gathering her things to leave for the day when there was a knock on her office door. "Come in!" She sounded tired.

"Good afternoon, Ms Myers. We know it's late, but we have some further questions to ask you." Jake smiled unnervingly at her.

Angela realised she wasn't going anywhere and sat back down at her desk. "Can I offer you anything?"

"No thank you. We don't want to keep you." Jake continued being his polite self. "Can you tell us who took over from Laura when she was called away on the seventeenth of May, please?"

"She wasn't. What are you talking about. Let me check my records." Angela tapped away on her laptop and turned it to show the Inspector. "You see, she wasn't called away. She completed her treatment on Sofia Bailey at two thirty pm." Angela didn't understand why they were asking her about Laura.

"Were you aware that Sofia and Lucy swapped rooms and treatments?" Jake asked.

"I was not!" Angela looked shocked. "I have to authorise anything like that; Laura isn't working today but I'll be severely reprimanding her in the morning!"

"There's no need," Claire jumped in. "Sofia Bailey told Laura that she had gone to your office and asked you. In her words, you said it was fine."

"Well, I didn't. Even if it was, I'd have to authorise it. I can't have staff just swapping guests!" Angela was struggling for breath.

"Who would have taken over from Laura when she was called away?" Jake asked her.

"I've no idea. If you look at this, all the therapists are busy doing treatments or setting up for treatments. I have to run it like clockwork," Angela said. "I don't understand!"

"I would like to ask you something personal," Jake smiled. "Are you having or have you had an affair with Jett Bailey?"

"Not you as well. No I have not had a flipping affair with Jett Bailey. Why would I be interested in him?" Angela looked upset.

"Ms Myers, it's just something that has been suggested," Jake said trying to calm her down. "Do you remember seeing Jett here on the day of Lucy's murder?

"I had that friend of Lucy's, the estate agent, in here yesterday accusing me of the same thing and no I did not see Jett here or anywhere else for that matter on the seventeenth of May!"

Jake acted thick. "Yesterday? Louise Smart was here?"

"Yes, and if she comes anywhere near me again accusing me of all and sundry, I'll be calling you and a lawyer. If anything, I bet she's the one having an affair with him!"

Jake rose to his feet. "Thank you, Ms Myers. You have been most helpful."

Outside Angela's office Claire said, "She didn't seem to know a thing about Sofia and Lucy swapping rooms!"

Jake said, "She's either telling the truth or she's a damn good liar!"

Peter and Dee had returned to the office. They were busy updating the evidence board when Mrs Walker stormed in. Dee quickly flipped it over.

"I would like an update as to what I am spending my money on!" Mrs Walker ordered.

Dee didn't say a word as Peter went over to her and offered her the chair closest to his desk.

"I read your lovely news interview this morning. It was very scathing towards the police and ourselves." Peter rose to his full height. "We'll charge you for the work we've done up to now, but as you feel we're not progressing, we're happy to part company!"

"Now you wait here. You said you would have Lucy's murder solved in days not weeks!" she stammered.

"No murder case like this is solved in days, and it has just been over a week, but once again Mrs Walker if you're unhappy with our services, we're happy to part company!" Peter was not going to stand down.

"And furthermore, now that we're not working for you," Dee said, "What were you doing at Wellsdale Hall on the day Lucy was murdered?"

Mrs Walker looked shaken. "I, I was…"

Dee and Peter continued to glare at her.

"I'm a member. I told that useless…Inspector that!" she stammered.

Peter said sternly. "The truth, Mrs Walker!"

"Oh, for goodness' sake. I was following Lucy. I thought she was seeing someone else," Mrs Walker said, hanging her head.

Peter and Dee returned to their desks.

"Explain further," Peter instructed.

"I thought she was seeing someone, having an affair, but she met up with those horrible friends. I sat and had a coffee and left."

"I know you think we haven't been doing anything towards finding Lucy's killer, but you do realise you're now in the mix!" Dee told her.

"What are you talking about? Mix of what?"

"Suspects!" Peter announced. "You failed to mention you were there. Keeping information from us and the police makes you look guilty."

"I didn't keep it to myself. I just didn't see why it was important!" Mrs Walker was going very red in the face.

"Do you have anything else you'd like to tell us?" Dee asked. "Like when you left Wellsdale Hall which exit did you use?"

Mrs Walker looked at her. "The front entrance. There's only one!"

"What time did you leave?" Dee continued her questioning.

"I've no idea. I put my head scarf on and sunglasses. I didn't want Lucy or her friends to recognise me!" Mrs Walker looked bewildered.

"I'll check the CCTV to confirm this," Dee said to her.

Mrs Walker stood and turned to Peter. "I apologise. Please continue to look into Lucy's death if only to clear my name."

"We will, Mrs Walker," Peter said, showing her to the door.

"So that's one we can cross off the list!" Dee said to Peter as he went to sit back down behind his desk.

"Not necessarily, Dee. Many a murderer tries to help the police in order to evade suspicion," Peter stated.

"She can stay on the board then," Dee replied, sticking the picture of Mrs Walker from the newspaper back on the evidence board under the title *Suspects*.

Jake, Claire and Tom had said goodbye for the evening. Tom was sitting in his car and he phoned Claire.

"Hi, it's me!"

"Hi me," she responded, sadly.

"Claire, Jake didn't mean to say you should have asked the right questions. We all should have, including him!" Tom said.

"Yeah, I know, but it was in front of Dee and Peter. It was embarrassing!" Claire said.

"It was for him too, if you think about it. Dee and Helen found out more in one afternoon than we've found out in a week!" Tom declared.

"Yes, I didn't think of it like that!" Claire's voice seemed to brighten.

"Still heading to Dee's tonight?" he asked her.

"Yes, I'm looking forward to seeing what she's done with the place," Claire said but then added, "I'm not looking forward to going through all that footage again."

"Hey, you never know. You might spot something that we haven't," Tom joked

"What like Mrs Walker being at Wellsdale Hall!" Claire said sarcastically.

"Exactly!" He laughed as he hung up.

Jake was busy preparing a meal for three, when there was a knock on his door. He opened it to find Vicky on his doorstep.

"Vicky, hi. What have you got there?" he asked her.

"I had a clear out. Thought these might come in handy!" she said thrusting a large box at him.

Jake opened it up to find it full of baby items. "I'm not sure what most of this is but Catherine will appreciate it. Thank you."

"You're welcome. It will give her a head start to get organised. Anyway, I've left the boys. I'd better get back."

Jake waved and closed the door. He left the box in the hallway so he wouldn't forget to give it to Ben and Catherine and returned to the kitchen to finish preparing the lasagne he was cooking for them.

It was early evening and Dee was showing Claire the changes she had made to the flat. She had chosen a soft grey for the walls, complemented by grey and pink curtains and coordinating cushions. The kitchen featured a white backdrop with dark grey accessories and matching door handles. Grey-upholstered dining chairs surrounded a glass table, topped with an elegant pink bowl as a centrepiece.

"It really is beautiful!" Claire declared.

"Thank you," Dee said. "I've got some non-alcoholic Prosecco to try!"

"We can give it a go," Claire giggled.

Dee had connected her lap top to her television mounted on the wall. "I find this easier," she explained as they sat down on the sofa together.

"Is the sofa new?" Claire asked.

"No, I dyed it!" Dee said turning the television on.

"You dyed a sofa?" Claire looked shocked. "I didn't even know that was possible!"

"I did my research." Dee rubbed her hand along the arm of the sofa. "I think it came out rather well!"

They clinked glasses as the CCTV footage began to play.

"Stop it there!" Claire shouted making Dee jump.

"What?"

"That's David's mother!" Claire stood up, went over to the television and pointed at the grainy figure.

"Yes, I know. That's when I saw her," Dee agreed.

"So, we have her entering Wellsdale Hall and we can now see her near the coffee shop, but then where does she go?" Claire asked her.

"No idea, Claire! Shall we have a top up?"

They continued to watch the footage.

After a while, Dee stopped it playing. "Look there she is."

"Who? Dee that could be anybody wearing a head scarf and sunglasses!" Claire said. Then realising what Dee was getting at. "That's your point; it could be anyone!"

"Exactly!" Dee said. "There's just one thing to check.

Dee went back to the time, Mrs Walker entered Wellsdale Hall.

"Why are we watching this again?" Claire asked her.

"Shoes!" Dee replied.

A couple of hours had passed, the Prosecco was finished, and the pair were now on their second cup of tea.

Claire was checking through her notes. "We can clearly see all of them waiting to be called for their treatments - Vicky, then Louise followed by Sofia and Lucy who were called at the same time by Laura."

"Yes, but one therapist can't do two people!" Dee said, "And we know Laura did Lucy's facial so who did Sofia's massage?"

Dee and Claire looked questioningly at each other. Claire scribbled down in her notebook to ask Angela.

"Let's fast forward. Most treatments can be forty to fifty minutes, maybe an hour," Dee said.

"Stop it there, look that's Vicky coming out first, and now look that's Louise," Claire said.

"They seem happy enough, chatting away. Looks like they leave at this point but no sign of Sofia or Lucy as yet," Dee said.

"There!" Dee pressed the stop button. "That's Sofia. It looks like she's looking for the others."

They continued to watch as therapists greeted guests and took them to the treatment rooms, several trolleys of fresh towels and robes came and went and even the Head Gardener Eric was seen watering the indoor plants, but there was no sign of Lucy.

"Here we are again!" Claire laughed.

"I know, look at us three. It's weird watching yourself!" Dee commented.

"Still no Lucy and she should have been out way before us. It just doesn't make sense!" Claire said, looking at the timings in her notebook.

They swapped to look at the pool and sauna CCTV footage.

"That's me!" Dee said

"Can we go back to the time we finished our treatments and look at the hour or so before that," Claire asked Dee.

They watched the screen intensely.

"None of them go into the spa pool area. Dee that's you!" Claire said frustratingly. "Lucy's already in the Cave Pool at this point!"

"We need to go back again!" Dee said already pressing the rewind button.

"Look there!" Dee was now pointing at the television. "That therapist is going to restock the towels outside the Cave Pool. Unfortunately we can't see clearly as she's hidden by the alcove where the water fountain and towels are kept. Did anyone go in or near the Cave pool before her?"

"A couple of people did, but they came out. Remember, Dee, you said yourself there was no one in there but you!"

"Claire, we need to enhance that." Dee went right up to the screen. "Look!"

Claire went and stood next to Dee and they both squinted at the grainy image in front of them.

"Are you seeing what I'm seeing?" Claire grabbed Dee's arm.

Dee nodded, her green eyes huge with astonishment.

Claire could hardly speak. "But it can't be, Dee. That's impossible!"

Chapter Seventeen

The next morning no one was more shocked than Peter to find Dee waiting outside the detective agency for him.

"What's going on?" Peter said as Dee opened the passenger car door.

"I knew you wouldn't be long. We need to go and see Vicky immediately!" and Dee jumped into the passenger seat of Peter's car.

"Okay, but you need to explain!" Peter said turning the car around.

"I will!" Dee replied putting on her seat belt.

"Good morning, Sir!" Claire greeted the Inspector as he put his head round their office door.

"Morning you two. I understand you were both here early." Jake was still wearing his outer jacket. "Give me five minutes and then will you both pop into my office please."

"Yes, Sir," Tom replied.

Alison had arrived early, anticipating a visit from Dee. As she changed the date on the little wooden calendar on the countertop to the twenty-sixth of May she could see Albert approaching the café through the window; his pace slow and deliberate.

Simultaneously, Paula from Flowering Fancies arrived with a van stocked with fresh flowers and Alison opened the café door greet her. Paula responded with a polite "Good morning," despite having her hands full.

Alison then held the door open for Albert as he neared the entrance. "Come on slow coach!" she joked as Albert reached the door.

"Less of the slow, one day you too will be as old as me!" he moaned at her.

As Alison closed the door behind him, she watched Peter's car pass. She could see Dee in the passenger seat. "I wonder where they're going in such a hurry!" she thought out loud.

"Talking to me?" Albert said taking his seat and opening his paper.

Alison didn't answer him.

Tom and Claire, sitting in Jakes's office, were looking at each other.

"Out with it, what's going on?" Jake asked them both.

Claire looked at Tom and he said, "Sir, there's a very strong smell of garlic in here!"

"Really, is it that bad?"

They didn't answer, but both nodded.

"I made a lasagne last night for Catherine. She has a thing for it at the moment." Jake went over to the office window and opened it. "Flipping Vicky came round with a box of baby things for her, and I couldn't remember if I'd added garlic or not, so I added it again!"

"Easily done, Sir!" Tom said.

"Sir, I know it's none of my business, but are we to assume that congratulations are in order?" Claire asked.

"Congratulations?" Jake looked puzzled.

Claire didn't want to speak. She felt from his tone she had already overstepped the mark.

Tom changed the subject. "Sir, Claire has something to tell you."

Jake sat down at his desk, opened his top drawer and retrieved a packet of soft mints. "Anyone want one?" he said, offering them to Tom and Claire.

Both declined.

"Sir, it's more that I have something to show you. Can you come and look at the CCTV footage in our office please. We've managed to enhance it."

"Have you two found something else?" Jake asked.

Tom replied, "Not me. It was Claire and Dee!"

Dee and Peter had arrived at Vicky's home and knocked on her front door. Vicky opened it red-faced.

"I wasn't expecting you two. Come in." Vicky ran her hands through her hair. "I've just got in from the school run, and was running the hoover round!" She looked embarrassed and moved the vacuum cleaner out of the way.

"I know it's early, but can you spare us a few minutes?" Peter asked her.

Vicky checked her appearance in the mirror over the fireplace. "Thank goodness, it's you two and not my lovely neighbour - or should I say neighbours!"

Peter and Dee looked at each other.

"I was surprised. I always thought Jake might have had the hots for you to be honest." She glanced over at Dee. "Oh well, as long as he's happy. Are you wanting tea?"

"Only if you have time?" Peter replied watching her walk over to the kitchen. "Dee, what is she on about?"

"Catherine!" Dee whispered.

Peter stared back at her, completely bewildered.

Vicky returned with three mugs of tea. Dee thought she was being unusually pleasant.

"Vicky, can we ask you, after your beauty treatments where did you all meet up?" Peter asked.

"I'm not following," Vicky said taking a sip of her tea "Meet who?"

Dee jumped in. "On the CCTV we can see you and Louise walk out of the treatment waiting room together after you had your massage or whatever you had done, but where did you go after that?"

"I've no idea. I think we went for a coffee. No, we went to the cocktail bar." Vicky looked confused. "Am I in some sort of trouble? Do I need to tell Jake this and not you two?"

"Vicky, as you know we work closely together. We'll inform Inspector Jones of anything said here today and no, you're not in any trouble," Peter assured her.

Vicky relaxed. "Do you know the more I think about it, that's where Louise and I went, but then Sofia joined us, and we all went to sit in a room near the shop. It had sofas dotted here and there and lots of magazines. It was cozy."

"Sounds lovely," Peter enthused and asked, "When did you realise that Lucy was missing?"

"She wasn't missing, was she?" Vicky sounded a little agitated.

"No, she wasn't," Dee interrupted. "When did you realise she might have gone home? I believe from your statement that's what you all thought she had done."

"Time went on, and she didn't come to meet us. We texted her to tell her where we were waiting for her, or should I say Sofia did, but she got no reply." Vicky paused for another sip of her tea. "Then Louise tried but nothing!"

"Didn't you think that was odd?" Peter asked her.

"Yeah, I did, but she'd said at lunch she had stomach pains so we all presumed she must have gone home."

Dee said, "Vicky when you realised there was a body found in the Cave pool, you did say - I was there at the time - that your friend wasn't answering any of your calls, but you thought she'd gone home."

"We did, but I guess you want to know why I thought it might be Lucy?" Vicky looked at them both.

"Yes, I was about to ask you that?" Dee answered her.

"I felt they were too quick to assume she had gone home. I couldn't imagine Lucy leaving without saying goodbye. It just wasn't like her. That's the bit I found odd!" Vicky put her mug down. "I don't know why I thought it could be Lucy if I'm honest. I wish I did!"

"It will come to you eventually!" Peter nodded.

"Vicky, did Sofia or Louise leave you at any point for a significant amount of time?" Dee asked.

Vicky looked deep in thought. "I'm trying to think; but no, no they didn't!"

"Are you sure?" Peter probed.

"Louise went to the toilet, but not for any major length of time. Oh hang on!" Vicky looked like she was having a lightbulb moment. "I remember Sofia checking her watch. She asked us both if we had any paracetamol as she could feel a headache coming on. I didn't but Louise did. She went to fetch her some from the changing room."

"Would you have any idea what time it was when Louise went to the changing rooms?" Peter looked at Dee.

"Yes, I do, because when Sofia checked her watch, I checked mine. I don't know why, but I remember thinking the boys would be finishing school shortly and going to their friends for tea." Vicky looked at them both. "So around three o'clock."

Dee had been making notes throughout their conversation. "Vicky, did you wear a swimsuit that day?"

"Of course I did. I've had two children!" Vicky looked shocked at the question and then said in a joking manner. "Unlike them three in their skinny bikinis!"

Peter stood up and Dee followed suit. "Thank you, Vicky. You've been really helpful," Peter thanked her.

"You will tell Jake you've been here this morning. I don't want to take up any of his time." Vicky walked them to the door. "He's got enough going on investigating Lucy's murder and your upcoming wedding I believe?"

"We haven't set a date yet!" Peter explained to her.

"I hope it's soon before the patter of tiny feet arrive!" Vicky was laughing as she shut her door.

Peter looked at Dee, shocked. "I can assure you; Helen and I have already had this discussion. We're both happy with Clara. There's no way I'm about to become a dad!"

"No," Dee said, trying not to look upset, "But your Best Man is!"

Ruth was sitting at her desk typing away. Robert looked across at her and winked. He was wondering how much longer to leave it before telling her. Ruth looked up and winked back. This was the happiest she had been for a while.

"Ruth, get yourself in here!" bellowed her editor from his office door.

Ruth saved what she was typing and headed in.

"What now? Don't tell me the lawyers are on their way again!" Ruth said sarcastically, rolling her eyes.

"Is this right? Sofia Bailey could have been the potential victim and not Lucy Walker?"

Ruth stood nodding with her arms folded.

"How on earth do you know this?" he squawked.

"I heard it with my own ears!" Ruth declared.

"Get me a comment from that Inspector chap Ruth and we will go to print!" Her editor was reading her piece for the second time. "This is bloody brilliant!"

"He's very hard to pin down!" Ruth said, irked.

Her editor looked at her grinning as he sat back in his chair and folded his arms across his large belly. "Ruth Watkins you've never had any trouble pinning any man down! Now get out of here!"

At the police station all three officers were huddled around Claire's computer.

"Fantastic work Claire. That was just the break in this case we were looking for!" Inspector Jones said giving her a pat on the back.

Claire looked at Tom and for once she was beaming. "Sir, I can't take all the credit. It was Dee too!"

"Yes, I will thank her," he said vowing that if ever got the chance to take Dee out to Mr Wangs for the Chinese he still owed her by way of an apology he would also buy her a small thankyou gift.

"Sir, are you okay?" Tom said interrupting his thoughts.

"I'm fine!" Jake stammered realising he had been daydreaming. "Let's go!"

"Where?" Tom asked.

"Sofia and Jett Bailey's salon of course!"

Claire laughed.

Dee and Peter had left Vicky to her hoovering and had now arrived at David's home.

"I hope you two haven't come here to give me a hard time!" Mrs Walker said as she walked them through to the lounge.

"Absolutely not!" Peter assured her. "But we do have some questions for your son."

David stood up and turned the television off as they entered. "I'm pleased you're here. Have you found anything else out. I really want to have Lucy's funeral." David looked down at his feet.

"Yes, but only the police can release Lucy's body, David. I'm sorry. I know you want this all over and done with as soon as possible. It's hard not being able to move on," Peter said putting his hand on his arm.

"Very," David said and then looked to his mum as he asked, "Are we having tea or coffee?"

"We're fine, thank you." Peter smiled at Mrs Walker.

Dee knew they needed a moment alone with David so she asked Mrs Walker, "Could I have a glass of water please."

"Of course!" Mrs Walker disappeared into the kitchen.

"David, we need to talk to you without your mother present. Maybe a walk in the garden?" Peter asked him.

"Yeah sure, this way," David said, opening the patio doors and leading them outside.

"Oh, a green house. Are you green fingered?" Dee asked.

"No, it's all Lucy. Let me show you." David led them into the glass construction.

Mrs Walker returned to the lounge with Dee's glass of water. The lounge was empty, but the patio door was ajar. She looked out into the garden to see where they had all gone and could clearly see them all deep in conversation inside the green house. She slammed the glass down hard on the coffee table causing a little of the water to spill over the top of the glass.

"Shit," she said under her breath. She was not referring to the spillage.

Ruth had arrived at the police station, to be told once again that Inspector Jones was unavailable.

"Does that mean he's here and won't speak to me or he's genuinely not in the building?" She was frustrated.

"Neither nor," came the answer.

She turned on her heels and as she headed back to her car she dialled Peter's number.

In the greenhouse David was proudly explaining. "Lucy grew all these herself. Then she would make remedies and face creams with them. Her and Sofia were always trying them out at the salon."

"What do you mean by remedies?" Dee asked.

"Lucy suffered with psoriasis. She had finally made a cream that really worked. Her skin was looking very good when I came home. Mind you maybe that could have been the baby hormones too." David touched one of the plants as he spoke.

"Lucy liked to experiment with different herbs?" Peter asked him as his mobile began to ring. He excused himself, leaving Dee and David inside.

David said, "I know what he's getting at. She didn't grow anything she shouldn't and the police have already been in here looking for Poison Ivy!"

"Have they now? How do you know that's what they were looking for?" Dee asked him calmly.

"My mother said," he replied.

Dee had another thought. "You said Lucy and Sofia tried creams out at the salon?"

"Yes, often. Lucy would spend hours on her hobby. As you know I've been away for weeks with work. Lucy mentioned it had given her the chance to get creative - her words not mine! She'd spent hours on the new autumn range - her best yet," David said as he walked towards the greenhouse door.

"I'm sorry, did I hear you right? Lucy said the autumn range is her best yet?"

"That's what I said."

"David, this sounds more than just a hobby to me. Where does – did - Lucy make all these skin creams?" she asked, following him out of the greenhouse and into the garden.

"Upstairs in the spare bedroom. I'll show you!" David said making his way back to the house.

Dee turned round to tell Peter to get off his phone and follow them, but he looked like he was arguing with the person on the other end, so she left him to it.

Sofia and Jett were going through their diaries together when Inspector Jake Jones, followed by Tom and Claire entered their office.

"We meet again Inspector. I hope you're not here to upset my wife?" Jett said protectively.

"No, but we do need to speak with you both," Jake said sternly.

Sofia offered them all a seat and picked up the phone. They heard her ask for them not to be disturbed.

"We needed to speak to you anyway so you've saved me the trouble of phoning you!" Jett went on to explain. "We think Sofia's life might be in danger!"

"There's no need to jump to conclusions, but we do need to know whether it was your idea or Lucy's to swap rooms?" Jake asked Sofia.

"Lucy's. She said she didn't want a massage," Sofia said, playing with the collar on her blouse.

"And I understand you checked with Angela that this was alright to do so?" Jake questioned.

"I did, but I didn't. I knew it wouldn't be a problem." Sofia shrugged innocently. "She wasn't in her office, so I wrote her a note."

"A note? Where did you leave it?" Claire asked.

Sofia turned to look at her. "In her office on the notepad I wrote it on!"

Jake felt Sofia's tone was bordering on the sarcastic.

Jett obviously felt it too. "Sorry about that!" he apologised to Claire. "Sofia and I have been under quite some strain since we found out what we did yesterday!"

Jake nodded. "Yes, I can imagine. We're wondering why none of this was mentioned in the statement that you gave us on the day of Lucy's murder."

Sofia looked aghast. "My best friend had just been dragged out of the Cave Pool dead, and you want me to remember every little detail!"

"Yes Sofia - Mrs Bailey," Jake corrected himself. "As you're aware swapping rooms with Lucy might be a significant detail rather than a small one!"

Sofia put her head down. "Yes I see that; sorry."

"Mrs Bailey, may I ask which therapist was going to do Lucy's massage or should I ask who did your massage?" Claire had her pencil at the ready to record the answer.

Jake smiled at her, pleased she had asked the question he had forgotten.

"I had Lori. She's good but not as experienced as Laura." Sofia answered confidently.

"I understand Laura normally does all your treatments?" Claire said.

"Yes, she usually does. As I say she's very good at them all. She's easy to train; one of the best therapists there is at Wellsdale Hall." Sofia smiled.

"Would you say you and Laura have a close relationship?" Claire asked. Jake and Tom looked puzzled.

"We get on very well, but we're not friends if that's what you mean." Sofia looked to Jett for confirmation.

"We have a purely professional relationship with all the staff at Wellsdale Hall. We like to keep boundaries when it comes to work," Jett announced.

Claire wanted so desperately to ask the next question as did Tom but they knew what was coming, and waited for Jake to ask.

"Is that true Jett? Is everything purely professional between you and Angela Myers?"

Jett jumped up. "You listen to me. Angela Myers and ourselves have worked together for many years. Who on earth would say something stupid like that!"

"There's always tittle tattle in our line of business." Sofia rolled her eyes. "If you believed the staff in here, Jett's sleeping with half our clients and I'm probably sleeping with the rest!"

Jake nodded to show he understood where she was coming from.

"Who said that?" Jett asked sitting back down.

"One of your friends."

Jake waited for the reaction.

Jett and Sofia looked at each other.

"Louise Smart," Jake answered.

Back at the Walker's house Dee was shocked at what she was looking at. "This is like a laboratory!"

"I know. Lucy took her hobby seriously," David said.

"Sorry about that, just a little problem to take care of!" Peter apologised as he came up to join them. "Wow, this is impressive!"

"This is where Lucy invented all her creams and lotions!" Dee said, hoping Peter knew what she was thinking.

"David, can we have a moment to look around. I can see it's difficult for you to be in here," Peter said ushering him out of the door.

"Yes, that fine. Lucy spent hours in here," he said as he turned to leave.

They waited for the door to close. Dee and Peter knew exactly what to do.

As Dee opened another drawer to go through, she asked Peter, "Problem on the phone?"

Peter was looking through a book that had lots of bright coloured post its sticking out of it. "It was Ruth, wanting to know if we were with Jake. I told her politely to get lost!"

Dee giggled "And what was her response to that?"

"Not pleasant!" He shrugged. "Jake can speak to her when he wants to!"

The mention of Jake's name stopped Dee in her tracks. She paused as she couldn't help thinking how wrong she had been about her feelings.

"Is everything all right?" Peter enquired, noticing that she was simply standing there.

"Just thinking!" Dee replied quickly.

"Penny for them?" Peter asked.

"Not this time. What I was thinking about isn't even worth that!" Dee said and then turned to face a calendar on the wall so Peter couldn't read her face.

Suddenly she took out her phone and started taking pictures of the calendar.

"What have you got there?" Peter asked coming over to have a look. "Hey, that's one busy calendar!"

"Sure is. Take a closer look at what's written in for May the eighteenth." Dee pointed at the day on the calendar.

Peter read it out loud. *"Meet AM - sign contract.* "I wonder what contract she was due to sign on the morning of the eighteenth? We can see if David knows anything on our way out."

"Peter, I've had another thought." Dee looked at him. "What if AM stands for Angela Myers?"

Chapter Eighteen

The morning had turned into afternoon, and following her phone call with Peter, Ruth was fuming. She'd sat outside the police station for quite some time waiting for Jake to return but he hadn't. Eventually a PC came out and told her to move on. Deciding on her next move, the only sound that could be heard was the tapping of her long, sharp nails on the steering wheel before she turned the ignition on.

Dee and Peter were outside the Walkers' house.
"Dee this is all getting very messy. We need to get back to the office and sort it out – timelines - who knew who. It's all very confusing. We need to think straight and stop guessing!" Peter's tone was one of frustration.
"Coffee Creams first?" she asked him. "Nothing like one of Alison's cakes to give us some brain power!"
"The way this is going, we're going to need more than brain power!" was Peter's reply.

Jake, Tom and Claire had left the Baileys, promising that if Sophia felt threatened in any way, they had to call him immediately and he would have a police officer stationed outside their door.
"I wouldn't want to be Louise Smart!" Tom said as they got back in the car.
"Me neither. The way them two reacted to that bit of information, we could have another murder on our hands!" Claire whispered in his ear.
"Back to the station!" the Inspector ordered as he got in the passenger seat of the police car.
"Yes, Sir!"

Alison was tidying up. She seemed to have had a sudden rush of customers for the last couple of hours. The bell tinkled over the door of Coffee Creams and Alison turned to greet her next customer.

"Ah, you two were in a hurry this morning. Where were you off to?" Alison smiled as Dee and Peter moved towards the table next to the window.

"We went to see Vicky," Dee answered her as Alison came over with her notepad to take their order.

"No need for that," Peter smiled. "Two coffees, please, and can you surprise us with two slices of one of your wonderful cakes!"

"Right you are!" Alison said making her way back behind the counter.

Albert headed over towards the pair. "Been talking to Miss Fancy Pants, my neighbour, have we?"

"Albert, are you still here? Thought you would be home by now." Peter winked at Dee.

"Nothing between the ears that one, mark my words!" Albert said.

"Albert, that's not kind!" Dee pulled a face at him. "She might know more than you think!"

"Nah!" Albert laughed. "Alison. I'm on my way. I'll see you tomorrow!"

Alison shouted, "Bye!," from behind the counter.

"The one thing Miss Fancy Pants does know, is that we're getting a new neighbour," Albert said as a parting shot.

Dee and Peter watched him leave, and smiled when he waved at them as he passed by the window.

"What's that about a neighbour?" Alison asked carrying a tray towards them.

"Vicky's told Albert they're getting a new neighbour apparently!" Peter grumbled.

"Enjoy these. One is almond and raspberry and the other chocolate orange. You can choose which one you want or share," Alison said as she put the plates down in front of them. "Anyway, I thought Jake was the new neighbour."

"He is," Peter said letting Dee choose which cake she preferred.

"Maybe he's taking in a lodger!" Alison suggested.

Dee opted for the chocolate orange cake and put a piece on her fork. "He's not getting a lodger. It will be his girlfriend!"

"Girlfriend!" Alison looked stunned. "Peter you've never mentioned Jake having a girlfriend."

Peter looked out of the window. "No I haven't. Turns out our Inspector is a bit of a dark horse!"

Tom and Claire were settled back in their office checking through recent reports when she received a message to go to the front desk.

"I won't be a minute," she said to Tom and headed out of the office.

Tom had been waiting for just such an opportunity. He quickly went over to Claire's desk, opened the bottom drawer - for once she had not locked it. It wasn't what he had imagined. He lifted the letter out and his mouth went dry. He knew there was something wrong. Why had she not confided in him. He quickly put it back and ran to sit back down behind his desk as he could hear footsteps coming back down the hall.

Alison was busy washing up in the kitchen.

"I'll just go say bye, and then walk back to the office. I need some fresh air!" Dee said.

"Right you are!" Peter agreed, sensing Dee wanted a quick girlie chat with Alison. As he opened his car to drive the short distance to his office, he recognised Ruth's car parked outside the agency. "Here we go!" he sighed!

Back inside Coffee Creams, Dee had picked up a tea towel and was helping to dry some pots.

"This is kind of you. Need to tell me anything?" Alison asked not looking at Dee.

"Yes, I need you to go undercover for me!"

"Me! Of course I will. I've been feeling a bit left out of this case after the last one." Alison sounded excited "What do you want me to do?"

"First I need you to phone here." Dee showed her a picture on her phone. "I've already sent you the photo. I need you to say you would like to rebook, you're now ready to proceed and can they give you some dates. Nothing more than that."

Alison nodded. "Okay, and I take it there's another thing?"

"Yes, can you and Jim go to Blacks Estate Agency and say you're looking to buy a house. Avoid Louise Smart. Only go in if Charles Black himself is there. Only speak to him and I've also sent you a list of questions I need you to ask." Dee's green eyes sparkled like emeralds.

"Are you on to something?" Alison asked.

"Maybe, maybe not, but this will really help!" Dee popped the tea towel back. "I'd best be going!"

"Just hang on a minute!" Alison shouted and ran after her. "Are you alright?"

"Alright, yes why?" Dee said, one hand holding the door to the café open.

"Jake having a girlfriend, I know that must be a bit of a shock, I always thought…"

Alison was interrupted by Dee. "Alison, if you want a real not only does he have a girlfriend, he's also going to be a father!"

As Dee closed the door behind her, Alison froze. The cup she was holding slipped from her grasp and shattered into pieces on the floor.

"Long time since I've been in here, Peter," Ruth said. "It looks much brighter than I remember."

"All Dee's work. She has quite the eye." Peter stood at the door as if he was keeping guard. "Ruth why are you here? I told you, I've nothing to say. I can't help you!"

"Peter, I need some sort of comment from our Inspector friend, or any update. I'm getting it in the neck from my editor!" Ruth sat on the edge of his desk, trying to look sexy.

"Ruth, quit that crap. I'll have a word with Jake and see what I can do," Peter said opening the door.

Ruth jumped up and thanked him.

"By the way, are congratulations in order?" he said as she slid past him.

"What on earth for?" Ruth said from halfway down the corridor.

"I understood there was an imminent proposal," Peter mocked.

Ruth knew immediately he had known she was at Bailey's salon the same day as he and Dee were. She turned and laughed. "Peter, piss off!"

Jake's mobile vibrated on his desk. He was relieved to see it was Peter.

"You read my mind, fancy a catch up tonight at the Star and Crown?" he asked.

"Sorry Jake, can't do tonight. I have a school thing with Clara. You'll find out all about that sort of thing in due course," Peter joked.

"Hope so!" Jake replied.

"Jake, do you and Catherine want to come to Gaitley Manor for dinner tomorrow night?"

"I'm sure she would love to but Peter we need to talk about the case. Would Dee be there?" Jake was hoping she would be.

"No, Jake. I think she has something on tomorrow night!" he lied.

Jake sounded disappointed. "I understand, but we're starting to build a case!"

"We definitely need a catch up tomorrow. How about we meet at Coffee Creams early?" Peter asked him.

"Yes, I'll let the others know," Jake replied.

"By the way, the reason for my call is that Ruth called me, and she's shown up here at the office today. Give her a comment Jake, or some sort of update. Get her off our backs." Peter said it in such a way that there could be little doubt he wasn't so much asking Jake as telling him.

"I hear you. Leave it with me. See you all in the morning!" Jake said and put the phone down.

Alison had finely brushed up the last fragment of the broken teacup when Paula from Flowering Fancies walked through the door.

"Hi. You don't have any breakfast muffins left do you? Oh, have you been having a smashing time?"

"Not so much smashing as shocking but never mind!" Alison shook her head. "Paula is there any chance you could come and cover for me around two thirty tomorrow?"

"I can't do two thirty, but I can do three, if that helps."

Alison passed her three muffins. "That would be great. Take them; they're the last of the batch. I have to be in early tomorrow; lots of baking to do!"

Paula thanked her, and then as she was leaving she turned and asked, "Going anywhere nice, Alison?"

"House hunting!" she replied.

Back at the police station Claire and Tom were in the staff canteen grabbing a coffee.

"Fancy a drink after work?" Tom asked her.

"I can do, but I can't be late. I have a date with the washing machine!" She laughed.

"Who was at the front desk?" Tom asked her.

"The bank manager from Gamblewood. He had some information for me," she answered flippantly.

"Care to share!" Tom said nudging her and causing a tiny splash of coffee to land on her white blouse.

"And now I have more to wash!" Claire playfully punched him.

"Tom, Claire, can you meet me in the conference room!" Jake called from the doorway.

"Sure, Sir. What's happening?" Tom put his cup down.

"Ruth from the Amberleigh Gazette is on her way!" Jake said as he rolled his eyes towards the ceiling.

Peter and Dee stood staring at the evidence board in front of them.

"This is giving me a headache. I can't think straight!" Peter stated, pretending to pull his hair out.

"Don't you have that school report thing for Clara tonight?" Dee asked him.

"I do, Dee. We're meeting Jake and the gang early in Coffee Creams tomorrow morning to go through all this.

Let's leave it till then," Peter said picking up his car keys. "Are you alright to let Alison know we're coming?"

"Sure. Won't be a problem. Alison loves us all turning up early!" Dee laughed sarcastically. She waited for Peter to leave before calling Alison.

"Hi Alison, it's me!" Dee said into her mobile.

"Dee, I made that phone call not long after you left. It was the weirdest conversation ever," Alison said.

"I thought it would be!" Dee acknowledged. "Did it go how I thought it would?"

"It went exactly as you said it would and to let you know Jim and I are going house hunting tomorrow!" Alison said excitedly.

"Thank you so much. You've done a great job," Dee praised her.

"I've written it all down for you. I'll keep it till you next pop in!" Alison said sounding really pleased with herself.

"About that, I need you to be discreet tomorrow morning." Dee was almost whispering into her phone.

"You do? Why? What's happening tomorrow morning?" Alison sounded intrigued.

"Alison, with your approval, we'd all like to meet for an early brainstorming session at Coffee Creams," Dee said tactfully.

"You know you're all welcome anytime. When we say early, how early?"

"Seven thirty okay, Alison?" Dee asked, fairly cringing on the other end of the call.

"Yes. Fortunately for you lot I have a lot of baking to do!" Alison sighed. "You mentioned the word discreet?"

"Please don't mention anything about the call you made or the house hunting if you follow my drift. I want to keep that on the quiet for now till I have all the facts." Dee paused. "Another thing - don't say anything to Jake about his girlfriend or the baby. He hasn't officially told anyone yet. Not even Peter!"

"Not even Peter? How do you know then?" Alison was confused.

"Vicky told me in the supermarket!" Dee explained.

"In the supermarket? Didn't know you knew what one was!"

Alison laughed.

Ruth was already waiting for Jake to join her in the conference room at the police station. "Sorry to keep you!" Jake said smiling at her.

To Ruth, Jake looked as handsome as ever with his thin clever face and cool blue eyes. She shook the thought of them in bed together out of her head. "It's fine." She smiled. "Hope you have something interesting for me?"

Jake passed her a piece of paper with a typed statement on it.

"This is the best you can do?" Ruth screeched.

Tom and Claire stepped forward, Jake raised his hand for them to stay where they were.

"Ruth, if you don't mind me calling you that, we're close to making an arrest. Please print what you have and nothing more," he said sternly.

Ruth didn't answer. She threw him a filthy look as she headed for the door.

The remainder of the day had been quiet for everyone. It was only five thirty and Tom, Claire and Dee were sitting having a drink in the window of the Cocktail Bar in Amberleigh.

"Thanks for asking me to join you both. You two come here a fair bit," Dee said taking a sip of her mocktail.

"I suppose we do!" Tom laughed looking over at Claire.

"It's fairly quiet at this time and it's not in Gamblewood!" Claire said.

"Yeah, I understand, Jake and Peter use The Star and Crown. I've been a couple of times with them," Dee said pushing back straggles of loose red hair that had escaped from her ponytail.

"Jake said we needed an early finish to recharge as we had such an early start!" Claire laughed.

Tom excused himself and went to the bar to place another order.

"Here, before he comes back!" Claire passed Dee an envelope. "It's a photocopy!"

Dee smiled. "Is it what we thought?"

"Looks like it is. Read it when you get home." She stopped. Tom was returning carrying more drinks.

"Isn't that the Inspector?" Tom said as he placed the drinks on the table.

They all turned to look out of the cocktail bar's window.

Jake was emerging from the jewellers next door to Natalie's Clothes shop. He was smiling and chatting to the attractive woman behind him. The three watched in silence as Jake hugged her and as she turned a baby bump was visible for all to see.

"Well, I never!" Tom spluttered

"I thought as much the other day," Claire said looking at Dee.

"Is that so?" Tom said still looking out of the window.

"Garlic, Tom!" Claire rolled her eyes at him. "He said Vicky had brought round baby things!"

Tom finally twigged what Claire was talking about.

Claire put a hand on Dee's arm. "Are you okay, do you know who she is?"

Dee nodded. "She's called Catherine."

After another drink Dee, Tom and Claire had all left the bar in Amberleigh. Claire was going home to do some washing, Tom had football practice and Dee wanted to snuggle up on the sofa in her coziest pyjamas so they said their goodbyes.

Dee was now at home. She looked at the time. It was eight pm. She'd already had a quick bubble bath and picked up her mobile to video call her Gran.

"Hello, love, how are things?"

"Developing!"

"With the case?" her Gran enquired.

"And other things!" Dee said. "I need to explain."

They enjoyed a good hour chatting away with Dee bringing her Gran up to speed on the case and telling her it looked like Jake would be announcing his engagement shortly.

"Dee, you don't know that for definite!" her Gran scolded her.

"Gran, she's pregnant and moving in with him. Vicky told Albert as much!" Dee was getting agitated.

"Things may not be what they seem!" her Gran sighed.

"I think they are!" Dee replied.

Dee's Gran could tell she was becoming upset and changed the topic. "You mentioned an envelope?"

"Ooh yes. Let me get it. Wait a minute. It's in my jeans pocket," Dee said throwing her mobile onto the sofa.

Her Gran smiled to herself as all she could see was the ceiling, but she could hear Dee running to the bedroom and back. "It's here!" Dee announced picking up her phone and holding it up for her Gran to see.

"Open it, dear. From what you've said, I hope you're right!"

Dee stopped talking and propped her phone up against some books she had decoratively positioned on the coffee table.

"Is it what you thought, dear?"

"Gran it's exactly what I thought. If Alison and Jim can see Charles Black tomorrow and ask my questions, then I believe we'll have our killer!"

Chapter Nineteen

Mrs Wood was busy fussing around in the kitchen.

"Morning!" Peter said.

Mrs Wood jumped. "You're up early; I haven't even started breakfast yet!"

"I've got a meeting with Jake and the others at Coffee Creams" Peter said.

"I can rustle you up something quick," Mrs Wood said reaching for the tray of eggs on the side.

"Honestly, I'm all good. Looking forward to tonight," Peter said with a cheery wave.

"Bye!" Mrs Wood called after him.

Dee was up early too, showered, and doing her make-up as sunlight streamed through the window, casting rainbows on the walls. She was unsure what to wear but then the tiny rainbows reminded her of a scarf she had not worn for a while. Dee went to her wardrobe and pulled out a pair of sky-blue pencil trousers and a cream top. She retrieved the scarf from the box under her bed and took a step back to look at her reflection. The waves of merging blues, creams and pinks of the scarf complemented the outfit and her red hair. Dee didn't have much real jewellery, but she did have a pair of her Gran's pearl stud earrings which got caught in her hair as she was trying to put them in.

"Flipping Eck!" Dee was now crawling around the floor trying to find the back of the earring she had dropped when she could hear Peter calling her from the office. "I'm nearly ready, one sec!" she shouted through the connecting door between her flat and the office.

Peter was taking yet another good look at the evidence board. He could see who but how still seemed to be a problem. He hoped Jake might be able to shed some light on that bit of the puzzle.

"Sorry, I dropped my earring and…" Dee said locking the door behind her.

Peter knew he was in for a longwinded explanation of her morning and found it easier to head for the door.

Alison had been at Coffee Creams busily baking away from six in the morning. The sought after breakfast muffins were in the oven, the croissants were cooling, and her second batch of cake mix was sitting on the side waiting for oven space. Alison checked her watch. It was ten past seven. She quickly went out into the café and checked there were enough chairs around the two tables she had put together and mugs for the pots of tea she had already prepared waiting for them all to arrive. Pleased with herself she returned to the kitchen to put the final touches onto a platter of morning pastries she had baked fresh for them.

Inspector Jones was already in the police car and driving to Coffee Creams with Tom and Claire. "Tom, did you pick up all the bank statements?" Jake asked him for the second time.

"Yes, Sir. Claire has the full file on the case. Are you okay, Sir?" Tom asked and then braked hard because the lights were changing.

"Yes, of course I am!" Jake replied twiddling with his collar. "Watch it Tom you nearly went through that red!"

Tom glanced at Claire through the rear-view mirror. Claire understood Tom's thoughts; the Inspector appeared unusually nervous.

The little bell over the door of Alison's café tinkled marking the arrival of Peter and Dee.

"Wow, you look stunning, doesn't she Peter?" Alison said as she greeted them.

Peter, uncertain of the appropriate response to both his employee and his fiancée's close friend, chose to respond with a polite smile and a nod.

"Love that scarf!" Alison said. "Really suits you. Dee. You couldn't give me a quick hand in the kitchen, could you?"

"Course." Dee smiled and followed Alison.

"Dee, I just wanted to check on you. You were rather flippant yesterday about our Inspector!" Alison whispered handing her the platter of pastries.

"Alison, I'm happy for Jake. Why wouldn't I be? It's fantastic news!" Dee said unconvincingly. "Remember we can't let on about anything. Are you and Jim still okay for this afternoon?"

"Yes, Jim's quite excited to do a bit of sleuthing!" Alison spoke quietly as the bell over the door tinkled.

Alison followed Dee out of the kitchen and into the café area. The others had arrived and were all shaking hands and swapping pleasantries when Jake noticed that Dee was carrying a tray. Alison watched as Jake took the tray of pastries from her. She noticed their hands briefly touch, and then Dee's eyes meeting Jake's.

"Good morning," he stammered, really wanting to tell her how beautiful she looked, but knowing it would be unprofessional. Instead he said nothing and placed the tray on the table.

"Help yourselves to tea," Alison said. She couldn't help thinking that from the way Jake looked at Dee, Vicky had to be wrong!

"Inspector Jones, I think it's only right that you start proceedings," Peter said once they were all sitting down.

Jake took a deep breath. "We're nearly ready to make an arrest."

"You are?" Dee jumped in.

Jake was caught off guard. "Yes, well…we're still missing the most important piece of the puzzle!"

"So, you're not ready to make an arrest then!" Dee jumped in again.

Peter gave Dee his look with the raised eyebrows. Dee knew what that look meant. "Sorry Jake, please explain," Dee said, playing with the handle of her mug.

Jake looked across at her. He had a million feelings flooding his system and he wouldn't mind if she interrupted him for the rest of his life.

"Sir!" Tom said trying to bring the Inspector back on track.

"We all know who, but not how and we believe Lucy was not the intended victim," Jake said glancing at Claire who picked up the hint.

"Yes," she said, "…the murder had to take place between one thirty and two thirty."

"Why?" Peter asked, already knowing the answer.

"Because we see Lucy and Sofia going into the treatment room just before one thirty and Sofia comes back into the waiting area at a little after two thirty." Claire took a breath. "Lucy's treatment should have taken roughly the same amount of time."

"There's no cameras outside the treatment rooms. What if Lucy never even had a treatment," Tom said.

"She definitely did. Laura started the treatment and left her when she was called away," Dee stated. "I think we can trust Laura's account."

"So, who don't we trust?" Peter threw out to the table.

"All of them!" Jake replied. "They're trying to confuse us. The only facts we do know, are location, time, the poison used and that Lucy was receiving money from the Baileys and Louise Smart."

"Are we talking blackmail?" Peter asked him.

"Maybe but why, and if it was, why would the Baileys want to use their blackmailer as a surrogate mother for their child," Jake asked.

Alison started to cough. They all looked over at her, Dee trying to hide a smile at her friend's earwigging.

"They wouldn't!" Tom said. "Also what did Lucy have on Louise Smart?"

"That's a million-dollar question?" Jake replied. "We're seeing her this afternoon."

"Are you talking to her at the estate agency, Jake?" Dee asked him, as innocently as she could.

"No, at the station. The Black Estate Agency, like Wellsdale Hall, insists on a legal representative being present." Jake looked at Peter, not trusting himself to look at Dee.

"Why do you ask, Dee?" Peter pried.

"Nothing. I would have liked to have been there, that was all," Dee said, glancing over at Alison who was bent down behind the glass counter pretending to clean it.

"What are your thoughts on how they poisoned her?" Jake asked them all. "Because to be honest unless the person responsible confesses, I have no idea!"

"We know it wasn't in the food, so it had to be in the treatment room," Tom offered.

"Maybe they put it in the water. I know they made me drink lots of it during and after my massage," Claire chipped in.

"Any thoughts, Dee?" Peter asked.

"Yes but no, not definitely. The more I think about it, that's a possibility." Dee was deep in thought.

Peter and Jake exchanged looks of confusion.

Jake took charge of the situation. "Let's all start at the beginning. Who was there, what time, and motives!"

Time ticked on as they talked over numerous scenarios and possibilities. Alison was keeping a close eye on the time knowing that Albert would be arriving shortly.

"I'm sorry everyone, but our best customer will be here soon and I don't think you'll want Albert seeing you all here together!" Alison said as she cleared the empty pastry tray away.

"Yes, fair point Alison," Peter said.

They agreed that after interviewing Louise Smart at the police station, Jake would let Peter know the outcome. "You can tell me tonight!" Peter said without thinking. Claire, Tom and Dee shared a knowing glance but didn't say anything.

As they made their way outside to leave, Dee hung back. She wanted to have a final word with Alison who was busy in the kitchen.

Jake waited for Peter to join Claire and Tom outside and then went over to Dee.

"Dee, I hope we can have this all tied up by the end of the week. Would you be free to join me at Mr Wangs on Saturday night?" He was crossing his fingers.

The bell tinkled over the door and Albert came bounding in waving his newspaper. "I'm surprised to find you two in here. Have you read this? Turns out Lucy was murdered by mistake. They were after that Sofia Bailey all along. You lot need to get a move on, or there'll be another murder. Mind my words!"

Dee looked at Albert then back at Jake.

"What's that racket Albert!" Alison came flying out of the kitchen.

"I'd best be going; looks like we both have a lot to do," Dee said looking up at the Inspector.

Jake followed her outside and Alison ran to the window. She watched as Dee and Peter walked away towards their office and Jake along with Tom and Claire headed to the parked police car.

"Bloody hell, Albert. Your timing couldn't be any worse!" Alison said to him annoyed, her hands on her hips.

Ruth was enjoying a morning coffee and the many compliments on yet another thought-provoking article. Robert watched her closely as she bathed in her colleague's appreciation. Ruth was aware he was watching her. "Dinner tonight?" she mouthed across the office.

Robert winked back in agreement as he ran his hand through his curly hair.

"You want to watch that one. He's a player!" The young journalist sitting at the desk next to Ruth's piped up.

"I'd remind you to mind your own business. I can handle him. He's child's play!" Ruth retorted, smirking.

The young journalist had been doing some investigating of her own. She looked back at the screen on her laptop, feeling sorry for Robert's wife and his two children.

Dee and Peter were back in the office, contemplating what to do next.

"I think we need to speak to Angela Myers again and Sofia Bailey," Dee thought out loud.

"We've all agreed we know who did it and why. It's just a matter of how they obtained Poison Ivy and administered it." Peter played with his pen as he spoke.

"I've a thought on that, but I need to go to Wellsdale Hall," Dee said. "Do you want to drive or shall I?"

"I'll drive," Peter offered.

Jake and the others had just arrived back at the police station when Jake's mobile vibrated, and it was Catherine.

"Hello, I have to be quick, Catherine. I'm about to go into an interview," he said turning away so Claire and Tom couldn't hear him.

Tom nudged Claire.

Catherine was asking what an appropriate gift for Helen and Sir Henry would be.

"Chocolates might be an idea. Catherine I'm rubbish at this, but don't take any alcohol as you won't be drinking any!" He laughed into his mobile.

"Dee was right!" Tom said to Claire as they walked back to their office leaving Jake chatting away into his phone.

"You know Tom, I'm sure there's a Catherine covering for Ann in forensics," Claire said as she opened their office door.

"Wouldn't know!" he replied.

Peter and Dee had finally arrived at Wellsdale Hall. The morning traffic had been bad, and they seemed to have hit every red light.

"Can you distract Angela, while I have a look around her office?" Dee asked.

"I can, but why?"

"I think I'll know it when I see it!" she said.

"Dee, you've been talking in riddles all morning!" Peter said.

"Please don't look at me like that. I've just got a feeling!"

"Now you're a proper detective, we all get that. Talking of which, don't you get your results soon?"

"Peter don't ask!" Dee knew the results of her Private Investigator exams would be arriving any day soon.

"Please come in," Angela said to them. "We don't have long as I have to prep everyone on the weekend ahead!"

"It won't take long; Angela would you be able to show me the kitchens, please," Peter asked her.

"I can but I can always ring down and let them know you're coming."

"I'd like to ask you some questions on our way, if that's okay?" Peter smiled.

"Sure," Angela replied.

As the three of them headed for the door, Dee made the excuse of needing to use the toilet.

"Use that one. It's for staff." Angela pointed to a door at the end of the corridor.

Peter speeded up and naturally Angela followed him. Dee kept her foot wedged in Angela's office door to stop it from automatically closing. She watched as they went down the stairs and out of sight.

Once inside, Dee opened Angela's desk drawers but there was nothing to be found of significance. In the corner Dee could see her coat laid over a chair. She picked it up to check the pockets but as she did so, she discovered Angela's handbag was hiding underneath.

She quickly opened it and peered inside. There were lots of receipts and a bank statement. Dee took several photos and then put everything back as neatly as she could. Dee was just about to leave when she heard footsteps coming towards Angela's office. She checked her mobile but Peter hadn't messaged to say they were on their way back. Dee found herself hiding under Angela's desk as the office door opened.

"Trust the silly bitch not to be here!" a female voice said.

"I'm sick of this. We need to take a stand. She's definitely lining her own pockets!" said another female voice.

"It's about time upper management knew what she's up to!" said the first voice Dee had heard followed by the words, "…Unfortunately they think the sun shines out of her arse!"

Dee heard the door close. Only then did she realize she had been unconsciously holding her breath. As she emerged from her hiding place, she inhaled deeply. Dee knew she had recognised one of the voices.

Louise Smart was sitting in one of the interview rooms at Gamblewood Police Station with her lawyer. They had arrived earlier than expected.

Tom had knocked on Jake's office door to let him know Louise had arrived. A few minutes later Jake and Tom entered the interview room. Claire was already standing at the back of the room near the door.

"We're going to be direct, Ms Smart, as we don't want to keep you. At what time did you finish having your treatment?"

Louise looked at her lawyer and shrugged.

"Could you speak up for the tape please!" Tom said loudly.

"No comment," came the reply.

"Is that because you don't know, can't remember or don't want to co-operate?" Tom asked her.

Louise looked at her lawyer for guidance.

"Louise, if it's okay for me to use your first name, you could make this so much easier for yourself," Jake said

"Are you arresting me?" Louise asked him.

"No, you're only here to answer some questions about the murder of Lucy Walker," Jake answered.

Louise looked at her lawyer once again; he nodded at her.

"We all had our treatments after lunch. Maybe they started around one thirtyish and finished around two fifteen. I can't be sure," she said.

"We understand that after your beauty treatment you and Vicky Wright then met up with Sofia Bailey, but Lucy didn't join you." Jake constantly watched her as he spoke.

Louise kept her head down; her perfect dark brown almost black sharp bob sheltered the view of her face.

"Yes, Lucy didn't come to meet us. That's when we started to become worried."

"We can see from your statement that you messaged her but got no reply. Is this correct?" Tom jumped in.

"Yes," Louise agreed. "We thought she must have gone home. She'd said at lunch, she wasn't feeling well!"

"Would it be unusual for Lucy not to let at least one of you know she was leaving?" Jake asked.

"Yes, but if she left during her treatment, we were all still having ours. She'd have no idea which rooms we were in so she couldn't tell us she was leaving!" Louise said.

"Yes, I see," Jake said taking a second to gather his thoughts. "Now, I need to ask, why were you paying Lucy Walker sums of money. We have traced these amounts into her bank account from yours!" Jake said it sternly, showing her the reports.

Louise looked at her lawyer. "No comment," she replied.

At Wellsdale Hall Peter and Angela had returned from the kitchens but Dee was nowhere to be found. "Thank you for all your help. Dee will probably be waiting for me in the car," Peter explained.

Angela really wanted to get on with the rest of her day and made an excuse that while they had been out an urgent e-mail had arrived. Peter took his leave.

"Peter!" called Dee as she saw him leaving.

"I thought you'd gone to the car," he announced walking back to join her in the foyer.

"No, but I've had an interesting chat with Chrissy. Turns out our lovely Angela Myers likes to charge her extra for displaying her products around the hotel and spa!" Dee said.

"So, you're thinking she charges everyone even the Baileys?" Peter said in a low voice.

"Definitely and their products are everywhere!" Dee said, her green eyes shining brightly.

"I wonder if Jake can pull her bank statements for us!" Peter said.

"He doesn't have to," Dee waved her mobile at Peter "I already have them!"

Jake was sitting back behind his desk. Tom and Claire watched Louise and her lawyer leave from his office window. Jake's frustration was clear to all of them. "This isn't going to be as easy as I hoped. I wanted to get this all tied up and make an arrest in the morning!"

"Sir, I need to check something on the CCTV footage. Is it alright if I go?" Claire requested.

Jake nodded and waited for them both to leave. He picked up his mobile and called Mr Wangs. "Hello it's Inspector Jones here. Please could I book a table for two on Saturday night around seven please."

Alison had spent most of the day clock watching. She was clearing a table when Paula entered just as Jim pulled up outside.

"Thank you for this Paula. I won't be long!" Alison said, removing her pink-spotted apron.

"It's fine, no rush. Hope you find what you're looking for," Paula said, putting on a clean apron.

"What do you mean by that?" Alison asked her abruptly.

"Houses; hope you find your dream house!" Paula said looking at her as if she was cuckoo.

"Yes, me too!" Alison left, realizing detective work was harder than it looked.

"We need to head to the Baileys," Dee said to Peter as they crossed the Wellsdale Hall Hotel and Spa carpark.

She felt her mobile vibrating in her pocket as she'd turned it to silent earlier. "Peter I'll be a sec!" she said as she saw Claire's number flashing on her mobile.

"Hi Dee, where are you?" Claire asked not messing around with small talk.

"We're at Wellsdale Hall. Just about to go see the Baileys. What's wrong?" Dee asked.

"I need you to go back and check something for me," Claire spoke quietly

Dee found herself whispering into the phone too. "Tell me what you need!"

Claire explained and Dee signalled to Peter she'd be back in a few minutes as she needed the toilet.

"Claire, you're right," Dee whispered into the phone a few minutes later.

"Hello. Why are you still here?" Angela Myers was right behind Dee who spun round surprised by the tap on the shoulder and quickly cut Claire off.

"I was just going to use the bathroom but Angela, while I'm here, did Peter ask you about signing a contract with Lucy Walker on the eighteenth of May?" Dee asked casually.

"No, but I wouldn't be signing any contract without head office approval." Angela looked puzzled. "Why would I be signing anything with Lucy Walker anyway?"

"No reason. It was just mentioned," Dee lied, "…That she was signing a contract. She liked to invent skin care, face creams that sort of thing. I wondered with her being a good friend of Sofia Bailey's if you were giving her a helping hand as they say."

Angela was scrolling through her phone. "No, I had a meeting with Sofia Bailey and Westwood Foods scheduled for that day, but that reminds me I need to reschedule Westwood as with what happened here at the Spa the day before I didn't make any of those meetings."

Angela's mobile began to ring. "Sorry I need to take this!"

In Amberleigh, Jim and Alison were happily mooching around outside Blacks Estate Agency. They pretended to look and point at houses for sale in the window, but they were trying to peer inside to see if Louise Smart was in the office.

"I think we're clear!" Jim said, enjoying himself.

"Let's go in," Alison said.

Charles Black sat happily sipping a cup of tea as the pair entered.

"Welcome to Blacks. Let me know if I can help in any way?" he told them

"We're looking for a three to four-bedroom home, with a decent sized garden. Can you recommend any?" Jim sound totally believable.

"Please come and sit down. How much is your budget and which area are we looking at?" Charles was already tapping away on his computer.

"Up to seven hundred thousand and it must be here or in Gamblewood." Jim smiled.

Alison nearly fell off her chair. Where on earth had he got that figure from.

Alison coughed a little. "I don't like to ask but what is your commission?"

Charles answered without looking up. "Two percent on sales, higher if you have joint agents. Do you have a house to sell?"

"Yes, "Alison said, checking the list of questions on her phone from Dee under the table. "Does that include marketing costs, photos, all that sort of thing?"

"Definitely. No hidden costs here. Now what do you think to this one?" Charles turned the screen to show them a cottage with an acre of land.

"That will do nicely!" Jim replied.

Dee and Peter had finally arrived at the Bailey's Hair and Beauty Salon.

"Hi there. Are Jett or Sofia here," Peter asked the blue haired receptionist.

Jett appeared seemingly out of nowhere. "I am. Sofia's at home. Do you want to speak to me?"

Dee jumped in. "No Jett, it was Sofia really."

"She's at home, playing with her lotions and potions!" He laughed. "Here's the address. I'll let her know you're coming."

"No need. We might not get there today, but thank you, Jett," Peter said waving the notelet in his hand.

Before Dee could say anything, Peter had ushered her outside. Opposite them, from where they stood on the pavement, Dee could see Alison and Jim leaving Blacks Estate Agency. She hoped Peter hadn't noticed them.

In order to distract him, she said, "Peter, we are going to visit Sofia at home, aren't we?"

He replied, "Of course we are. I just don't think we should give her the heads up that we're on our way!"

Jake sat tapping his pencil against his chin. He questioned what he was missing. He felt he was running out of time. He checked his watch. He would need to leave soon and he wanted to grab a nice bottle of red for Sir Henry on his way home and flowers for Helen.

"Sir, you wanted to go over the evidence again. The vital piece we're missing is where the Poison Ivy came from and how was it administered," Claire said stating facts.

"Yes, Claire, I've been thinking about that. Can you pull me Laura's and Angela Myers statements immediately!"

Dee and Peter were flabbergasted by the enormity of the Bailey's home.

"There's money in hair and beauty that's for sure!" Peter said as he rang the doorbell.

There was no answer. He tried again. Still no reply.

"Dee, I don't like this. You go that way, and see if you can see her. I'll check round the back!" Peter ordered.

Dee, following instructions, ran round to the kitchen patio doors. Sofia was not in the kitchen. She peered in again, but still couldn't see her. She could hear Peter shouting Sofia's name so Dee did the same.

"What the hell's going on?" Sofia appeared out of a fancy garden building wearing a lab technicians coat.

"Sofia, we were worried something had happened to you!" Dee called across the garden to her just as Peter came round the corner of the house.

"Thank goodness, I thought the worst!"

Sofia disappeared back into the building. Peter nudged Dee and quickly made his way across the garden to the wooden structure, where he knocked on the door but didn't wait to be invited in. Dee followed closely behind.

"This is very impressive!" Peter announced.

The setting closely resembled Lucy's hobby room at home, albeit on a significantly larger scale. Rows of empty jars were arranged in neat rows prepared for use, while a labelling machine operated efficiently nearby. Jars containing various herbs and spices were methodically organised, and Bailey's hair and skincare products were displayed throughout the entirety of the garden house.

"Wow, I didn't realise you did all this by yourself. I thought you would have it all made in a factory," Dee said.

"We were getting ready to take the plunge, but we're a small business, and I can cope, although it was easier with Lucy's help," Sofia said picking up a pipette.

"Looks very scientific. What are you doing?" Peter asked.

"I'm currently adding oil to the lavender for the massage blend," she explained as she continued her task. "Would you mind waiting outside for just a minute, please?"

As they headed towards the door Dee noticed a desk with a cork pin board behind it.

Peter made his way out into the garden first. The scent inside the garden house had got up his nose and he started to sneeze.

Dee had stopped to look at Sofia's desk and what was pinned on the cork board when she was interrupted.

"That goes for you too!" Sofia shouted at her.

Eventually after waiting some time, Sofia joined them, and they all marched up the garden together and into the house.

"Have you always made your own skincare range?" Dee asked.

"Course I have!" Sofia snapped. "Why are you really here? As you can see, I have an order to get out and I'm rather busy!"

"Did you know Louise was paying Lucy sums of money a month?" Dee asked her outright.

"No, why?" Sofia looked puzzled.

"We were hoping you could tell us that!" Peter said trying not to marvel at how modern and well thought out the kitchen was.

Dee was trying her best to concentrate. She too really wanted to ask Sofia for a tour of her amazing home but instead asked, "Do you know if Lucy was due to sign any contract with anyone, especially on the eighteenth, the day after she was murdered?"

"Lucy? A contract? I wouldn't think so. Was it a work thing? Contract at the bank maybe?" Sofia shrugged.

Dee changed the subject. "Did you come up with all your own formulas for the creams and oils?"

"Yes of course. Lucy would help sometimes. We often tried out new ideas together," Sofia responded. "I miss her."

"Yes, I'm sure you do," Peter chimed in sympathetically.

"Did Louise help you sometimes?" Dee asked looking towards the dining area of the kitchen.

"Not so much help but she would keep me company in the garden house if I or we - as in Lucy and me - were in there playing with our lotions and potions. That's what Jett calls it. Playing!"

"Did you pay Lucy for her time, when she helped you out?" Dee asked her.

"Sometimes, but nothing major. More of a thank you if you know what I mean. Now, if there's nothing else, is it alright if I get on?" Sofia said ushering them towards the door.

"Yes, of course," Peter stammered. "Dee do you have anything further to ask Mrs Bailey?"

"No. Oh just one thing. I wanted to say what a lovely photo of you and Louise." Dee pointed to the bookcase in the dining area of the kitchen. "Where was that taken?"

Sofia followed Dee's gaze. "In the Bahamas. We go every February!"

"You both look like you're having a great time!" Dee said.

"Lucky you!" Peter added just before Sophia closed the door on them.

Walking to the car, Dee turned to Peter. "There's a thought - The Bahamas. You could get married abroad!"

"We might have some news for you on that!" Peter laughed, tapping the side of his nose.

"You're finally going to set a date?" Dee said as they got into the car.

"Wheels are in motion!"

Peter laughed again as he started the car.

Claire and Tom sat in their office gathering all the information together. Jake had told them he felt they were on the cusp of catching Lucy's killer.

"Do you agree, Claire?" Tom asked her.

"Yes, but there's just the disappointment of not finding a pot of Poison Ivy somewhere. The Walker's didn't have any in their green house, the Head Gardener said it doesn't even grow here and…" Claire stopped talking.

"And what?" Tom asked her. "It's not like the killer is just going to leave it out on display for us all to see!"

"I'm just going outside to phone, Dee!" Claire said ignoring his last remark as she rushed past him.

Ruth was having her hair brushed and brushed again by Jett Bailey.

"You're becoming a regular. What do you do for a living again?" he asked, making small talk.

"I'm a writer," she lied.

"Wow, would I have read any of your work?" he asked as he picked up the hairdryer.

"Maybe!" Ruth laughed to herself.

"Where are we going tonight?" Jett asked, not that he was particularly interested.

"Just out for a meal. Not sure. Robert said it was a surprise!" Ruth felt a warm fuzzy feeling come over her as she said his name.

Peter and Dee were making their way back towards Gamblewood talking through the case.

"I imagine the evidence would be long gone," Peter sighed.

"You mean the poison?" Dee said as her phone vibrated. "It's Claire!"

Peter listened as Dee answered her mobile. "Hi…Yeah, sure…Where?...Mine…Okay, I'll see you later. Bye!"

"That was short but sweet!" Peter commented.

"Claire's popping round tonight. She wants to run something past me," Dee said pulling a puzzled face. "I hope Jake hasn't upset her again!"

"Me too. She's going to make Inspector herself one day. I know a good detective when I see one!" Peter declared.

"Do you now!" Dee laughed.

Jake was on his way home with a pounding headache. He was frustrated at himself and with his team. They had their suspect, but the nagging itch was back. What had he missed to bring it all together? He pulled the car over as Peter was calling him.

"Hi, just checking you and Catherine are still alright for tonight?" Peter asked him.

"Yeah sure, looking forward to it. Is Dee with you?" Jake enquired.

"No," Peter replied. "I've just dropped her back at the office. Claire's popping round to see her tonight."

"That's nice," Jake said.

"Jake, you haven't upset Claire have you. You've been pretty hard on her lately!" Peter said.

"No, Peter, I haven't but why do you ask?"

"Nothing," Peter replied. "Dee thought it might be about work, but it must be about something else."

Jake didn't comment. He reached over to check that the little gold box was still in his glove compartment.

"Are you still there?" Peter shouted into his phone.

"Sorry Peter, I was just checking something, see you shortly," Jake said pressing the end button on his mobile.

Peter smiled to himself as he arrived at the gates of Gaitley Manor. The case was now at the back of his mind as he was hoping Helen would have some news for him on a completely different matter and if so, he was excited to share it with the others.

The afternoon had turned into evening, and Dee was chatting to Alison on the phone about her findings when Claire arrived.

"I have to go, Claire's here!" Dee said. "Remember not a word. There's a couple of things I need to check in the morning, but please say thank you to Jim for me too."

Dee opened the door and Claire waltzed in carrying a bottle of Prosecco.

"That's nice. Are we not driving tonight?" Dee asked her.

"Tom dropped me off; he's still outside. Look," Claire said making her way over to the window.

"Would he like to join us?" Dee asked Claire.

"I think not. He's picking me up on his way back from rugby practice," Claire said nonchalantly.

"That's really kind of him. Not a bit out of his way Claire?" Dee said with sly smile.

"Stop that!" Claire laughed. "We're good friends; it's not like that!"

"Are you now!" Dee teased as she fetched two glasses.

Catherine and Jake stood on the steps of Gaitley Manor.

"I'm a bit nervous Jake, it's lovely of Peter to invite us both," Catherine said shifting from one foot to another.

"I know, I was a bit surprised myself when he invited us. Do you remember Peter?" Jake asked.

"Of course I do. I bet he hasn't changed a bit!" Catherine smiled as the door opened.

Mrs Wood invited them in and showed them into the drawing room where Peter, Helen, and Sir Henry were happily chatting away as they entered.

"Welcome!" Sir Henry went over to shake Jake's hand. "I believe you must be Catherine."

"Yes," Catherine stammered as Sir Henry kissed the back of her hand.

"Ignore him; he's being silly. Let me take your coat. Would you like a drink?" Helen asked the pair.

"These are for you as a thank you for inviting me!" Catherine passed Helen the box of chocolates as she took her coat off to reveal a baby bump. "No alcohol for me!"

Peter and Helen exchanged glances. "When are you due?" Helen asked.

"End of August, if I ever get there. I swear this one seems to be in a hurry!" Catherine smiled putting her hand on her bump.

"Sit down, my dear girl!" Sir Henry ordered.

Catherine did as she was told. Jake went to sit next to her handing over the bottle of red to Peter and the flowers to Helen at the same time.

"I'll just pop these flowers into the kitchen and ask Mrs Wood to get you a juice or water?" Helen asked.

"Would I be okay to have a soda and lime if you have it?" Catherine asked sheepishly.

"You can have whatever you like!" Sir Henry roared.

Mrs Wood entered with a tray of canapes and placed them down on the coffee table in front of Jake and Catherine.

"Oh, I'm so sorry. I was not informed. Is there anything you're not eating, or don't like at the moment?" Mrs Wood asked Catherine. noticing her pregnancy.

"Gosh no, but that's really thoughtful of you, thank you. If anything, I'm eating like a horse at the moment!" Catherine giggled.

Helen followed Mrs Wood out of drawing room and into the hallway where she whispered to her, "Looks like we'll have a little guest at the wedding!"

Claire and Dee were busy going over the CCTV footage once again.

"Do you see it?" Claire asked her.

"Yes, I do, but there's something bothering me. It will come to me!" Dee replied. "Have you searched the garden house at Sofia's?"

Claire looked perplexed. "No, we thought that was a summer house, outside bar that sort of thing!"

"No, it's like a laboratory in there, Claire. It's where they make their skin and hair care products. Lucy had a smaller version of it in her house upstairs!" Dee explained.

"You're joking. I'll check it out first thing with Tom!" Claire was looking at her phone. "Tom's on his way!"

The pair sat quietly for a moment.

"Dee, I've something else to tell you, before Tom gets here," Claire said solemnly.

"I knew you did," Dee replied topping up her glass.

"Dinner is served!" Mrs Wood announced to the drawing room.

Sir Henry offered his arm to Catherine. She graciously accepted, and they walked in ahead of the others.

"You most certainly kept that quiet!" Peter said to Jake.

"I thought it would be a nice surprise for you!" Jake laughed.

"You're not kidding!" Peter said as they entered the grand dining room.

Throughout dinner, they exchanged polite conversation and shared plenty of laughter. Then, quite unexpectedly, Catherine doubled over.

"Catherine!" Jake shouted, jumping to his feet.

Helen ran round to the other side of the dining table to help but their guest was already sitting up.

"Sorry about that. It's passed!" Catherine explained catching her breath.

"It will be the Braxton Hicks!" Helen told her.

Catherine nodded. "Yes, they seem to be getting stronger by the day!"

"The doctor told you and Ben you were over doing it. You need to take it easy!" Jake scowled at her.

"Ben? Is it a boy?" Helen asked returning to her seat.

"We don't know what we're having. Ben is bump's dad!" Catherine said. "He's Cami's brother, Peter."

"I'm sorry, you've totally lost me!" Helen looked to Peter for clarification.

"Are you saying the baby isn't the Inspector's?" Sir Henry looked shocked.

Catherine looked at Jake for help. She was becoming as confused as everyone else.

Peter jumped in. "I think there's been some misunderstanding, Jake. We thought you and Catherine were together as a couple and having a baby!"

Catherine burst out laughing. Jake too looked startled.

"No, Peter. We were close once after Cami's death. That was such a long time ago. Mind you, you weren't called Jake Jones then!" Catherine looked at Jake and smiled at the table rubbing her baby bump as she continued. "Ben and I have been together for a fair number of years now; he's in the Met. Once I've finished covering for Ann, I'm going straight on maternity leave and then in a year I'll be joining Ben, but in Forensics you understand!"

Helen drank deeply from her glass of water. Silence enveloped the room.

"Here you go, Tiramisu!" Mrs Wood announced proudly as she entered the dining room.

Sir Henry cheered as Helen leaned over to ask Peter "Why did Jake change his name?"

"I'll explain later. It's all to do with the bank robbery in Amberleigh that I told you about," Peter whispered to her.

Mrs Wood was serving generous portions of dessert to Jake and Catherine when she asked, "I know you can't say too much, but may I ask how the case is going?"

Sir Henry had overheard, Mrs Wood. "Yes Jake, Peter, please tell us are you any closer to making an arrest?"

Jake was reflecting on how anyone could have perceived himself and Catherine as a couple when he noticed that everyone's attention was now directed toward him. "Apologies, could you please repeat the question?" he asked.

Peter smiled at him. "Jake, Sir Henry and Mrs Wood were asking about the case?"

"Yes, we're near to making an arrest. In fact if it wasn't for the one missing piece of the puzzle I would have had this murder solved already!"

"Explain young man," Sir Henry said gesturing for Mrs Wood to take a seat at the table.

"Yes, maybe we can help," Catherine said.

Jake and Peter explained as much as they could about the case without revealing their main suspect.

Helen jumped in. "So the missing puzzle piece is the Poison Ivy itself!"

"Yes, Helen, it is," Jake said, nodding.

"Flowers and herbs do have Latin names," Catherine chipped in.

Mrs Wood announced, "Toxicodendron radicans is the Latin name for Poison Ivy it means poison tree; to take root I believe."

"That rings a bell!" Catherine said thoughtfully "Yes, it's part of the cashew family!"

"How knowledgeable you both are!" Sir Henry praised them.

Peter stood up and announced he was going to the library.

"Why Peter?" Helen asked surprised at his announcement.

"Mrs Wood, you were looking at a book the other day. Can you remember the one I mean about toxic plants?"

"Yes, I'll come with you!" Mrs Wood said.

"We all will!" Sir Henry announced.

Helen waited to help Catherine and show her the way. "Congratulations to you and Ben. Peter told me all about the robbery and Cami losing her life. I'm so sorry for what happened to your friend," Helen said as they walked slowly to join the others.

"It affected them more than me. Peter left the force, and Jake had to move away and change his name due to death threats. It changed all of us. I secretly hope this one is a little girl so I can pop Cami in there as part of her name," Catherine said proudly.

"Or Cameron for a boy and shorten it to Cami!" Helen suggested.

"That's brilliant. What a great idea. Now let me ask you something." Catherine paused to take a breath. "Who's the special person in Jake's life?"

"Special person? Well, we thought it was you. I don't know of anyone else!" Helen looked stumped.

"I helped him pick out a pretty bracelet at the jewellers the other day. He said he was taking someone very special out for dinner on Saturday night!" Catherine said as they approached the library door.

"Honestly Catherine are you sure it's not you he's taking out for dinner!" Helen asked her.

"Absolutely not; it's mine and Ben's anniversary weekend. We're going away one last time before this one puts in an appearance!" Catherine laughed as Helen held the door open for her.

As they entered the library, Sir Henry was pulling books from the shelves and placing them on the table next to Peter and Jake who were busy thumbing through them as quickly as they could.

"What are they looking for?" Helen asked Mrs Wood as she came to join them.

"No idea!" Mrs Wood shrugged.

"And there you have it. I'll be damned!" Peter said elated.

"What have you found, Peter?" Sir Henry asked.

Jake looked at Peter then back at the book on the table "I don't see anything that we don't already know!"

"Bahamas!" Peter announced to them all.

"You're not making sense Peter. The Bahamas?" Sir Henry asked shaking his head at Mrs Wood and Helen.

"Peter, you mentioned The Bahamas earlier; you said Dee was saying we could get married abroad, something like that?" Helen looked to Peter. He nodded and winked.

"How on earth did The Bahamas come up?" Jake asked.

"Dee noticed a photograph of Sofia and Louise in Sofia's kitchen. She asked Sofia where it was taken. Turns out they holiday in the Bahamas every February," Peter replied.

Jake's face changed as the realisation of what Peter was saying dawned on him. Peter instantly recognised the look on Jake's face.

"Gotcha!" Jake announced to the group.

Chapter Twenty

"Morning Dee, where are you off to in such a hurry?" Peter asked her as she passed him in the corridor.

She didn't stop. "Alison's. I'll pick you up a coffee. I'll be back soon!"

"Hope so!" he said as he entered the empty office "I wanted to tell you about last night!"

Ruth was hammering away on her laptop when her editor called her into his office.

"What's going on with the murder of Lucy Walker?"

"Not much more than we've already printed, but I've had a tip off they're about to make an arrest!"

"What are you doing here then!" he shouted at her.

"I'll be on my way, once I know it's going to happen. I'm taking Robert with me!"

"I don't care when you go or who you take with you; just get me that story!" He was yelling again.

Ruth went to sit back down at her desk.

The young journalist next to her said, "He's in one of his moods I see!" For once Ruth agreed with her.

At the police station Jake sat in his office updating Claire and Tom on the previous night's events.

"Sir, I take it we are ready to make an arrest?" Tom said taking a sip of his morning coffee

"Yes, but Sir, I understand that Lucy and Sofia both had some form of labs at home where they made creams and things. Shouldn't we take a look first?"

"You and Tom go though I don't believe you'll find anything," Jake said as his mobile rang. "I have to take this!"

Alison and Dee were deep in conversation about Alison's investigation at the Black's Estate Agency when Albert entered Coffee Creams.

"I hope I don't have to wait long for you two to finish your nattering!" he grumbled.

"No, Albert" Dee smiled at him. "I've got everything I need!"

Alison handed over two coffees in takeaway cups and Dee left shouting a goodbye.

"Just watching that girl exhausts me!" Albert said to Alison who nodded in agreement.

Tom and Claire were on their way to the Bailey's house hoping to find them at home.

"Claire, I want to talk to you about something, but I don't want you to think I've been prying." Tom looked straight out at the traffic in front of him.

"I know what you're going to ask, and no I'm not too sure what we're looking for. We'll have to use our instincts!" Claire said.

"I wasn't going to ask you about the case. It was about…"

"Tom, we're concentrating on this right now. If you want to go for a drink later I can but right now let's focus!" Claire interrupted him.

Tom went quiet as he drove, and Claire looked down at her notes, checking them once again.

Back in the office Peter was busy swapping a few of the notes and names around on the evidence board.

"Here you go!" Dee said handing him his coffee "What are you doing now?"

"I need to tell you about last night," Peter said taking a sip of his coffee.

"That reminds me, I need to phone Helen!" Dee was already making her way towards her flat door. "I'll call her from in here; girlie stuff that's all."

Peter shrugged returning to his desk. Thirty minutes later Dee reappeared.

"Helen is so lovely. You're such a lucky man!" Dee said to him on her way over to her desk.

"That I am. Good chat?"

"Yes, very informative!" Dee replied, upbeat.

Peter felt relieved. Helen must have explained the situation with Jake and Catherine to Dee meaning he didn't have to.

"Dee, I need to tell you about the discovery we made last night regarding Poison Ivy."

"Helen told me everything, Peter we need to go to the Walker's," Dee said excitedly.

"Now?" Peter said

"Now," Dee replied .

Claire and Tom arrived at the home of Sofia and Jett Bailey.

"Where's that Inspector chap?" Sofia asked Claire and Tom on the doorstep.

"He's busy at the station. He asked us to pop down to take a look at your garden house," Claire smiled.

"Do you have a warrant?" Sofia asked.

"No, but if you've nothing to hide, I'm sure you won't mind!" Tom said sternly.

"Of course, I've nothing to hide. Come with me!" Sofia said closing the door behind her.

The garden house surprised both Tom and Claire. "I thought this was a guest house or a bar in your garden not a factory," Tom told Sofia.

"Jett doesn't like all the smells of the herbs and oils especially when I make the candles, so we built this for me to work from," Sofia said proudly.

Claire was over by a shelving rack with various herbs and plants stored in jars on it.

"You have quite the selection. Are any of these dangerous? Claire asked innocently.

"Nothing is dangerous if they're used correctly. Everything here is homeopathic," Sofia said.

"Tom made his way back towards the door. "I see what Mr Bailey means. The smell is quite strong in here!" Tom said holding his finger to his nose.

"I'm sure you've seen enough. I need to get to the salon. I have clients today," Sofia announced.

Claire and Tom followed Sofia out and into the fresh morning air.

Dee and Peter rang the doorbell of David's home. As predicted Mrs Walker answered.

"I was hoping you would have an update. Please come in," she said politely. "Tea?"

They both declined and asked if David was around.

"He's in the greenhouse watering Lucy's plants. That horrible Sofia said she would be stopping by over the weekend to take them," Mrs Walker explained.

"I suppose you have no use for them now," Dee said.

"No and with David heading back to the oil rigs soon, there'll be no one to take care of them all," Mrs Walker explained.

"David is heading back to work? I thought he might need more time," Dee said.

"I agree with you. I think he's rushing back, but he says he wants to go as soon as the funeral is over." Mrs

Walker looked across at the photograph of Lucy and David on the mantlepiece. "Here he comes now!"

Peter stood up and shook David's hand.

"Do you have any news for us? Inspector Jones called this morning. We'll be able to have Lucy's funeral in the next week or so, fingers crossed." David smiled as best he could at the mention of Lucy's name.

"David, would you be able to show me Lucy's hobby room again please. Have you touched or moved anything at all?" Dee asked him.

"No, I don't like going in there. Is it alright if I stand outside?" David asked.

"Of course it is," Dee replied as she followed him upstairs.

She found herself once more amid a collection of test tubes, herb pots, and spatulas. Checking the calendar again, she was glad to see that nothing had been erased.

"David did Lucy have a book or anything like that; something she would write her creations, recipes, formulas in for her creams," Dee called through the door.

"Yes, it's an old thing. Looks like a gardening book. It's usually on the shelf over near the window," he shouted back.

Dee went to look and David was right. She took the book and joined David on the landing.

"Can I take this? Just for today and I'll bring it back in the morning," Dee asked him.

"Of course you can. It's of no use to me although Sofia was asking about it."

Dee smiled at him. 'I bet she was!' she thought to herself.

Back at the Bailey's house Tom wasn't happy. "I think that was a complete waste of time!" he said once they were back in the car. "The Inspector was right. What on earth were you hoping to find?"

"No, Tom. Sometimes it's more about eliminating something than finding it," Claire explained.

"I have no idea what you're talking about but I've had a message from Jake. We're to head to Wellsdale Hall." Tom looked across at Claire. "He's ready to make the arrest!"

In the Walker's house, Peter had been waiting patiently with Mrs Walker for Dee to come down and explain herself.

"While you've been upstairs, Inspector Jones has called. He would like us all to join him at Wellsdale Hall," Peter said. The raised eyebrows were back.

"Us too?" David questioned.

"Yes. He has an update for all of us!" Peter said calmly.

"I'll get my handbag," Mrs Walker announced leaving the room.

"We'll follow you," Peter declared as David locked his front door.

Once in the car Dee asked, "What's going on?"

"Jake is ready to make his arrest, and he doesn't want these two going anywhere!" Peter said as he started the engine.

"I see," Dee said opening the book on her lap and thumbing through the pages.

"What have you got there?" Peter asked as he tried to stay as close to the Walker's car as possible.

"Just what I've been looking for!" Dee smiled.

Jake had already arrived at Wellsdale Hall to find Angela Myers occupied fluffing the cushions in the jigsaw room, as they hadn't been arranged to her preference.

"Hello Inspector, will in here do?" Angela asked him "You seemed very cryptic on the phone."

"Perfect. The others will arrive shortly!" Jake said looking out of the window and down towards the tennis courts.

"Others?" she questioned, not having a clue what was going on. "I can go to the kitchen and ask for a platter of sandwiches if that would be helpful?"

"I think that would be kind of you, but can you stay here. I'm sure you have the head chef's number in your mobile."

Angela nodded and sat down in one of the armchairs. "I wish you could tell me more about what's happening."

"All in good time!" Jake replied.

Charles Black put the phone down and went across to Louise's desk. "We have an important client staying at Wellsdale Hall," he said.

Louise looked up from her computer screen. "Do we?"

"Yes, he's leaving tonight. Can you take all the brochures over the million mark to show him, and do your best sales pitch. This is a second home he's looking for, and you never know, he might want a third!" Charles Black was always excited at the thought of a sale.

"I'll head there now. What's his name?" Louise asked gathering her things together.

"Mr Huntingdon, flown in from Jersey!" Charles informed her.

"I'm on my way!" Louise said, grabbing her laptop as an afterthought.

The thin haughty man on the reception desk at Wellsdale Hall popped his head round the door of the jigsaw room. He didn't speak but nodded regally at Jake.

Jake smiled and mouthed a thank you.

Louise Smart was on her way!

At the Bailey's house Jett and Sofia were busy loading the completed order into Jett's car.

"Is that the last of the boxes?" Jett asked Sofia.

"Sure is. How long are you going to be. I don't like being here on my own after you know what," Sofia explained.

"Come with me. Then we can go straight to the salon from Wellsdale Hall. I'm only dropping these in to Angela," Jett said closing the boot of his car.

"Yeah, I will. Let me get my bag and I'll go and lock up," Sofia said disappearing into the house.

Jett started the engine and checked his mobile for messages. Sofia jumped into the passenger seat and locked her car door.

"We can't hang around at Wellsdale Hall, Sofia. Mrs Barker is due, and you know what she's like!" Jett laughed as they made their way down the drive.

Angela thanked the young man who carried the large platter of sandwiches and nibbles into the jigsaw room. He said he would return shortly with tea and coffee.

Jake checked his phone. Peter had texted to say they were only minutes away so Jake popped his head round the door again and was giving the man on reception a heads up as Claire and Tom arrived.

"Hello, you two. There's a sandwich over there and a cup of tea on its way," Jake told them.

Claire and Tom thanked him and went to take their positions, Claire by the large window that looked out onto the front lawn of Wellsdale Hall and thus gave a clear view of who was coming and going while Tom took up a position by the door.

Dee, Peter, Mrs Walker, and David all walked in together. Jake greeted them with handshakes. He then courteously invited the Walkers to take seats on one of the sofas beside Angela while Dee and Peter went to stand by the huge fireplace.

"What is all this about?" Mrs Walker asked Angela.

"I'm sorry, I have no idea!" Angela replied shaking her head.

The young man returned with a large tray of tea and coffee. Claire went over to him, offering to pour out the tea, but only Mrs Walker accepted.

"Hello, I'm Louise…" She stopped in the doorway and half turned round. The man from reception was right behind her, Tom stayed behind the open door "What the…"

"Ms Smart, please come and join us. You may leave your things over there. You won't be needing them!" Jake advised.

"I'm in the wrong place. I'm here to meet a Mr Huntingdon from Jersey. He's looking to buy a second home!"

"Please take a seat. There's tea, coffee and sandwiches if you'd like any." Jake pointed her at the other sofa opposite David and Mrs Walker.

As Louise sat down, she threw Angela Myers a dirty look and asked David what was happening. He shrugged his shoulders by way of reply.

Claire, who was back at the large window, looked across at Dee and motioned her head towards the door.

"I'll be back in a minute!" Dee whispered to Peter.

Peter nodded and Dee left the room.

"Vicky, over here!" Dee called across the foyer.

"What's this all about. Jake said it was urgent. Has someone else died?" Vicky asked, her eyes as wide as saucers.

"No, he's about to make an arrest, but we want you to go in last. Stay here with me. We're just waiting for Sofia and Jett to arrive," Dee told her.

"Oh my god. I have kids. I hope you're not going to arrest me!" Vicky was starting to sound hysterical. "I haven't done anything!"

The man on reception came over and ushered them through the door behind the reception desk. "I think this will be preferable!"

Dee and Vicky found themselves among coats and uncollected suitcases.

"Vicky, of course we aren't going to arrest you, but as Lucy's friend it's only right you're here," Dee said trying to calm her down.

The woman grabbed hold of Dee. "I know we'll never be best friends but thank you for this!"

Jett had gone to the rear. The laundry doors were wide open, and while he started to unload the boxes, Sofia stayed in the car.

"Angela is wanting a quick word with you and Sofia." said one of the girls working in the laundry room.

Jett tapped on the car window and Sofia wound the window down.

"Angela needs a quick word with us both," Jett told her.

Sophia got out of the car, remarking caustically, "This had better be quick!"

They cut through the laundry room into the Spa and then walked through to the foyer. They were just about to go up the stairs to Angela's office when Jett heard the man from reception call his name and issue the instruction that Angela was waiting for them in the jigsaw room.

Sophia entered the jigsaw room first. "What the hell is this? Angela, Louise - someone better tell me!" she barked, looking around the room.

Jett followed her in equally confused. "Angela, I thought you wanted to see us?"

Angela stayed seated and shook her head.

Jake took a step forward. "Please help yourselves and if you wouldn't mind sitting here, we would be much obliged!"

"I'll sit where I want!" Sofia said and then thought better of it as she saw at the scowl on Mrs Walker's face.

In the foyer Dee heard a gentle tap on the door.

"You're fine to go in; they're all here!" the receptionist told them. He then pretended to write something on a notepad, so he didn't have to engage with them further.

Dee pushed Vicky who looked like she was about to faint out of the cloak room. "Don't say anything, Vicky. Not one word and don't talk to Jake at all when we go in!" Dee warned her, worried she would throw herself at the Inspector.

Vicky couldn't utter a word; she was a bag of nerves.

Ruth had received the tip off she had been waiting for.

"Robert, we need to get to Wellsdale Hall now. It looks like they're about to make an arrest!"

Robert grabbed his camera and his jacket from the back of his chair. Ruth was already heading for the lift.

The editor stuck his head out of his office door and shouted across at the junior Journalist "I take it they're heading to Wellsdale Hall?" he barked.

The young journalist looked up and nodded.

"About bloody time!" He slammed his door.

Ruth had left her lightweight jacket over the back of her chair. The junior journalist had been waiting for the right opportunity. She looked around the office but everyone was occupied and when she felt no one was watching, she popped an envelope into Ruth's jacket pocket for her to find.

The mood in Wellsdale Hall's jigsaw room was tense as Vicky and Dee walked in. Dee noticed an empty chair beside Jett and Jake pointed Vicky towards it.

"Thank you all for coming today. I know for some of you this is not why you thought you were here." Jake looked across at Louise. "However for your own safety we didn't want to alert anyone to the update we have to make."

"Are you saying you've made an arrest?" Mrs Walker was wide eyed.

"If you could bear with me, Mrs Walker, I'll be happy to explain it all." Jake smiled at her.

Dee went over to sit in the window seat and Claire joined Tom guarding the door.

Jake watched Dee as she sat down in the bay window. The sun caught her scarf and tiny beads of light sparkled around her. He knew he was staring. Dee smiled as she made eye contact with him, waiting for him to continue.

Jake did a fake cough to look as if he was clearing his throat. "As we all know Lucy was found by Dee Firth unresponsive in the Cave Pool and was pronounced dead at the scene." Jake paused. "At first we believed this was a terrible accident but after forensic analysis it turned out that Lucy had died of anaphylactic shock from Poison Ivy which is when we started to investigate Lucy's death as a murder!"

"We know all this Inspector!" David said, "Do you have to go over it again?"

"I appreciate this is difficult for you, David and indeed for the rest of you." Jake looked around at them before continuing. "We know the murder took place between one thirty and two thirty, when four of you were having your treatments. This is because we can clearly see each of you arriving at the treatment area but only three of you leaving when your treatments had finished."

"We thought Lucy had gone home!" Louise interrupted him.

"Yes, that is so, but only two of you messaged her to find out where she was when she didn't join you. Vicky why didn't you message Lucy?" Jake had walked behind the others to be near Peter.

Vicky looked over at Dee for support. "I don't know!"

"Is it because you knew she was already dead?" he asked her sternly.

"No Jake, Inspector. I didn't know. I don't know anything!" Vicky was going a shade paler than she already was.

Jake watched as the others all turned to stare at Vicky.

"It turns out you're not the only one who didn't message her either!" Jake announced changing his position in the room. "Louise Smart, we've checked your phone records. You lied when you told us you had sent Lucy a message."

"I did not. Here check my mobile. Maybe it didn't go through!" Louise was on the edge of the sofa.

Jake turned his attention to Mrs Walker. "You lied to us all too. You were here on the day of Lucy's murder. You can be clearly seen entering Wellsdale Hall. However, it was difficult to check when you left; that's if you did leave. We have received a report that states your car left the carpark at twelve thirty, providing no one else was driving it - David?"

"You hang on here a minute, I left when I told them, two and you, I did and I can assure you David was not in the car with me!"

"Mrs Walker, you also said you were a member here, and that is not true. Ms Myers here checked for me."

Mrs Walker looked down at her hands. "No, that isn't true, but the rest is."

David sat still, he didn't say a word.

Jake ignored her and moved once again around the room.

"Now we come to you, Ms Myers." Jake took a deep breath. "You knew Sofia and Lucy had swapped rooms, Sofia here told us she had left you a note. The question is why would you want to murder Lucy?"

Angela squirmed in her chair. "I wouldn't, I didn't even know her!"

"This is true but let's say you never received the message, and you were already on your way to what you believed to be Mrs Bailey's treatment room. You could easily call away Laura and take over the treatment yourself. Was it a case of murdering the wrong person, and your intended victim wasn't Lucy."

"This is ridiculous. Why would I want to kill Sofia. What a load of rubbish!" Angela was shaking and bright red in the face.

Sofia finally spoke up. "Perhaps because I was going to tell the owners here, that you have been charging us to display our products around the hotel and Spa. I wasn't the only one. Chrissy was going to tell them too. You've been taking money from this place for years!"

Angela turned on Sofia. "I'd like to see you try and prove that one. You signed the contracts you stuck up…"

Louise interrupted. "Lucy told me you were having an affair with Jett. That's another reason!"

They all turned to look at Jett.

"I was no more seeing her than the man in the moon!" he said sarcastically.

"Give over, we've made out many times in my office you piece of shit!" Angela spat out.

"I knew it. You told me you weren't seeing anyone and I just knew you were!" Sophia said quietly.

Jake made a loud cough. "I think we're digressing. As we all know, Lucy was pregnant. She was acting as a surrogate for Jett and Sofia, although we believe Sofia didn't know that Lucy was pregnant. Is that true?"

"Yes, they were going to tell me on my birthday," Sofia said.

"Sofia you were heard arguing with Lucy in the saunas. Once again why?" Jake asked her.

"It wasn't me!" Sofia shouted. "I've told you this!"

"No, it wasn't you was it. Louise?" Jake looked at her, taking an educated guess.

Dee and Peter exchanged glances but Louise didn't answer.

"You were paying Lucy sums of money to keep her quiet. I believe Lucy was blackmailing you. We won't go into the reasons why." Jake looked across at Dee and, as quickly, looked away. "Sofia, you too were paying Lucy sums of money. We understand the payments for the surrogacy as we've seen a contract that backs up those payments but for the others was Lucy blackmailing you too?"

David stood up. "My Lucy wouldn't blackmail anyone! You've got this all wrong. If you know who killed my wife spit it out!"

Jake turned and asked him to sit back down and Tom, who had taken a step forward, returned to his place by the door.

"Yes, we're not going to take up any more of your time. We have clear CCTV which shows several therapists pushing the large blue trolleys back and forth from the treatment rooms to the laundry room at the side of the spa. We also have clear CCTV footage of the spa and once again therapists can be seen pushing trolleys back and forth between the spa and the laundry room at around the time Lucy was murdered." Jake paused and took a deep breath.

"Are you saying Lucy was murdered in the treatment room, taken from the treatment area to the spa and then dumped in the Cave Pool by one of my therapists!" Angela was aghast.

"It most certainly looked like one of your therapists, but it wasn't. We know this person was in both areas at the correct times. The first was when Lucy was murdered as they were supposed to be having their treatment and secondly at the time when Lucy's body was put in the Cave Pool to make it look like an accident. That person is seen entering the spa area at three pm, and seen pushing a trolley to the entrance of the Cave Pool. Your hairstyle is undeniable," Jake said, turning to look at Louise. "So, Louise Smart, we're arresting you for the murder of Lucy Walker!"

"I haven't done any of those things. This is ridiculous. I went to the spa to get her…" Louise pointed to Sofia,

"...some headache tablet's not to put Lucy's body in the Cave Pool. Tell them Sofia!"

Sofia kept looking down at her hands.

"And where on earth would I get Poison Ivy from?" Louise shouted. "I don't even know what it looks like!"

"The Bahamas," Jake answered. "We'll discuss that with you in the interview room. Tom please read Ms Smart her rights!"

Dee stood up and moved away from the window, over to Louise's side. The woman burst into tears as Tom approached her and Dee signalled for Tom to move back where he was.

"Yes, Sofia. Why did you send Louise to fetch you headache tablets at three pm?" Dee asked her.

Sofia looked up. "I'm not saying anything. What would you know? You're not even a real detective!"

Dee looked at Jake. "I'm going to have to start at the beginning!"

Peter jumped in. "Dee, what are you doing? We all can see it's Louise on the CCTV footage."

Dee gave him a smile. They had encountered this very scenario before. Peter glanced over at Jake who appeared stunned.

"It's about, masks, swimsuits and shoes!" Dee declared.

Peter knew better than to question Dee's thought process and let her continue.

Claire smiled at her.

"You see, Mrs Walker - and I must give credit to DC Brown for the idea of looking at her shoes. You're clearly seen walking into Wellsdale Hall and having a coffee in the café, but we didn't see you leave." Dee paused. "You told us you left wearing a headscarf and sunglasses once you realised Lucy wasn't meeting another man but her friends that you don't like very much and you didn't want to be recognised."

Mrs Walker agreed that she had because she didn't care for Lucy's friends.

"However, any one of you could have worn that disguise. Mrs Walker might have tried to change her appearance but not her shoes. Fortunately that means that Mrs Walker did leave at the time she said and can be clearly seen doing so on the CCTV footage."

Mrs Walker thanked her and commented on how observant they had been.

Dee turned towards Louise. "Now, you're guilty of misleading your clients. You've been putting a marketing charge into the contracts and keeping it for yourself. Lucy found out when she worked at the branch in Gamblewood. She checked your accounts, and the Blacks Estate Agency accounts so she could see the money going from one to another."

"How do you know this?" Jake asked Dee.

Dee looked across at him "A contract fell on the floor when Peter and I went to ask Louise a couple of questions. I saw the amendment next to the commission charged and I guarantee you that was not on the contract when it was originally signed."

Jake said, "I see!"

"Furthermore, I believe Lucy checked her own sales contract and Louise had added a marketing fee to theirs. This has been going on for years, hasn't it, Louise?"

Dee waited for an answer but Louise didn't make a sound.

"Alison." Dee started to speak again.

Peter jumped in "Alison?"

"Yes Peter, I asked Alison to go house hunting, and speaking to Charles Black, he said there were no hidden costs and you would only ever be charged the agreed commission!" Dee turned her attention back to Louise "I think Lucy approached you and asked you to stop, but instead you offered to give her a percentage and for personal reasons, Lucy agreed."

"Louise Smart not only are we arresting you for the murder of Lucy Walker, we're also arresting you for fraud!" Jake announced.

"Not so quick Jake!" Dee looked at him horrified. "I haven't finished!"

"You haven't?" Jake turned to look at Claire and Tom.

"I do feel a bit sorry for you, Angela. Jett did have a dalliance with you, but it was only to use you. The one true love in his life was Lucy." Dee turned to look at him.

"So, it was Lucy you were seeing you…" Sofia spat at him.

David interrupted, shaking his fist at him. "I always knew there was more to you two - friends indeed. You're lucky there's officers here or I'd come over and punch your lights out!"

"Steady on there, David!" Jake warned.

"What do you mean he used me!" Angela asked, a tear falling down her face.

"Sofia was about to sign a contract not only with you but with the whole hotel chain. It was very lucrative. Jett used you for information and it gave him access to your office."

"I did tell Jett about the contract. I didn't know it was a secret!" Angela said. "But why would having access to my office have anything to do with it?"

"Jett do you want to explain or shall I?" Dee looked at him folding her arms as she waited.

Peter went to stand next to Jake.

"You shouldn't have swapped rooms, you bitch!" Jett jumped up from his seat and went for Sofia.

Tom ran over and shoved his arm up his back. Sofia stayed sitting, smirking at Jett.

Dee spoke a little louder. "You see Jett had used you Angela to check your computer to find out which room Sofia was going to have her treatment in. Laura said she saw Jett here at Wellsdale Hall on the day of Lucy's murder, but Claire and I could not find Jett on any of the CCTV footage!"

"Shut up. It's all her fault!" Jett shouted.

"You watch your mouth!" Jake snapped at him "Go on Dee!"

"Jett used one of the wigs from the salon that the girls use to practice doing Jett's signature bob!" Dee unfolded her arms and pointed at Louise's hair. "He then took one of the therapist outfits and a trolley from the laundry room, and blended in, keeping his head down. Jett waited for Laura to be called away and then he went in as the replacement therapist to kill Sofia not Lucy!"

"Hang on a minute Dee, how did Jett know Laura was going to be called away?" Peter asked.

"Jett knows as much as Sofia does how all the treatments are done. There is always a brief period when the therapist steps out of the room after the mask is applied. Helen confirmed this happened to her during her facial. Jett told Laura she had a call, or maybe passed her a note?"

Jett did not respond but his face was seething.

"Jett entered the room and placed Clingfilm over the masked body believing it to be Sofia. Clingfilm was found on Lucy's earring, Jake?"

"Yes, it was!" Jake answered, blown away by what was occurring.

"He then put her in the trolley he had left outside the room, covered the body with the used towels, and waited for the appropriate amount of time to pass. After that Jett pushed Lucy to the spa and then into the Cave Pool. I think it was only then that Jett realised it was Lucy and not Sofia!"

"You tried to set me up, looking like me!" Louise screamed at him. "You bastard!"

"So how do you know for definite it's Jett and not Louise pushing that trolley?" Jake asked calmly.

Dee nodded at Claire.

"It's all to do with shoes, Sir," Claire said as they all turned to look at her. "The therapist who looks like Louise is not wearing the same footwear as Louise on the CCTV footage. Louise is wearing flip flops, Sir. The so-called therapist is wearing trainers - those trainers!" Claire pointed at the trainers Jett was wearing. "Once you notice it, it's clear to see on the CCTV. That's what I was checking earlier, Sir. You see all the therapists wear clogs. They're comfy and do not slip easily! Dee checked for me too. No one wears trainers, Sir."

Claire had gone a nice shade of pink. Tom mouthed a *well done* at her.

Jake was about to read Jett his rights when Jett started screeching and Peter went over to help Tom keep a hold on him. "Sofia, you're the one who should be dead. You made me kill my Lucy. You made me kill my baby. I hate you!"

"There's just something bothering me," Jake interrupted in a loud voice looking first at Claire and then at Dee. "Lucy died from poisoning not asphyxiation!"

Dee moved behind Mrs Walker.

"Jett, did Lucy put up a fight when you put the Clingfilm over her face or should I say over the mask?"

"No, it was all very quick!" Jett's eyes began to fill with tears.

"Jett, you didn't kill Lucy. She was already dead!" Dee announced.

The room filled with expletives and gasps!

"Dee you better know what you're saying?" Peter said letting go his hold on Jett.

"I do Peter. Sofia Bailey killed Lucy!" Dee said confidently.

"I did not. It was him!" Sofia said pointing at Jett.

"No, it wasn't Jett, it was you!" Dee walked back to the fireplace. "You orchestrated the whole thing. I'm not sure how you found out Jett's plans to kill you. I'll let Inspector Jones work that one out!" Dee took a breath "First of all with the exception of Vicky, you made sure you wore the same bikinis - just a slightly different shade of green. That way if any of the bikini was showing when Jett entered the room, he would still think it was you."

"You bought us those bikinis; you gave them to us as a surprise!" Louise blurted out pointing at Sofia. "In the changing rooms!"

"Thank you for clarifying that." Dee smiled at her "Sofia, you said you went to Angela's office to leave a note to tell her you were swapping rooms, but you didn't. You used that as an excuse to take the key that unlocked the connecting door between the two treatment rooms."

"Oh my god!" Angela let out.

"When Lori had left you to relax, you knew you had several minutes before Jett would swap places with Laura. You waited for Laura to leave. As Helen remarked under that mask her face was set rigid. Lucy's would have been the same. You used a pipette filled with a mixture of oil and the Poison Ivy and thrust it into her mouth. Lucy would have died quickly."

Jake interrupted her. "There was ash found on her body, Dee?"

"Yes, just for good measure, Sofia burnt Poison Ivy over the air holes for her nose. I believe some ash may have fallen on to her. Lucy would have struggled," Dee answered him.

"But the air would be toxic to anyone entering that room, Dee?" Peter said.

"Yes, Sofia had already opened the window. It's as simple as that as it's next to the connecting door!"

"Are we saying it was Sofia who brought back the Poison Ivy from The Bahamas not Louise?" Jake asked her.

"That's correct - Lucy discovered that by using a highly diluted form of Poison Ivy in her homeopathic creams, her psoriasis had almost completely disappeared. It's all here in her book!" Dee picked up Lucy's book of formulas, which she had left on a table by the fireplace. "As is every formula for the Bailey's Hair and skin care range!"

"I never liked you!" Mrs Walker said to Sofia. "You're one nasty cow!"

Sofia started to stand up but Louise pushed her back down on to the sofa. "Why Sofia? I don't understand," Louise said.

Sofia with a rigid politeness told Louise to never touch her again!

Dee cleared her throat. "It's all because of the contract that Sofia was due to sign the next day on the eighteenth of May. Lucy and Sofia were arguing in the sauna because Lucy had been asking for a bigger cut. After all it was her work. Sofia was just the face of the product. She never invented a single one of the Bailey's hair and skincare range. Sofia used to pay Lucy as to use her work, but for once Lucy wanted what she truly deserved, money and the recognition. Sofia was not going to let that happen!"

"That scheming bitch wanted sixty percent!" Sofia said under her breath.

"She was carrying your baby, you witch. Didn't you think about that when you were killing my daughter-in law!" Mrs Walker was on her feet shouting at Sofia.

"It wasn't my baby, you stupid idiot, it was theirs!" Sofia pointed at Jett. "She was going to leave your David for Jett and the two of them were going to take my company with them!"

"What do you mean it's their baby?" David too was now on his feet.

Dee intervened. "All sit down!" she shouted taking Jake and the others by surprise. "There was a congratulations letter from the clinic pinned next to the calendar in Lucy's hobby room. It stated that while their services were not needed at this time, help would be available in the future if required. Lucy never visited the clinic, which Alison confirmed.

Peter wanted to ask what Alison had done to confirm anything but decided not to.

"I cannot believe you both pretended to go; it was hilarious to watch! When I found out that day in the salon from the stupid receptionist who works at the clinic how wonderful it was that I had manged to get pregnant naturally, you were lucky I didn't kill you on the spot, you bastard!" Sofia shouted at Jett. "The two of you were a scheming, thieving pair of rats. You even took my money for a surrogacy that was never going to happen!"

"I don't care about any flipping baby or money!" David rose to his full height and looked Sofia straight in the eye. "You killed my wife!"

"She flipping deserved it!" Sofia screeched back at him.

Jake moved forward and declared, "Sofia Bailey, you're under arrest for the murder of Lucy Walker!" He signalled to Claire to recite Sofia's rights.

A little while later Ruth was interviewing Inspector Jones outside the grand entrance of Wellsdale Hall. Robert took pictures as Sofia and Jett Bailey were taken out in handcuffs and placed in separate police cars by the officers who had been waiting outside on standby. A female officer escorted Louise to a different police car.

Dee and the others had remained sitting in the jigsaw room.

"I'll have some fresh tea brought in!" Angela Myers said.

"You're not going anywhere, Angela," Claire said. "The company are sending their lawyer to speak with you. You have a great deal of explaining to do. It will be interesting to see if they want to press charges!"

At that moment, the thin receptionist entered the room. "I will bring you all fresh tea and sandwiches shortly," he announce. Picking up the tray he glared at Angela, and laughed as he left the room.

"It's Helen. I'll take this outside!" Peter said waving his mobile at them.

Claire and Dee watched the flurry of activity outside from the window.

"You did it Dee, well done!" Claire said nudging her.

"It was both of us, Claire. I didn't work it out all on my own!"

Peter and Jake returned followed by a young man carrying a new tray of sandwiches and pots of tea and coffee.

"Mrs Walker, David - the press would like to ask you a few question. How do you feel about it?" Jake asked them.

They both agreed it was better to face the music. Then they were going to have the weekend away to avoid any further intrusion.

"Vicky you're free to leave, thank you!" Jake smiled at her.

Two police officers escorted the Walkers out as the lawyer representing Wellsdale Hall arrived and briskly escorted Angela to her office. Two police officers on Jake's command followed them.

Claire poured out tea and handed round sandwiches.

"You two were amazing," Jake said proudly to Claire and Dee. "I don't know how you do it Dee, but I look forward to reading your full statement and as for you DC Brown I'll be putting you forward for your Detective Sergeant exams!"

"I'll pop into the station tomorrow. Is that alright?" Dee asked Jake.

"No rush," he replied unable to take his eyes off her.

"Congratulations," Tom said to Claire. "You deserve it!" He gave her a big hug.

Claire walked away and took the transfer letter out of her pocket. Tom watched her closely as she tore it up and threw it in the bin.

Peter walked back into the room to make an announcement. "Helen and Sir Henry would like to invite you all to Gaitley Manor around five thirty for a celebratory drink on Saturday. Is that okay with everyone?"

They all gave nods of agreement.

"Dee it's time for us to take our leave," Peter said.

"We'll walk you out," Jake said as they headed towards the main entrance.

Jake let the others go ahead so he could grab Dee's arm which took her by complete surprise. "Dee please meet me at Mr Wangs on Saturday night seven o'clock," he whispered.

Dee didn't get the chance to answer as a barrage of reporters were surrounded them and shouting, "Inspector Jones. Inspector Jones!"

Chapter Twenty-One

Peter and Dee had called into Coffee Creams to tell Alison all about the arrests on their way back to the office. Peter had thoroughly enjoyed listening to Alison's accounts of her and Jim's sleuthing escapade over a cup of tea and a slice of cake.

"I'll drop you back, Dee," Peter announced as he picked up his car keys. "Don't forget about Saturday Alison - Gaitley Manor at five thirty!"

"Jim and I will be there. Looking forward to it!" she said as she cleared the table.

They said their goodbyes and as Peter dropped Dee at the door to their agency, he congratulated her once more.

Dee watched as Peter sped away Only then did she open the door to find the envelope lying on the floor.

The results of her private detective exams had arrived.

Friday morning passed in a whirl of paperwork for all.

"Done!" Dee announced to Peter across the office, passing him her typed report of the previous day's events.

"I'll check it for you and then on my way home, I'll drop it into Gamblewood Police Station for you."

"Ta Peter. Doing anything special tonight?" Dee asked.

"No, we're going to have a film and pizza night." Peter was already reading Dee's report. "By the way have you had your exam results yet?"

Dee was just about to answer when Paula from came through the door holding the most beautiful bouquet of flowers.

"For you, dear," Paula said placing them on Dee's desk. "I think you'll want to read the card!"

Peter came and stood beside Paula as Dee opened the little envelope.

"They're from Jake!" Dee looked a little taken aback "He's thanking me for all I did to help solve Lucy Walker's murder."

Paula was already making her way to the door. "I'd best be off. I've another bouquet to deliver to DC Brown!"

No sooner had Paula left, when Mrs Walker arrived with David in tow.

"Hello. Those are beautiful and well deserved!" Mrs Walker announced, on seeing the bouquet on Dee's desk.

Peter asked them to take a seat and after pleasantries said, "I thought you two were going to have a weekend away?"

Mrs Walker answered. "We're on our way to the coast, but we didn't feel we got the chance to thank you both properly. I'm hoping you have your invoice ready for us and we wanted to pop in and give you this."

David handed Dee an envelope. It was a thank you card and as she opened it to read the inside, something fell out on to the floor. Dee bent down to pick it up.

Peter passed Mrs Walker the invoice he had done for them that morning. "If you would like to check it, you can forward the payment next week; no rush."

"No need!" Mrs Walker bellowed taking out her cheque book. A moment later she was handing a completed cheque to Peter.

Holding the slip of paper that had fallen to the floor, Dee, flustered, let out a gasp. "David, Mrs Walker; I can't accept this!" It was a second cheque, this one for five thousand pounds and made out to Dee.

"Yes, you can. Without you, I might have been in serious trouble and someone else could have been wrongly arrested for Lucy's murder," Mrs Walker said firmly. "You were brilliant and so clever! We both told that journalist woman as much yesterday," David added.

Dee didn't know what to say. She looked across at Peter who was beaming at her.

Mrs Walker and David thanked them once again and took their leave but not before Dee had given them both the biggest of hugs.

"Well Dee, let's call it a day. By the way your report is spot on. Jake will be pleased."

Dee smiled at him. "Will you please thank Jake for me; the flowers are beautiful!"

Peter picked up his car keys. "You can thank him yourself tomorrow at Gaitley Manor!"

Saturday had arrived but was passing too swiftly.

Mrs Wood had devoted much of her day to baking and organising food for the party only belatedly hurrying upstairs to change her clothes after checking the time.

Dee stood in her dressing gown deciding what to wear to Gaitley Manor. After bringing her Gran up to speed on all the arrests and the generosity of the Walker's, Dee had spent the rest of the day cleaning her flat and the office. She pulled out a summer dress but promptly put it back. Instead long white trousers caught her eye as did the pale green blouse which matched her eyes. Dee quickly got dressed. She didn't want to be late.

Tom, Claire and the Inspector had finally left the station after another intense day. Fortunately, they had all brought a change of clothes with them. Tom and Claire were in the police car behind Jake.

"You look lovely," Tom complimented Claire.

"As do you," Claire said nudging him cheekily.

"Claire, I saw you throw something away yesterday at Wellsdale Hall. Was it what I thought it was?" Tom asked not daring to look at her as he drove.

"Yes, it was. I'm not going anywhere, Tom. I'm here to stay!" she replied.

At Gaitley Manor, Helen, Peter and Sir Henry waited for their guests to arrive in the drawing room.

"They'll be here any minute!" Helen said excitedly as Peter kissed her.

The doorbell rang and they could hear Mrs Wood inviting people in. Inspector Jake Jones, followed by Claire and Tom had arrived. Mrs Wood showed them into the drawing room. Sir Henry greeted them all and invited them to help themselves to canapes as Peter poured their drinks.

"Helen, can I have a quick word," Jake whispered in her ear.

"Of course," Helen replied making her way over to the window where they could see Alison, Jim and Dee arriving.

"I'm meeting someone very special at Mr Wangs around seven, so I'm sorry but I'll have to leave early. I hope you don't mind. I want to be there before they arrive!" Jake explained.

"Of course, it's no problem at all!" Helen said, not wanting to pry.

Dee followed by Alison and Jim came in to join the others. Once again Sir Henry was on his feet greeting the trio. Peter poured more drinks and just as Mrs Wood was about to head to the kitchen, Sir Henry tapped his glass to get everyone's attention.

"Firstly, congratulations to you all and especially to Dee and Claire. I also understand even Alison helped with a little sleuthing too!" Sir Henry raised his glass in the air.

"As did Mrs Wood and Helen!" Dee chipped in.

"Don't forget your Gran, Dee!" Helen added.

"Congratulations to you all. Marvellous work!" Sir Henry repeated raising his glass in the air once more.

Mrs Wood was just about to fetch more canapes when Peter asked her to stay as they had an announcement to make. "Helen and I have set a date for the wedding. It is to be in October - on the fourteenth!" Peter smiled and gave Helen a kiss as Clara came running into the room.

Alison asked, "Are you having the wedding here?"

The room fell silent.

"No, we're getting married at a friend of Sir Henry's," Helen answered. She took a deep breath. "You're all invited to the beautiful island of Kefalonia!"

As they were cheered and congratulated, Jake caught Helen's eye and slipped out.

Helen glanced around at the delighted faces; her cheeks flushed with happiness. "It's going to be absolutely magical," she added. "The villa overlooks the sea and there are olive trees everywhere. I can't wait for you all to see it." As laughter bubbled up among the group, Peter squeezed her hand, clearly as thrilled as she was.

Dee let out a polite cough. "I have some news too; I passed my exams!"

"What a night for celebration!" Sir Henry announced.

They all hugged and congratulated her. Dee looked for Jake. She hadn't had the chance to thank him for the flowers, but he was gone.

"Where's Jake?" Dee asked.

"He's meeting someone special at Mr Wangs!" Helen said.

"Oh, that will be Catherine," Dee said to the group.

"I don't think so. Catherine and Ben are having a last weekend away before the baby arrives!" Peter told her.

"What!" Alison said surprised. "Are you telling me Catherine isn't Jake's girlfriend?"

"No, Alison. Where did you get that from?" Helen asked her.

"Vicky told Dee that she'd met Jake's girlfriend and she was expecting!" Alison said. "Dee, Vicky had it wrong this whole time!"

Peter butted in. "Catherine is here covering for Ann in Forensics, and she's about to go on Maternity leave. Catherine is the girlfriend of Ben, Cami's brother. Do you remember me telling you all about the robbery that Jake and I were involved in when Cami lost her life."

Dee stood motionless. "But I saw them coming out of the jewellers together. We thought they'd got engaged, didn't we, Claire?"

"Yes, we did."

"No. Catherine was helping him choose something for someone special!" Helen said.

"Oh, my word! I've messed up!" Dee blurted out. "Jake asked me to meet him at Mr Wangs tonight!"

"What time?" Alison asked her.

"Seven. What time is it now?" Dee asked them.

"It's quarter to. Oh Dee, you are the someone special!" Helen exclaimed.

"Go, hurry. I'll phone Mr Wang!" Peter said and they all watched Dee flee from the room.

Robert and Ruth were enjoying a meal together at the cosy Italian restaurant in Amberleigh. They clinked their glasses as Robert congratulated her on another incredible scoop.

When they'd finished eating, Robert excused himself and made his way to the gents. Ruth checked her coat pocket for her keys and found an envelope in it. She pulled it out and opened it.

Robert returned and sat down and Ruth promptly stood up and to the delight of the other diners poured her entire glass of wine over his head, shouting, "Married with two kids. You make me sick!"

"I'm separated. She left me for another man. We're getting a divorce!" Robert shouted after her as she made her way dramatically towards the exit.

She shouted back across the restaurant. "Likely bloody story!" and left.

Sitting in Mr Wang's Jake checked his watch for the fourth time. It was now seven thirty. He popped the gold box back in his pocket and made his way to the toilet.

"I'm sorry Mr Wang, I don't think she's coming," he explained as he passed him.

Mr Wang watched the Inspector go into the gent's toilet as Mrs Wang came over to tell him that Mr Peter was calling again and wanted to stay on the phone till Miss Dee arrived.

Just then Dee ran into the restaurant somewhat out of breath. She looked around but couldn't see Jake. He must have left. Without saying anything Mr Wang handed the phone to his wife, took Dee by the hand and led her to the table where Jake had been sitting.

"Okay Mr Wang, I will stay for a bit!" Dee said as her eyes began to fill with tears.

Jake exited the men's room and made his way directly towards the door but Mrs Wang quickly stepped in front of him, gesturing towards the table where he'd been sitting. His heart missed a beat.

Mr and Mrs Wang held hands aware that Peter was still on the phone. They watched Jake make his way over to the table. Dee didn't look up as he sat down opposite her, lifted her face to look into his and with a gentle hand wiped away a tear as he slid the bracelet in its pretty gold box across the table.

Meanwhile everyone had gathered around Peter's phone waiting patiently. Suddenly the halls of Gaitley Manor echoed with cheers and the sound of glasses clinking as Mr Wang finally declared, "We have lift off!"

Printed in Dunstable, United Kingdom